A Light in the Shadows
A Shadow and Ash Novel
By Emily Grey

Copyright 2025 Emily Grey
ISBN Paperback: 979-8-9892881-1-3
ASIN e-book: B0DTBZJXBH

Cover Design by Ever After Cover Design
Edited by Emily Martin and Ramona Mihai
Interior art by Emily Grey via Canva

A
LIGHT
IN THE
SHADOWS

Shadow and Ash Vol. 1.5

Emily Grey

To anyone that's ever looked beyond

their cage and longed for more.

Chapter One

It should have struck me as odd how, as a creature of blazing fire, I had spent over a year of my life drowning in this lake. It was a near perfect image, foreign enough to the fabric of my being that it prevented me from trying to see it for what it was: a glamor, concealing my memories.

Now, I once more swam along the bottom of my being, my memories riding in the steady flow that raced down my back. The further I swam, the more I remembered. The waves moved like the passage of time. My earliest memories were hazy, swept away in the languid current. Hard to picture and harder still to recall with the decades had passed. The tide picked up, and I was no longer swimming but being carried away on the waves. I barreled toward the very end of my old life, flowing seamlessly into the start of my new beginning.

Where the old Aria had died, now replaced with this hollow version.

I watched those events unfold, each piece of my life building to the crescendo that had left my soul in tattered pieces beneath this glamor.

Children danced in the streets beneath the bursts of fireworks in the sky, a display lit in honor of my tenth birthday.

From my tower window, I watched with my silver wings drawn close, longing gripping my heart. With each burst of red and gold fireworks, shrieks of joy filled the air. I observed absentmindedly as they danced with shimmering fire sticks, chasing one another amid playful protests and laughter. Their small black wings carried them aloft, careening gracefully through the revelry.

"Aria?" my mother's voice came softly from behind.

My gaze lingered on the celebration for a few beats longer before I peeled my eyes away, locking on my mother. I forced a small smile, my gaze roaming over her face, searching for any sign that she was drifting again, slipping from reality and into the deep blue of her mind. Her gaze was distant, but clearer than it had been in days. I noted the artificial flush of rouge on her cheeks, the same color painted across her wan lips.

My mother might have been beautiful, once. Some still considered her to be, but I always imagined she was beautiful in the way one of my dolls was beautiful: painted, poised, and utterly hollow inside.

"Are you ready?" she asked softly, her eyes scanning my blood red gown. I slid off my seat on the windowsill, walking over to the mirror to take in my reflection. My long, unruly hair had been combed and tugged into a coronet on my head, my scalp still tingling from the abuse inflicted by the nimble hands of my lady's maid.

The dress I wore was crimson, layered with silk ruffles of deep golds and burned oranges, all tapering into a flaming red hem. The gown looked to be crafted of fire, marked entirely by my father's gift. Made to represent the magic   he hoped I would inherit tonight.

The symbolism and hope made the gown feel all the heavier, weighted down with expectation.

I hated the color.

They were our royal colors, but it never suited me. My hair was more white than gold, my skin flushed cool. My silver wings always stood out so starkly against the brassy gold, their delicate iridescence clashing. My mother stepped behind me, and I met her gaze in the mirror.

"What if I fail?" I said softly. It was a stupid question born of fear, a question I already knew the answer to. I didn't seek truth by asking it but rather comfort in her reply.

My mother flinched, her blue gaze darting behind us, where the handmaidens shuffled about in the shadowed room. When her gaze swept back to meet mine, it was fractured. Tears lined her lids, silver and bright. She was afraid, but not for the same reasons I feared the strike of midnight.

"If you fail, he will kill you." She didn't mince words, the directness in her tone startling me. My mother had always been soft, attentive, and caring, but as my birthday approached, something had shifted within her.

It was as if all the years of abuse and sorrow had finally broken her, now that she stood mere paces away from the finale. If I did not inherit both my mother's and father's magic tonight, my mother would be forced to produce another child. She would endure ten more agonizing years of being this child's everything—another night of anxious pacing as the child stood where I now stand, waiting to learn if their creation was a success or a devastating failure.

And if I inherited magic... my mother would be relieved of her duties as a mother. I would become my father's ward, being passed off into the care of his many governesses and trainers to shape my magic and my body into the weapon he always planned for me to be. My mother would be free to crumble into the despair she had long since fought off, only for my benefit.

I wanted to kick and scream and fight against the inevitable separation, to cling to my mother's skirts like a small child and weep. But... she had distanced herself for months now, no longer catering to my every whim or indulging me as she used to. And I had begun to feel less like her daughter and more like a burden she was no longer strong enough to bear.

I knew my disappointment and fear were plainly written on my face, yet she paid no heed. I watched my mother step away, murmuring softly with her lady-in-waiting, Amabel. Shifting my focus back to my reflection, I saw my eyes dim as I stared at the stranger in the mirror.

I drew in several slow, deep breaths, before plastering an easy smile on my face, set beneath two blank eyes.

Even as I turned away and allowed the party to lead me from my chambers, I fostered a small spark of treasonous hope I would fail.

At midnight, beneath the three full moons of my birth night, I longed for the magic to remain absent from my veins. I thought of the children in the streets as I followed my mother to the great hall. Of their cries of joy, their playful demeanor was born only from a life of low expectations and ease.

If I failed, if magic skipped my bloodline, then my father's machinations would have all been for naught. He would cast me aside as a failure. He might strike me dead tonight... or he might hesitate in his rage, and I could flee.

I could flee and he wouldn't have cause to pursue me. Why would he, when I was a failure anyway? I could fly until my wings could carry me no further, and then I might be free. I only felt a small stab of sorrow when I thought of leaving my mother here, at his mercy. But I thought of the distance growing between us, the way I had begun to feel less like a daughter and more like a job she was desperately ready to quit, and I swallowed around the sorrow.

How my faithless heart prayed for just that one moment before the doors to the hall opened before me, midnight would pass and I would remain the same. That magic would refuse to enter my veins, would refuse to surface for my father's gain.

I offered the small prayer up to the fates, begging for this last chance to be free of this life.

To be free of him.

I stood to my father's left, tucked a few paces behind his mammoth throne of black marble. Three *serpenttus daemonium* circled my father's feet, their leathery bodies and whip like tails twisting as they paced at the foot of his throne. My father holds a certain love for these particular demons, as one might love a common house cat. Their slitted nostrils twitched, scenting the air, as black saliva dripped from their rows of needle-like teeth.

My eldest brother, Perceval, sneered down at the puddles of drool by his boot, glaring at the hungry demons. "Shall we send Aria to fetch your pets some dinner, Father?"

My father glanced up at Perceval from where he lounged in his throne. "Perhaps I'll send you to retrieve a rag from the laundress so you can mop up their drool, if it bothers you so much."

I hid my smile in the sleeve of my gown, averting my eyes from Perceval's white face before he caught my gaze. It was never good to be in his line of sight when he was slighted; he had a tendency to lash out at whoever was closest.

I turned my attention back to the mingling crowd below with mild interest. My father had sequestered me away for most of my life, never allowing me to attend any formal events until tonight, but I had more than enough practice at my governess's behest. I kept my chin level, eyes disinterested, and my tongue clenched tightly between my teeth.

A fallen princess did not speak unless first spoken to, and even then only under the supervision and direction of the king or the heir apparent. So I did just that, and I was eternally grateful to the goddess that all addresses in my direction merely demanded a small dip of my chin or a saccharine smile as a response.

It was not lost on me, however, how drastically my position in this court would change after tonight. My father had finally done what the entire continent had believed impossible—sired a child with an archangel. A practice that had been illegal until it became the only way for the fallen to break the treaty forced upon them at the end of the dark war.

When the High Witch had called for light and dark to mingle within the soul of one being, for death and life to live in harmony, a near impossible task made Alexandret Alvar's curse a death sentence. Until now.

Until me.

I watched the crowd coalesce in the hall, their soft murmurings flowing with the lilting orchestra in the corner until it all sounded like the same song. Everyone wore the royal colors in honor of my birthday. Beneath the candlelight, the crowd looked like a gilded river of blood, snaking through the black marble room.

My eyes snagged on the clock above the throne room doors, watching the minutes tick by to midnight. Each hour passed heightened the anxiety in my veins, dampening my palms and quickening my heartbeat. I only hoped my father couldn't sense it.

"Aria, this is Duke and Duchess Ashford of Ilenora, and their son, Lord Kellen." My father's deep voice sent a jolt through my body, and I snapped my gaze to the three figures kneeling before us. They rose at the dismissive wave of my father's hand, offering me tight-lipped smiles that didn't lighten their cunning eyes.

I dipped my chin in acknowledgement.

I knew of the Ashfords; their Dukedom was located in the northern regions of Arkala, in a small valley in the eastern mountains. Their son I often saw in the halls of the castle. He was two years older than me, and we rarely spoke.

"We wanted to wish you a happy birthday, Princess. And good luck with the ceremony tonight, we are all eager to see what gifts finally present themselves." The duchess grinned.

I forced a smile. "Thank you, Duchess."

The duke pushed his son forward a step. "We hoped to introduce you to our son before your lessons begin tomorrow. The training arena can be brutal, we hope to offer you an ally to help you with the transition."

Kellen's gaze locked on mine, his crimson eyes filled with an open warmth that was so startling my own smile faltered.

He bowed shallowly, his dark hair shifting with the movement. "It would be my honor to assist you in any way I can."

My eyes darted to my father. He dipped his chin, the only sign of approval he would give.

I turned back to Kellen and curtsied. "Thank you, my lord."

My father nodded to the duke in dismissal, and the Ashfords bowed once more before clearing away from the dais.

My father shifted in my peripheral, his gaze sliding toward me. I kept mine fixed on the dance floor below, on Kellen Ashford's retreating form until the glittering crowd swallowed him whole.

"The Ashfords offer you more than a simple alliance with their son."

My throat went dry as I finally peeled my gaze away from the dance floor, my eyes locking on my father's. His face was always so neutral, neither bordering on contempt nor indifference. Blank, void of all feeling. Thoroughly analytical.

It was how he expected all of his children to present as well. My emotions were always as strong as an ocean tide, threatening to drag me under the waves, but I was never allowed to let them break the shores of my features. It would be a dishonor to my father, one would never go unpunished.

"I wasn't aware that such propositions were entertained yet," I replied flatly.

Perceval snickered beside my father, his lofty gaze fixed on a fallen woman fluttering her lashes up at him. "People have been making such propositions for your hand since you were in your mother's womb."

I merely blinked, turning my gaze back to my father as if Perceval hadn't spoken at all. He was my eldest brother in title alone. No fondness existed between us. He was to be the heir to the throne, and I was destined to be his righthand should tonight go in my father's favor, but our relationship was as formal as an advisor to a king.

I had two other older siblings, Benedict—whom I spoke to even less than Perceval—and Orella. Orella had always been my favorite, mostly because she had been the only sibling to pay me any mind as a child. Not to mention that she appeared to be the only one with a sense of humor.

My younger sister, Ralia, was technically closest in age to me, but as she had not yet turned ten, she wasn't out in society yet. She was just as locked away as I had been my entire life, kept in order by a governess in a separate part of the castle. I've seen her only about a dozen times since her birth.

"He speaks the truth," my father replied nonchalantly, his gaze darting after Kellen once more. He moved with ease through the crowd, laughing freely with the other nobles' sons and jesting in a way filled me with an aching longing. What must it be like to move freely?

"And was his proposition one that intrigued you?" Nausea churned low in my gut, but I barely allowed a grimace to coast over my lips.

My father rested his chin on his jeweled fist, examining me once more. "It stands to be seen if the power Kellen Ashford inherited two years ago continues to grow. And if power is compatible with your own, to ensure that the union is strong. I would be a fool to hand you off to anyone whose power didn't rival your own."

My gaze hardened, and I almost felt that invisible collar around my neck now, biting against my skin and held taught in my father's iron fist.

I glanced once more at the clock above the doors.

Four more hours until midnight, until my fate was sealed in blood.

Until I knew if I would be the catalyst for another war, or another failure for my father to cast aside. Just a few more tedious hours of posing atop this dais like a sculpture at my father's side, until the chains he had locked me in at birth would either tighten around me, or if I might have a small chance to break free of them.

Ten minutes to midnight, I stood before the altar far above the gathered crowds in the temple. Moonlight from the three full moons beamed down upon us, a symbol of good fortune and prosperity. I traced my eyes over the carving of the Goddess of Death before the altar, her harsh features limned in silver light.

The High Witch, Corvinna Alcherwynn, stood at the foot of the dais. She wore white robes, her lilac hair gleaming beneath the torch-light. I stared down at her, my heartbeat quickening in my chest at all raw power in her veins. All magic, was contained within her lithe form, held smoothly within her control.

Being close to the High Witch always filled my chest with a buzzing sensation, a being meeting its maker. In more ways than one, she was my true goddess. She orchestrated my conception, placing all the ingredients to the humans' downfall into my father's greedy hands. She led the capture of my mother, daughter of the archangel Mikkael, and heir to the life magic now might flow in my veins.

The key my father needed to bring our people home.

A ripple of power skittered through the room, the darkness in the corners of the chapel thickening. It effectively silenced the onlook-ers, all eyes locking on the High Witch.

When the witch spoke, her voice slithered through the crowd unnaturally, filling our minds as much as it did our ears. "Centuries have passed since we lost the Dark War. Centuries in exile, Arkala's borders reduced to whatever scraps the Alvars deigned to give the fallen in the treaty. For too long, your people have suffered. As have my own." At the mention of her people, the witch paused.

When she spoke again, rage cut through her words like a razor. "Our two kingdoms, brought low by the Alvar lineage and forced to kneel before our lesser, have united as one. I created the treaty for Alexandret Alvar when I believed him to be an ally. The Alvars were fools to betray the Witch Kingdom, and they were fools to bring the Fallen Kingdom to their knees."

Murmurs of agreement, of centuries of rage and hatred, drifted through the chapel. My father tilted his chin, his crimson eyes near glowing in the dim light.

The High Witch raised her arms in the air, her dark skin shimmering in the moonlight. *"This treaty shall hold true and strong through the centuries, barring any further attack against the human empire by the fallen people. Should either party make an attack, the treaty will dissolve and the soil your kingdoms rest upon will rot, laying waste to all of Corvale. This curse will stand until light and dark coexist in the same being, and water mingles in the veins of fire without extinguishing its flame.*

"That treaty, called for a Child of Light and a Child of Dark, a child born to Khalios, the God of Life, and Xerexes, Goddess of Death. Such a child has never been allowed to live, a being born of both lineages with the ability to harbor death and life within their veins. Alexandret Alvar believed it to be an impossible key to this curse, believing that he had built his new world on a foundation that could not crumble." The witch turned her luminous silver eyes to me, stepping away to leave me beneath the weight of the crowd's gaze behind her. Crimson and obsidian black eyes filled with varying degrees of awe and pride, rage and injustice, as they stared up at my small frame. I was but a child, yet they looked upon me as if I were more.

I nearly buckled under the weight of all hope, all those expectations. But my gaze locked on my father's, and I held my chin high.

And I selfishly clung to my last shred of hope that I was not this miracle child, this salvation, for my people. How I longed to sink into the floor and melt away from here.

"I call upon Khalios and Xerexes to bless this child, and to bring our peoples home!" the High Witch bellowed in a voice that was anything but human, the darkness in the corners of the room leeching into her palms, thickening the air.

Fireworks lit up the sky again, and my eyes darted toward the golden display.

I wanted to be there, under the stars. Deep within my coward's heart, I begged the fates to let me be normal. To let me go.

The clock struck midnight, every toll of the bell ricocheting through my bones.

The room held its collective breath as silence settled once more.

I welcomed the pressure in my chest as I refused to draw in air. And I waited. Not a spark, not a thrum, not so much as a flicker of power stirred in my fingertips. I slowly released my breath, afraid to feel the relief welled behind the damn in my soul. My eyes locked on my father's, expecting to find rage and horror, but… he was calm. *Smiling*.

And that was when I felt it.

Not a tingle or a flutter, but a roar in my gut. Like a swirling wildfire trapped in the pit of my being. It felt as if I had swallowed kerosene and set fire to my innards. My veins *burned*.

I opened my mouth to scream and fire billowed out on a torrent. The flames were violet, burning the same purple as my irises and the color of my veins beneath my pale skin. They tore through the night sky in a burning display, to slam into an iridescent ward. The flames spiraled around the ward, swirling through the dome to find an escape. There was none to be found.

The blood drained from my face, my breathing escaping in ragged pants as I tried to draw the flames back into my body. They still raged on, racing toward me now. I opened my mouth to scream, but… I felt the heat, nearly searing my skin, but there was no pain. I looked down to find the flames swirling around my arms, weaving between my legs, recognizing me as its place of origin.

I gulped down air, calming my racing heart, and the flames responded to the shift in my fear. They dwindled, reduced to little more than a glow beneath my skin once more.

The only sound for several heartbeats were my ragged breaths. My eyes locked on the witch, and she dipped her chin as she approached me.

Held within her slim hands was a small, white dove. I had prepared myself for this part, over and over in my head, but I couldn't help the pinprick of tears behind my eyes. I loathed myself for them, swallowing thickly to press them back into my bleeding heart before my father saw.

The small bird struggled as the witch held the creature down on the stone.

I bit my tongue as she raised a jeweled blade, piercing the bird's heart.

The screech that escaped its small beak ripped a hole in my heart. That desire to fail, to have failed to inherit the magic of my mother's lineage, died with the dove. As I watched, the dove's small chest rose once more, fell, and stilled. The witch stepped away, revealing me to the crowd, but I couldn't tear my eyes from the fading light in the dove's eyes.

Instinct drew me near the bird, the small well of blood filling the grooves of Xexeres' alter. With small, shaking hands, I placed my fingers over the wound in the bird's chest. I wasn't sure what I expected, but heat raced to my palms.

Violet filled my veins, lighting my skin. A small glimmering thread of it raced into the bird's still heart.

I watched in mixed horror and awe as the wound in the creature's chest healed. The magic filled the bird's veins, lighting beneath its thin skin until I watched the creature's first few, pulsing beats.

In a flash, the bird launched into the air, flying up through the skylight above. I watched the small creature vanish, my heart pounding so loudly in my ears that I barely registered the applause.

Time seemed to slow as I lowered my gaze to my palms, where small smears of red lingered from the dove's fatal wounds. The applause grew into a roar of weeping and exultation as the fallen aristocracy welcomed their savior.

Slowly, I found my father's gaze, the solitary still figure in the celebrating crowd. His crimson eyes held mine, a cold smile twitching at the corners of his lips. And, in that moment, I could have sworn I felt that invisible collar around my neck tighten.

Chapter Two

10 Years Later

"Please, Your Royal Highness. I didn't mean any harm." The whispered plea echoed off the vaulted ceilings. I looked down the dais at the crumpled form of the male before us, his wings bent grotesquely on his back. He pressed his sweat slick brow to the floor, his body wracking with fear and pain.

The only sound for a long moment was the steady drip of blood from his broken wing, splattering on the floor. The black marble, run through with thick veins of red, concealed the pooling blood beside him.

The injury must've been excruciating.

The candelabras on the pillars flared, the male flinching at the sound of the rising flames. I stood to the left of my father's throne, watching as he tapped his jeweled fingers along the arm rest casually; a cat toying with its prey.

My father's tapping stopped abruptly, and he leaned forward in his throne. "We have been searching for you for quite a while, Cormac Tywyrn. You have given my men more trouble than your pathetic life is worth." His crimson eyes raked down the sniveling male's form, distaste twisting his mouth. "When our source informed Captain Ashford that you were a high-ranking member of this supposed 'thieves' guild,' I expected to be presented with a man who held himself with more dignity than this."

Cormac mumbled something indecipherable into the tile floor.

My father leaned back in exasperation, waving his hands at the shadows by the throne room door. Kellen Ashford strode forward, stooping down to pick up the sniveling thief. The man let out an agonized groan as his wings shifted, the steady drip of blood flowing faster now. "I would suggest," Kellen said softly, patting the male on his shoulder condescendingly, "speaking up this time, if you wish to plead your case."

Kellen stalked away, leaning against the doorframe to the throne room once more. His eyes connected with mine, and white teeth slashed through the shadows in a grin.

I glared at him, just as I felt a small brush against my mental shields. I internally groaned, stepping up to the wall around my mind and leaning against it. I could feel Kellen's presence on the other side. I opened a small crack, just enough for his words to pass through.

Never enough to allow his presence into my mind, to overwhelm my senses.

You look gorgeous in those leathers today, Princess, his voice purred into my mind.

I rolled my eyes. *You should focus on your job, Lord Ashford.*

A soft chuckle coasted down my arms, sending a shiver down my spine. *You can't blame me for being distracted.*

No, but I can blame you for distracting me. I slammed my mental wall down again, ignoring his grin across the throne room as I turned my attention back to the man before us.

"Your Royal Highness, I am not the leader you seek. I merely served them. I don't really know what the leader's true identity is, but I can assure you it was not me," Cormac stumbled through an explanation, his stammering words visibly grating on my father's already thin nerves.

"After hearing you speak, I have no doubt about that. You were, however, close with the leader?" my father mused.

Cormac nodded vigorously. "Yes, yes, I was close to the leader—"

"Yet, not close enough to know their identity or sex?"

Cormac flinched. "Well, no, sir. They're a shifter, no one has ever seen their real face."

My father waved him off. "If you plan to plead for your life, you better offer more than that."

He blanched, his jaw opening and slamming shut as his eyes darted around the throne room. "I... I could lure them out! Say that I had information on our next raid, schedule a meeting—"

My father cut him off with a snarl, the flames on the pillars flaring once more. "Do you really think," he said, his words dripping with venom, "we have not already tried that? My men have been chasing your band of thieves and their leader for two years. The closest we can get to this leader of yours was *you*. We got your name from the last sniveling idiot we picked up, right before the princess," a gesture toward me, "slit his throat in this very room."

Cormac looked nearly ready to pass out as he glanced down at the floor beneath his feet, as if he might spot the bloodstains from the last victim.

My father leaned back in his throne, rubbing the bridge of his nose with his forefinger and thumb. "Do you have anything of use for me, Cormac Tywyrn, or are you just another dead end?"

Cormac's lips quivered, spit dripping down his chin as he fumbled over his words, searching for the answer that might keep the contents of his throat from spilling across the floor. My father waited a generous three seconds before gesturing for me to step forward. "Be done with him, Aria. And next time you and Lord Ashford find it fitting to inform me you have information on the thieves tormenting my people," my father snarled, "be sure you are not mistaken."

My father rose and left the throne room.

Perceval yawned, stretching his arms as he pushed off the pillar he had been leaning against. "What a waste of time."

I rolled my eyes. "Ah, yes, we all know how precious your time is, Perceval. My sincerest apologies for interrupting your... antics."

Kellen had found him in a broom closet with a servant, trousers around his ankles, twenty minutes ago. He was meant to attend a war council meeting but skipped it for a quick tryst with the maid, who looked downright horrified when caught. The tongue lashing he had received from father was honestly pathetic; if it had been me in that broom closet instead of on duty, I would have been beaten within an inch of my life.

But never dear, perfect Perceval.

Perceval glared at me before stalking out, shouldering past a snickering Kellen.

Cormac was sobbing by the time the throne room doors slammed shut.

For a few heartbeats, no one moved, and the only sound was his sniveling in the center of the room. It filled me with distaste, watching this traitor weep for his life mere moments after he had scrambled to disclose the identity of his leader. The guild that had been terrorizing the wealthiest neighborhoods in Calasera, stealing their goods to sell off in the slums, normally employed highwaymen with more resolve than this.

Or more honor, at the very least.

Kellen pushed off the wall, his slow, swaggering footsteps ringing out in the large hall. I rolled my eyes at his dramatics, walking down the dais to meet him. Kellen pulled Cormac to his feet once more before he looked up at me, his crimson eyes latching on to mine. Awaiting the command.

I sighed, dipping my chin in agreement, and watched as Kellen's silver magic slithered free from his palms. It slipped into the man's ear like a thread. Cormac let out a muffled sob, a small plea, before his face went entirely slack. His eyes, once nearly black, lit silver from within. Kellen cringed at whatever he saw in his mind, and with a flick of his wrist, he severed something vital within the man's head.

Cormac's lifeless body swayed and flopped forward like a rag doll, collapsing in a heap. Dead before his body even hit the floor.

I snapped my fingers, setting the body ablaze with violet flames. I watched for a moment as tendrils of Kellen's silver power danced among the fire, our magic twining together in keen, curious spirals. I drew the flames back into my veins, leaving the body in a neat pile of ashes as we left the throne room.

"Where are you off to today, Princess?" Kellen asked cheerfully, as if he hadn't just shattered a man's mind mere seconds ago. He slipped his hands into the pockets of his long jacket, tossing me a sideways glance.

I ran my fingers through my hair, twisting it in a loose bun at the nape of my neck and tying it off with a few pins I'd tucked into my pocket. "Seeing as I have completed all of my duties to the crown today, I'm off to enjoy my afternoon."

"Do you maybe want to—"

"Nope."

Kellen pouted in my peripheral. "You don't even know what I was going to ask."

"Whatever it was, I'm not interested." I smiled sweetly.

"It involves tea and pastries."

"Bribery? You're so transparent, Kellen. I'm not going to the castle guard meeting with you."

He turned to walk backwards before me, clasping his hands in supplication. "I beg you, don't leave me here alone."

"You'll be fine!"

"You don't know that."

I snorted. "I am certain that you'll get through it. It's only two hours."

"I think I might die."

"If you die sparring with the castle guards, then you'll deserve your death."

Part of Kellen's duties at court involved lending his expertise to aid in training the castle guards, something he loathed. It wasn't that they were bad per se... not on the same level as the warrior training Kellen received his entire life in Illenora. His family kept to the ancient way, operating as more of a warrior clan than a modern city, and his skill was undeniable.

Kellen stopped walking suddenly, and I nearly slammed into his chest. "I beg you, come and entertain me."

"Stop pouting, it isn't very noble of you."

"Fine, if I can't convince you to entertain me, how about you meet me for dinner tonight?"

I cringed internally. "I'll be getting home pretty late..."

"A drink?" he persisted, his eyes scanning mine.

There it was, that small glint of... *something* in his gaze. Eager-ness? Longing? Whatever it was, I shrank from it quickly.

"Can't tonight, Kellen, I'm sorry!" I cut around him, jogging down the hall toward the open window at the end. The breeze off the ocean filled my nose, and I smiled as my wings unfurled from between my shoulder blades.

"Have fun!" I called lightly over my shoulder as I leapt up on the windowsill.

"I hate you," Kellen quipped back.

"No, you don't!" I laughed before I spread my arms out and fell off the side of the castle.

My favorite way to visit Calasera was from far above. The capital city was nestled between the foothills of the eastern mountains and the rocky coast of the Paramana Sea. The castle, perched atop a cliff high above the city, had an eastern side jutting out over the rough, dark ocean. Every window offered breathtaking views of the jagged coastline with its ceaseless crashing waves and the shimmering cityscape spread out in the valley below.

Still, I preferred viewing the world from way up here, keeping everyone in the capital at a distance. Few fallen choose to fly through the valley, instead spiriting away their wings and enjoying their time walking through the crowded city streets. When the city reaches the boundaries of the eastern mountains, flying becomes essential as paved streets give way to buildings and homes carved into the solid gray rock of the mountainside. Only accessible to those with wings.

Many of my father's inner circle live in mountain top estates, preferring the drafty, dark stone buildings to the manors that line the upscale neighborhoods beyond the castle. The truly elite preferred to live far away from civilization.

I, however, hated our mountaintop manor and praised the Goddess Xerexes that we rarely visited. It was cold, dark, and silent in a way that has less to do with peace and more to do with isolation.

I watched as the landscape below shifted, as the glimmering upper-class neighborhoods and markets gave way to the grayer portions of the city that line Calasera's northernmost side. Mansions turned to small homes, morphing to apartments until finally dissolving into rundown shacks. I banked higher, ducking between the clouds to conceal my presence.

My wings were the only silver wings in the city. On the continent, assuming there weren't other secret half-fallen half-angel children hiding about. It made me stick out like a silver beacon in a part of the city where a princess was not supposed to dwell.

I circled the slums, ensuring I was truly alone before finding the small house near the fish markets. Portions of the home's sun-bleached, green-tiled roof were disintegrating from decades of strong weather and neglect. The rainy months were approaching, and I wasn't sure this roof would make it another season without major leaks seeping through.

I added it to my mental list of things to fix before landing softly in the small garden in the backyard. I retracted my wings immediately, hiding deep within my heavy black hood and cowl, obscuring my features completely.

Slipping through the backyard, I pushed open a rounded wooden door into the cramped hallway of a tidy kitchen. The scent of lemons and herbs wafted off the stove from a lower simmering pot as I walked past the wood burning stove. My eyes strained to focus past the candle lit kitchen into the dimly lit living room beyond, scanning for movement.

A growl started, deep and throaty from the dingy foyer beyond the staircase. I rolled my eyes, leaning against the counter and helping myself to a pastry left on a chipped plate.

"You're not funny," I called out in a sing-song voice, biting into the pastry as I squinted into the shadows.

A massive black shape prowled forward, stepping into the beam of sunlight streaming in from the curtained windows. A wolf, larger than any I'd ever seen in the wild, glowered up at me through large, golden eyes. In a blur of movement, the wolf shifted, and Rhea stood in its place.

Short black hair remained from her wolf form, now curling thickly just above her shoulder and shaved on one side. Delicately arched ears peeked through her curls, and small braids pulled her fringe away from her up-tilted, golden eyes.

She leaned forward, snatching the pastry back with a feral growl. "Don't you have better pastries in that fancy castle of yours, *Princess*?"

"Please don't call me that," I groaned, Kellen's face flashing in my mind. I shoved the image away, handing the rest of the pastry off to Rhea.

She shoved it in her mouth, eyeing me curiously. "Who got under your skin?"

I gave her a deadpan stare. "No one. Everyone." I shook my head, swinging my satchel up on her counter. "Do you want your shit or not?"

Rhea didn't even glance at the pack. "Is it that hot friend of yours?"

I glowered, tugging the straps of the bag open. "No."

"Oh, so it totally is. What's his name again? Kelly?"

"Kellen." I sighed. "And I'd rather not talk about it." I'd rather not talk about the sudden shift in our relationship, a friendship morphing into something that I wasn't sure I wanted.

Rhea rolled her eyes, finally turning her attention to the pack.

I pulled out canned foods, jars of medicine, loaves of bread, and bags of dried meat. I raided the castle stores as often as I could without being noticed, smuggling as much as I could to Rhea. Being trapped in the slums of Calasera was a death sentence; you'd never get a reliable job living here. Not an honest one, anyway.

Rhea gave me an appreciative smile as she looked over the goods. "As always, you don't—"

"Have to do this, I know. It's been nine years, don't you think you'd hand over that last shred of pride and say 'thank you' by now?"

She rolled her large eyes, slinking around to the kitchen. Rhea rummaged through the cabinets, producing a wine bottle and two mismatched cups a moment later. She poured the red liquid in each glass, filling it nearly to the brim before passing it over to me. With a small, classless clink of our glasses, we both took a deep drink. "Thank you."

I gave her a small smile, taking another sip of the sweet wine.

"I'm assuming you're also here with some news?" Rhea looked at me expectantly.

I grimaced. "Yeah, we caught one of your guys. Kellen executed him less than an hour ago."

"Ah, fuck. Who was it?"

"Cormac Tywyrn."

Rhea rolled her eyes. "He was a stupid, arrogant bastard. I should have turned him down when he asked to join."

I sank onto her worn, faded green couch. "He didn't give up any identifiable information about you. As always, you're just some shifter that no one can ever nail down."

"I'm sure that pissed your father off." Rhea snickered.

I fiddled with the wineglass, staring up at the hairline cracks tracing across her ceiling. "I'm sorry I had to kill him."

"Don't be," Rhea said, swinging sideways into one of the cushioned chairs across the coffee table. "It isn't like you did it for sport. That honor would belong entirely to your bastard of a father."

I shot her a warning glance, but she merely raised a brow and took a long sip from her glass.

"As if you don't agree," she muttered.

It wasn't a question about whether I agreed my father was, in fact, a bastard. It was more the overwhelming discomfort that grew in my chest when I acknowledged anything negative about him. As if the air in Calasera had ears, and it would carry all my damning words back through the castle corridors.

Even if simply being here was breaking more than enough rules to water down the dishonor of uttering insults about him.

"Was he working for you when we found him?" I asked.

Rhea sighed, running her long fingers through her hair. "No. Cormac was out on his own. He went out to rob a few of the drunken aristocrats the other night after I had already sent out the order to guild to lie low. I knew your father's men were circling the streets in packs, and it wasn't safe."

"I can't blame him, not wanting to go hungry." Gods, I hoped he didn't have a family at home. I didn't have the nerve to ask. My heart ached at the thought, a dull, useless throb in my chest. There wasn't anything I could do about the starving people here. I was   as much at the mercy of my father's wrath as they were.

"I can. It was moronic."

"It was desperate."

"Desperation turns men into morons."

"Need I remind you," I leaned forward in the chair, planting my feet on the ground and placing my glass on the side table, "how you and I met."

Rhea snorted. "First, I was fourteen. Second, and most importantly," she pointed her glass at me, a lopsided grin tugging at her lips, "I would have kicked your ass if you didn't pull out those flames of yours."

I laughed, settling back against the couch. I could still see that day if I closed my eyes for a moment. Rhea, scrawny and covered in filth, unwittingly trying to lift the coin purse of the Princess of the Fallen in the market streets. In her defense, I was out of the castle when I wasn't supposed to be, and there wasn't any way she could have known who I was.

"I'm not so sure about that. All it would have taken was a single shout to get the attention of everyone in the market. There would have been a riot."

Rhea snorted. "That never would have happened. Even after you won and I took off running, you *chased* after me. You and I both know your father would've kicked your ass if he found out where you were."

"He would've kicked my ass if I returned with an entire bag of gold missing!"

"It's your fault for roaming the streets of the slums with gold coins."

I threw up my hands in exasperation. "In your words, I was fourteen!"

"And your street smarts have come a long way since then, love," Rhea said. "Mostly because of me, of course."

I laughed, my chest feeling lighter than it had when I flew here. "Either way, I won my coin purse back and somehow made a friend in the end. I wouldn't have changed it for anything."

Even with the risk her friendship brings, I wouldn't take a moment of the last nine years back. Rhea's life had been so vastly, startlingly different from the life I had grown to hate in the castle. I had everything I could ever need, yet nothing that I ever truly wanted. But Rhea... she fought for everything she needed, yet she was far happier than any of the miserable courtiers that schemed beneath my father's nose. Happier than any member of my family could ever dream of being.

Rhea was the one choice I made for myself, clinging to a friendship that never should have been, and I would sooner die than give her up. In more ways than one, this felt like my true home.

She was the only one who ever saw me for who I was, not what I could offer her.

Rhea gave me a false pout, her golden eyes widening. "Aw, stop being so sentimental. You can't be that drunk yet."

I grinned and finished my first glass, staring into the embers still flickering in the fireplace. Summer was creeping to an end, and the first crisp fall air had already drifted in off the eastern mountains after sunset. With half a thought, I lit the fireplace in a blaze of violet flames.

Rhea gave me a small, grateful smile. "Do you know if our be-loved king has any other leads on the guild?"

I shook my head. "He isn't even close to deducing that it's you, Rhea. He's gotten close with some of your associates, but the moment he catches one, he's enraged to discover   you've evaded him again. Or they kill themselves in prison, or somehow escape, the en-tire thing has him fuming beyond belief, but he has no real leads on your guild. You know…" I trailed off, hesitating as I debated adding more.

Rhea loosed a sigh. "Let's hear it." She set her glass down on the table between us, raising her brows.

I toyed with the tassels at the end of the thread-bare throw blan-ket beside me. "I could get you a job in the castle—"

"They would never allow a half-elf half-fallen shifter to work there. If anything, they'd want to kill me, despite your recommenda-tion based on my work ethic. Any other brilliant ideas?"

"I could pull a few strings, move you out of the slums—"

"And leave everyone here that now depends on me to starve?"

"Yes."

Rhea raised a brow. "That's cold."

"That's life. You need to look out for yourself."

She sighed, throwing her head back and massaging her temples. "I am looking out for myself, Aria. I also happen to be in the position to look out for others here, too. I started an entire godsdamned guild of thieves—"

"Yes, you surround yourself with criminals to rob the rich and feed the poor. You're very noble."

Rhea sat up, her golden eyes sharpening. "You have no idea how fucking difficult it was to start, Aria. To scrounge together every so-called criminal—"

I threw up my hands. "You're right, I'm sorry. That was a low blow. I just…" I sat up, placing the pillow in my lap. "I worry about you." I gestured to the cracks above us for emphasis.

Rhea's eyes trailed up to the ceiling, cringing. "Yeah, I need to fix that."

I sighed and abandoned the loose thread I had been toying with. "I hate this."

"It's life, Princess. If you hate it, change it."

I laughed harshly. "I wish."

Rhea glanced sidelong at me. "You could, you know."

I only shook my head. This wasn't the first time she and I talked like this, fantasizing over all the different shades we'd paint the world if given the chance. Rhea believed I could seize control, and I merely laughed, rubbing my neck and the invisible collar that always tugged me back into submission.

We sat in comfortable silence, Rhea refilling our glasses, drinking and contemplating all the troubles our short lives had already thrown at us. And as I flew home that evening, I watched the landscape far beneath me shift away from the crumbling slums, flowing toward middle and upper-class neighborhoods in nearly crystal-clear lines. It was jarring, watching Rhea's world fall behind me as I flew into my gilded cage, resting at the top of the city.

Chapter Three

"I like when your attention is on me, Princess," Kellen goaded. Sweat gleamed along his brow, his crimson eyes bright with exertion. He flipped the blade in his hands, watching my every move like a predator.

I didn't risk rolling my eyes, knowing that taking my gaze from him for even a moment would be a mistake. Kellen knew every button to push, every small thing to say or do to distract me enough to land the killing blow. Even if his flirtatious taunting made me want to throw my knife at his smirking face.

"Doesn't it bother you that I only give you attention when I'm pointing my sword at you?" I smiled sweetly, taking a few carefully placed steps to my right. He followed the movement, the lines of his powerful body shifting beneath his leathers.

His lips spread into a feral grin. "Quite the opposite. I prefer your attention when you're covered in sweat and aiming to bury a knife in my chest. I find it oddly flattering." He winked, and I lunged.

Our blades collided with a ring of metal, our breaths mingling in one exhale before I pushed off the blades and spun away. He didn't miss a beat, swiping his blade toward my side. I blocked with my own, following with a low strike he easily dodged. We danced around the training arena, kicking up dirt in small clouds of dust as we circled each other.

After a decade of training together, we had become nearly equal in skill. When one of us feinted, the other barely flinched, instinctively preparing to counter a strike from the opposite side. Every step and every calculated move was all too familiar. This was the birthplace of our friendship, endless hours trying to best the other during training. He morphed from a mentor to my greatest competition these past ten years.

He was the only one that pushed me to be better, to fight harder. To train late at night when I was alone just so I could find a new way to undermine him the following day.

He picked up his speed, coming toward me in a flurry of metal and rage that I smoothly deflected. Sweat beaded along my brow as I wholly focused on each blurring movement of his blade, each step of his feet as he advanced relentlessly toward me, until—

Until my back pressed against stone.

With his blade resting at my throat, a satisfied grin settled on his face. He clucked his tongue, leaning in close, the smell of sweat and dirt barely concealing the scent of his skin.

"I win this time, darling."

"You're so sure about that?" I smiled sweetly, my eyes flicking down between our bodies.

His gaze followed, his grin only growing when he found my dagger pressed against the soft leather of his inner thigh, right near his groin. He dragged his eyes back up to mine. "Ah, then no one wins here."

"No one? You don't think I could kill you in this position? One small slice and you'd bleed out."

"Not before I spilled your throat on the ground."

"I suppose whoever made the killing move first would be the winner, then."

He loosed a breathy laugh. "So bloodthirsty and practical, all in the same breath."

"Would you two either fuck or get out of the ring?" Perceval's voice called from behind.

Kellen lingered for one second longer before pulling away. He sheathed his sword down his back, walking out of the training ring in a few powerful strides. I followed moments later, sheathing my blade and sticking my tongue out at Perceval as I passed. Perceval gave me a distasteful glare before stepping into the ring, followed shortly by Orella.

Ralia and Benedict reclined on one of the amphitheater benches outside the ring. They only deigned to enter and train when either our father or their tutors were overseeing practice. Benedict had his eyes glued to a large tome in his lap and hadn't so much as looked up in the two hours since his 'training' had begun. Ralia lay on the bench beside him, her eyes closed blissfully in the sunlight. I slid down next to her, nudging her foot over as I reclined to watch.

The age gap between us all was wide, with Perceval being the oldest at one hundred and fifty. Orella followed half a century later, Benedict another four decades after that. I came a little over forty years after Benedict, followed five short years later by Ralia. All of us were half-siblings, born to different mothers. My father never claimed a queen, instead taking various fallen women as he saw fit and only elevating them to the status of a declared mistress if they ever bore him a child.

All except for my mother, that is.

My eyes flicked to the west wing of the castle in the distance, my mother's tower a white pillar against the blue sky, guilt twisting low in my gut. I didn't make time to see her this morning, waking up late after drinking far too much wine the night before. I wonder if she bothered to get out of bed today, or if she had merely rolled over and refused to greet the sun when I didn't show up with her morning meal.

"How's that going, by the way?" Ralia's soft voice cut through my thoughts. I peered down at her, her dark hair splayed over the bench. She shaded her obsidian eyes with a hand.

"How's what going?" I replied absently. I leaned back on my elbows, closing my eyes against the glaring sun.

"Your courtship… ?" she trailed off as if it were the obvious conversation point.

I started, "What courtship?"

Ralia rolled her eyes. "With Ashford?"

"We aren't courting."

"No," Benedict chimed in lazily, flipping a page of the book in his lap, "they're not courting, they're only fucking, Ralia."

I choked. "We aren't doing that either. Not that it would be any of your business if we were."

Ralia blinked up at me before settling back against the bench. "Why?"

"Why isn't it any of your business?"

"No," she said slowly, "why aren't you fucking or courting yet?"

Because falling in love with Kellen felt a hell of a lot like a wild animal accepting their cage. Even if it wasn't his fault that Kellen's family placed him in the pool of suitors upon my birth, vying for the chance to marry into the royal family. Even if Kellen wasn't the reason I felt caged and trapped in this life to begin with, he was still a male that my father would happily hand my leash over to in the form of marriage. Something deep inside of me rebelled against this idea of another fallen male inserting himself into my life, forcing me into submission like every other noble woman before me.

I wasn't stupid; I knew that the suitors were circling me at court like sharks. Waiting for my father to give the word, to unleash a string of courtships and negotiations to find the match that would best serve him. I was still young, and therefore I had maybe another five years of freedom before I was sold off to the highest bidder. When that time came, perhaps it would even be easier to let myself fall in love with Kellen, to maybe seek a kernel of happiness in a situation that was otherwise beyond my control.

But... another, larger part of me wants to gnaw at the bars of my cage. To rebel in whatever small way I can. It was the part of my soul that clung to my friendship with Rhea like a lifeline, that stared off at the ocean and wondered what it would be like to simply fly away and leave it all behind.

Keeping Kellen at arm's length felt like exerting control in a world where I had none.

"Because I'm not interested," I drawled, stretching out my limbs under the heat of the sun. "Besides, I don't need to worry about courtships right now. Orella still hasn't had a consistent suitor." It was a flimsy cover, but the only one I had. Fallen nobles typically married off their daughters one at a time, and while there wasn't an explicit rule against skipping an elder daughter over for her younger sibling, I prayed it would be years before father found an advantageous match for her.

"Well, if I were you, I'd be grateful he was an option."

I choked on a laugh. "I should be *grateful*?"

Ralia nodded solemnly. "We might not all be so lucky."

"Oh, spare me. Kellen Ashford is arrogant and entitled, and the only reason his parents propositioned Father was to further their own cunning agenda. Marrying into the royal family is all that the Ashfords have wanted for centuries."

Ralia chewed on her lower lip, cocking her head to the side as she examined Kellen from across the arena. I followed her gaze, watching as he stood over the match between Orella and Perceval. Besides serving his mandatory ten years in the fallen army, his commander recently assigned him the task of overseeing our training, whenever our private tutors were indisposed. I watched his cunning red eyes as he examined each move they made, noting each moment of weakness for them to improve upon once the match had finished.

"I think he is kind," Ralia said after a moment.

I wanted to deny, but found that I couldn't force words from my mouth. He was kind, our friendship growing through the years almost too easily. It made it that much harder to push him away.

I pushed my hair from my face and stood up. I leaned against the chains around the arena, peeking up at Perceval just as Orella disarmed him, his blade clattering to the ground. I snickered, a sound that did not go unnoticed. Perceval spat in the dirt, pacing toward me.

"Something funny, you half-breed bitch?"

I crossed my arms, smiling sweetly. "You left your right side open that entire time. I find it funny that Orella didn't bury a blade in it."

Orella straightened, flipping her golden braid over her shoulder. "I did not wish to maim His Highness's body and his ego all in one match."

Perceval spun around, swooping up his blade and pacing around the ring once more. "You're claiming you went easy on me?"

Orella crossed her arms, not intimidated by his show of rage. "Hardly, seeing as I won."

He pointed his blade at her chest. "Rematch me."

Kellen cleared his throat. "Aria is right. You left your right open, and you were sloppy with your footwork early on."

Perceval ignored him, his jaw clenched tight as he took up position across from Orella. She yawned blandly, taking a lazy stance and casually holding her blade before her. I watched them spar for a few moments before Kellen stepped in front of me. "Your meeting with your father is in half an hour. Go get cleaned up, you know how he laments when you enter his office smelling like shit."

"You think I smell like shit?"

Kellen closed the space between us, startling me enough that I took a faltering step, the backs of my knees pressing against the bench. He leaned in close, my heart stuttering in my chest as he inhaled deeply. "I think you smell positively delicious, but I'm nearly certain your father won't agree. He doesn't hold the same biases I do."

Ralia snorted behind us.

I ignored the curling feeling low in my gut as I held his crimson stare, refusing to balk under its weight. I grabbed my leather satchel off the bench, bowed sarcastically to Kellen, and made my way out of the training room. Perceval's bitching resumed, now aimed toward Kellen, but I didn't hear his response.

And I did my best not to look back, not as I felt his gaze on me the entire way out of the training room.

I lingered by the door to my father's study, listening to the muffled voices arguing on the other side. The deep tenor of my father's voice was easy to pick out, as was the cool, feminine one he argued with. The High Witch—Corvinna Alcherwynn. I wasn't at all surprised to hear them bickering in hushed tones; they rarely seemed to agree on anything these days.

She was the only being in this entire godsdamned kingdom that could actually argue with my father and live to tell the tale.

I rapped lightly against the door, abruptly halting their argument. Footsteps on the wooden floorboards approached, and Corvinna opened the door a moment later. The witch's silver eyes were bright, her smooth, brown cheeks flushed. I gave her a nod as I walked into the study.

My father reclined behind his carved wooden desk, the top neatly organized to a point of near obsession. "Aria, how was your lesson this morning?"

I took a seat, glancing back at Corvinna. The witch remained standing, her back rigid and her fists clenched. "Decent," I replied casually as I turned back to face him. He didn't truly care to know, so I didn't elaborate further.

"Corvinna and I have been discussing your progress in training for a few weeks now, and I have decided it is high time you are now a part of these meetings," my father began.

Corvinna paced behind me. "No, you decided you would not win me over to your side, so you called her in for backup."

My father blinked slowly, as if he were trying to dispel the stirrings of a headache before it could take hold. "I don't need backup, witch. And I think Aria is more than capable of partaking in these discussions and joining in on the war council as our preparations begin."

"Our preparations?" I asked slowly, glancing over my shoulder to find Corvinna chewing on the tip of her sharp nail. It was a nervous habit, standing so at odds to the fearsome being she was. It was so... *mortal*.

"Yes, our war preparations. It is finally time to make our move against the human kingdom."

I stilled, my heart skipping a few vital beats in my chest. He wanted to start the war again. Now, when I had only had my magic for a little over ten years.

For a fallen, that was nothing. I was still a fledgling as far as any magic wielder was concerned. Mastering one's magic had as much to do with age as it did self-control.

"As you might have guessed," Corvinna drawled, finally halting her pacing to stand beside me, "I told your father his asinine plan is only going to ruin everything he's worked so hard for. All because he cannot simply be patient—"

"I have been more than patient, witch, as you will do well to remember," my father said with quiet menace.

My spine straightened at his tone, hands clasping tight to hide their tremor. That tone always preceded a violent punishment, one I had been on the receiving end of far too many times to not heed it for the warning it was.

Corvinna rested her hands on the back of the chair beside me, leaning forward with predatory intent. "We have all been patient. This victory is not yours alone."

I cleared my throat. "May I ask why we must act now?"

They stayed locked in a stare for several trembling heartbeats longer before my father broke first, looking back down at me. "Our people grow restless, Aria. I brought you in here because I thought you'd be more than aware of how vital it would be to act as soon as we can."

"Don't patronize her." Corvinna huffed, resuming her pacing.

"Is there no other way to placate the aristocracy? I understand that no one was satisfied with the loss of land their territories took once we lost the south and the flatlands, but surely they understand that it isn't worth the risk to start the war prematurely."

"It has been two hundred years, Aria. They are eager to see their lands and wealth fully reinstated. And to see the humans driven from our lands like the cockroaches they are." My father's tone was condescending, as if I couldn't possibly understand the reason for the unrest. What was my twenty years of life in the face of their centuries on this plane?

He probably assumed I couldn't grasp the magnitude of the situation. He was sorely mistaken; twenty years has taught me plenty. I know how the aristocracy schemes. I see their cunning eyes and hear the whispered rumors of the Duke of Illenora being favored to take the throne next. The dwindling support for my father's schemes has been more than apparent these past five years alone, and it was no secret that the Elway claim to the throne was only supported because Amaros Thain had failed us in the Dark War.

But I wasn't ready. He had to understand that I simply wasn't able to do what he was asking of me, not yet. So there must be a reason why he couldn't just simply put an end to the scheming, kill a noble bloodline to pull the rest to heel while all of my father's plans took the time they needed to come to fruition.

Boldly, I asked, "Is there a reason why we have to act now? Something I need to be aware of?"

Corvinna peered down at my father when he remained silent. "*Has* something changed?"

My father's jaw tensed, his gaze darting between us before he reclined in his chair once more. "It is time for us to act. That is all either of you need to know."

The witch crossed her arms, arching her brows. "If something has changed, it is in your best interest—"

My father slammed his fist on the desk, rattling the quill in its inkwell. "It is in your best interest to remember your place here in this court, witch."

Shadows grew in the corners of the room, stretching ominously to obscure the sunlight beaming in through the windows. "My place is not within your court, Adriel Elway. It would do you some good to remember who it is you speak to," she replied softly, despite the churning ocean of silver power in her gaze.

This pissing match was going nowhere.

I leaned forward, the movement drawing my father's gaze back to mine. "If you need me to be ready, I will be. Is that all for today?"

The shadows faded so swiftly the sudden burst of sunlight nearly blinded me as it flooded the room. I blinked to clear my vision, carefully avoiding Corvinna's incredulous gaze. My father smiled at me, sharp as a razor. "Yes. And, as I mentioned earlier, I will add you in on our war council meetings as the time comes. Once your part in breaking the curse is over, I'll need your abilities out on our front lines."

I dipped my chin and rose, walking toward the office door.

"Oh, one last thing," my father called after me.

I turned around, raising a brow.

"The Ashfords have asked to host an intimate dinner in honor of your twenty-first birthday at their mountain estate at the end of the week. I'll send an escort to collect you around seven."

Since when do the Ashfords care about my birthday? I merely nodded, finally exiting the office and drawing in a full, steadying breath.

I walked down the hall as calmly as I could manage, despite the burning desire to run filling my limbs. I hoped he couldn't sense my pounding heart or the sweat dampening my palms. Corvinna was right; I wasn't ready yet. The life magic was foreign in my veins, even after a decade of training with it. Fire came naturally to me, but the small drop of water from my mother's heritage… it was unstable. As if it fought against the dark blood in my veins, raging at such an unholy beast trying to command it. It always lashed out, sucking from my own life force when I drew it forth.

And it was so weak, so fleeting, I had little hope the magic would settle into anything close to what I needed to end the curse and still hold on to my life.

Angry footsteps followed me out, and I didn't have to turn to know Corvinna was pacing after me. "Aria Iveliesse Elway, do you truly hate yourself enough to die for his cause?"

My eyes fluttered briefly, but I kept walking. "It would be an honor—"

"Cut the bullshit and look at me." Her taloned hand gripped my arm hard enough to prick the flesh beneath my tunic.

I looked back at her, my jaw clenched. "You know as well as I do, I have no choice."

"You have every choice, my phoenix. Every choice. Do not allow these men to delude you into believing you exist solely for their conquests and vengeance."

"Don't I, though?"

Unadulterated rage contorted her features. "You do not. You were created with a purpose, but you and I both know you have more power in your veins than any of these preening, egotistical men who claim to be your superior. You could overthrow them in a moment."

"That's treasonous, Corvinna. I'd watch what you say in these halls."

She barked a laugh. "I'll scream my thoughts from the highest mountain peak, and they still would not come for my head. They know I would lay waste to their precious city long before they ever reached me with shackles in hand."

I pulled from her grip, shaking off her words and whatever they tried to ignite in my gut. Smothering it, crushing it down with a flash of my mother's face in my mind's eye. "I was created for a purpose, and I am more than willing to bleed for this cause. You, of all people, should understand. You created me, Corvinna... did it never cross your mind I might yield my life to this?"

The witch's face went cold, her lips tightening. I studied her for a moment, wondering at the enigma that was the High Witch. Her vendetta against the humans ran deeper than my father's. The witches yielded their lives and ultimately their entire kingdom during the dark war, betrayed by their human allies at the bitter end.

"If you disagree, why don't you stop him?" I challenged softly.

"I allied myself—"

"Why? Why ally yourself with anyone?" I stepped closer, my jaw tight. "Why not   burn the entire world to ash and claim your vengeance alone? You claim your witches wait for you back home, wherever that is now. Why not call them to come to your aid, and be done with my father entirely? I cannot, for the life of me, understand why you suffer the displeasure of allying with him when you clearly wish to spike his head on our front gates."

I flinched as soft, shuffling footsteps echoed further down the hall, a spike of fear flashing through my core at the thought of being overheard.

"I have my reasons," the witch hissed.

"You're as much a prisoner to his whims as I am."

I was the key to regaining all they had lost. So I wasn't sure why she looked at me like that now, with a glimmer of despair in her eyes, as if I might be worth more than she ever expected me to be.

"You don't have to be," she said softly.

"You created me for one purpose. You don't have the right to rail against my purpose now."

I didn't have the right to want anything more for my life, not when it was never my own to begin with. Not when my life was as intertwined with my mother's fate as her own beating heart. When her existence only continued so long as I stayed in line, ever the obedient child. Not when our growing population and restrictions on trade was creating widespread shortages, our poverty lines blurring until it seemed there was only the aristocracy and everyone else scraping by beneath it.

And the only way to fix everything, to end the suffering of my people, was to fulfill this one purpose. What I wanted couldn't matter, not the way it did when I was a naïve girl who dreamt of a life where I was free of the burden of responsibility.

I walked away, drawing my wings to the surface as I paced toward the open window at the end of the hall. Corvinna didn't follow this time.

I found my mother in the aviary.

The large room had a glass dome for a ceiling, allowing filtered light to beam down upon the lush green foliage. It looked as though my father had sliced a center of the Kaliyah Jungles out and arranged it inside the humid building, laying it in large pots and raised garden beds set between the black and white tile paths.

My mother stood in the center, gazing up at the dome's peak. I observed her for a few moments, taking in her delicate frame draped in a shimmering gray dress. Over the years, her body had lost its soft curves; her shoulders now cut sharply through the fabric, as if she were little more than flesh stretched taut over bone.

Like she were slowly wasting away, decaying while her heart still beat stubbornly in her chest.

Her dress didn't have the same slits in the back to accommodate her wings should she need them; she didn't bother to bring them out anymore. The delicate muscles where the white feathers of her wings met skin were ruined, carved up with rippling scar tissue.

"I did it for you."

I squeezed my eyes shut tight against the memory of my father's voice. That had been his response when I asked him about it one day. I had been so young and innocent, and I thought it would be safe to ask him the question I had been too nervous to voice to my mother.

"Why does Mama have those scars on her wings?"

He regarded me cooly. "So she can never leave us. I did it for you, Aria. A girl needs her mother, after all."

I opened my eyes and made a small noise in the back of my throat to alert my mother to my presence.

She flinched, her lithe muscles tensing. Her gaze pulled away from the peak above us, dragging slowly down to my face.

Her eyes were once the ocean blue of clear water, capturing golden rays in its shallows. Now, they were the murky blue of an ocean during a storm, resting above two permanent dark circles. A small smile tugged at her lips when she recognized me, her body relaxing. "Don't you have training right now?"

I walked toward her, taking a seat on the lip of the raised garden bed. "I had a meeting that ended early, so I thought I'd stop by to see you."

She made a small noise in the back of her throat. "On what business?"

"Can't a daughter visit her mother outside of her normal schedule without a reason?"

"A daughter can, *you* cannot. Everything you do is calculated. If you wished to see me during your training hours instead of waiting for tomorrow morning, I'm sure you have a pressing reason for it."

"Calculated?"

Her eyes dimmed. "Yes, much like your father."

The blow glanced off the armor around my heart I was always so careful to keep intact around her. She didn't really mean it… she had days where she was too lost in her own grief to filter her words.

"Amabel says you aren't eating," I said.

"Amabel needs to mind her own business."

"She is your lady, her business is you."

"Yes, *me*. Not reporting to *you*."

I shifted, perching my hands beside me. "She only cares for you and wishes you would take better care of yourself. Amabel is wise enough to share her concerns with me so I can help."

My mother paced away, her unbound white hair swishing around her shoulders with the movement.

I tried again. "Please eat, Mother. I don't want to supervise all of your meals, but if that's what it takes, I'll clear my schedule three times a day."

"A daughter shouldn't make demands of her mother," she spat.

"A daughter shouldn't have to watch her mother try to starve herself to death."

A daughter shouldn't be responsible for ensuring that her mother's grief and madness didn't consume her whole, but here we were anyway.

My mother stiffened. She cast her gaze to the peak of the dome once more, the tension in her shoulders dissipating. "I will do my best to eat more."

It was all I could hope for. If Amabel kept her word, she would report before I had to take more drastic measures.

I finally followed my mother's gaze.

There, fluttering at the highest part of the glass dome, was a small, white bird. The bird flew against the barrier, desperately searching for a way out. Small thumps sounded, followed by a small, angry screech when the glass didn't give way. When the bird remained trapped in the dome, locked away from the blue sky and the freedom of the breeze.

I drew my eyes back down to my mother, another broken dove locked far away from the freedom of the sky.

Chapter Four

"Y ou're not trying." Corvinna seethed.

Sweat poured down my temples, the heat spiking my temper. It was an uncommonly hot day, the slight chill that had been rolling down the eastern mountains subdued by the relentless sun and the lingering traces of summer. The autumnal equinox was in a month, and it honestly couldn't come quickly enough. I despised training in the summer.

"I am trying," I replied through clenched teeth.

"Then you're trying too hard."

I threw my hands in the air, pacing away to grab a drink from the flagon of water by the wall of the training arena.

"Both things can't be true." I drank the cool water deeply, feeling rivulets trail down the corners of my lips and drip across my heated skin.

"I second the notion you're trying too hard, if you need someone to settle this." Kellen's deep voice came from the arena's darkened doorway. I squinted against the sun, shading my eyes with my hands to make out his form lounging against the wall.

"How long have you been spying on me, creep?"

He straightened, swaggering into the arena with raised brows.

"I'd hardly call watching a training session in a public arena spying."

I glowered up at him. "I'd call it spying when you have no business being here. Your sessions are always in the morning."

And this session was taking place at the miserable after lunch hour, at my father's behest. He nearly tripled my magic training sessions after our meeting yesterday, as if he could simply beat the magic in my veins into submission. His thought process was at least predictable; he beat everything else in his life until it bent to his will, why would this be any different?

Kellen smirked, a shallow dimple appearing in his cheek. "Ah, so you know my daily schedule? I'd say that classifies you as the creep, darling."

I raised my middle finger high above my head as I paced away from him, facing the High Witch once more. "How do I draw on the magic without trying 'too hard?'"

We had been attempting to wield my life magic for over an hour now, to force the full extent of the power to flow through my hands. There were ways to manipulate and multiply magic, things witches had apparently done for thousands of years. Corvinna had compiled a list of them all after the meeting with my father: refracting the magic through a witch glass, channeling it through an amplifier, drinking tinctures and potions to temporarily increase the life magic in my veins.

Despite the promising list, her expression had done little to inspire confidence inside of me. She had read the list and looked at me as if she were listing out desperate, outlandish treatments to a terminal patient.

Nevertheless, we chose to try to funnel it into an amplifier. It had seemed like the most practical of the options, sending the magic through a small, enchanted amulet hoping it would strengthen and contain the life magic. But first, I'd have to draw the ability to the surface, and without the threat of a dying being at my feet, that was proving to be extraordinarily difficult.

I shook off the dark spiral of my thoughts, waiting impatiently for the witch to respond. Corvinna perched on a barrel, her eyes contemplative. "Let it come to you. You've spent ten years trying to force the magic to yield control, like your flames. But it doesn't belong to you the same way your fire does. It isn't going to suddenly bend to your will... you have to coax it out with the water magic in your veins."

"I don't know what that means."

Her eyes flashed. "It means, you irreverent girl, that like calls to like. The magic in your veins is from your archangel lineage, a lineage of ice and water. From beings with shimmering blood and pure intentions, so the mythology goes. Your veins run black, drawing heavily from your father. It's a miracle a drop of life-giving magic entered your veins at all, with how much your fire rages through you. Your water born magic balks at the torrent of flames you carry with you. Show it some of that pure archangel heritage, and it will come to you. Once you draw it out, channel it into this." She pointed a sharp nail at the golden amulet resting on the ground between us.

"In other words, close your eyes and get in touch with your angel blood, Princess," Kellen called, now perched on the railing with his wings fanned wide behind him. I glanced back at him, unable to ignore how the sun gilded his dark hair, drawing out the deep brown and red strands. Or how it glanced off his ebony wings, each feather gleaming a dark-toned rainbow in the sun.

I shook my head, clearing the image rapidly from my mind. I paced over to the edge of the ring, sitting down in a small patch of shade. Pressing my back against the wall, I drew in a few deep breaths and closed my eyes.

The fire was always easy to feel. But the small drop of water, clinging to life in the torrent of flame, was so hard to find. It only rose to the surface when it sensed pain or death, rearing its meek head in answer.

When I was young, long before my father had beat the empathy from my bones, I couldn't stand to see anything in pain. Watching a small creature suffer would reduce me to tears, filling me with the desperate desire to help. So it always felt fitting that the only bit of magic I possessed that was good, rooted in something pure, felt like the fragments of my inner child.

I found it after a few moments of deep breathing, the small thread of golden magic glimmering like the peak of a wave.

I reached for it softly, drawing on memories of the girl I used to be, crying over the broken wings of butterflies. The magic responded, drifting to the palm of my hand, recognizing something familiar in my gaze.

I drew it to the surface, opening my eyes to find my fingertips glowing with the same energy. I ignored everything else in the arena, blocking out Kellen's gaze and the witch's intense stare. I spun the thread of magic from my fingertips, spiraling it in a wave of glimmering gold. It flowed freely at first, building as it searched for the creature that needed help. The life it desired to save.

Instead, I funneled the magic toward the amulet. It arced through the air, glittering in the bright sunlight, and for a moment I thought it would spiral through the amplifier. But the moment the magic touched the cool metal, it recoiled. I watched, deflated, as the thread of gold dissipated, the amplifier lay empty and useless on the ground.

I loosed a groan, looking over at Corvinna. Kellen had taken up a spot beside her, their arms crossed and gazes thoughtful, near mirrors of each other.

"Yeah, you're definitely trying too hard," Kellen said after a moment.

I let out a growl of frustration. "You two are insufferable."

I shot to my feet and stalked out the door.

"Why don't you let me help you relax, Princess." Kellen fell smoothly into step beside me as I entered the castle.

I rolled my eyes, pushing through the wooden doors and into the entrance hall. "If this is some sort of lewd offer, I'll pass."

He placed his hand over his chest, false indignation dripping from his features. "How you wound me with your nonchalance."

I ignored him, pacing up the stairs toward my chambers. I desperately needed a cool bath, the sweat drying down to a sticky film on my body.

Kellen grabbed my arm, halting me in the middle of the staircase. "Come on, Aria. Let me help." All the arrogant, cool joking left his voice. I finally looked up at him, surprised to find a slight pleading edge in his gaze.

I pulled out of his grip, crossing my arms defensively. "Why?"

"Because if you don't get this power under control, you're going to let it kill you."

I glanced around the stairwell, noting the potentially prying ears shuffling past us. "It would be an honor—"

"Cut the bullshit, Aria. There is no honor in death."

I raised my brows. "What a sentiment coming from one of the great warriors of the fallen army. From the future Duke of Illenora, no less." I spun around, holding his gaze. "You should be careful what you say, less the people of this court overhear and think you're standing against our own best interest in this war."

"I fervently support the war efforts, Aria, everyone knows that. Illenora has been one of your father's greatest supporters, and I am proud to call you, the cursebreaker herself, my friend. What you're doing is important."

My gaze hardened. "So you, of all people, would understand the sacrifice that might be needed to see our lands restored."

Or to see that my father's vendetta has been appropriately sated. I support this war for our people, for the sake of our future, but my father is more concerned with his bruised ego and his tarnished crown.

I will happily die to see our people return to their homeland and flourish once more, but I've never been able to make peace with the fact I'd also be dying to support my father's need for tyrannical control. For his bloodlust, his desire to soak the soil of Corvale with the humans' blood in the name of vengeance.

Kellen glowered down at me. "Death is sometimes an unavoidable necessity. We dress it up as an honor to soothe the sting, to remove the brutality of it and to paint it into something grand. The cruel, cold reality is that death is a fucking waste. And your death would be a travesty to this realm, Princess. Let me help you."

I searched his gaze, at whatever lay burning in it that remained unspoken.

I found quickly I wanted to look away, to put distance between our bodies with cruel jokes and jabs at his sentimentality. But I didn't pull away. I didn't look down or draw up a cruel remark meant to smother the flame in his eyes. I allowed myself to feel close to him in a way I had previously deemed unwise.

"Fine."

Kellen's crimson eyes widened in surprise. "Fine? No snarky remark, no scrunched nose at the thought of spending time alone with me?"

"I do not scrunch my nose."

"You're doing it right now."

I became uncomfortably aware of my facial muscles as I

smoothed out my expression. "Do you want me to take my answer back?" I snapped.

His responding laugh tugged at my own lips as I followed him out of the castle, back into the heat of the sun.

"You have got to be kidding me."

Kellen led me down the cliffside behind the castle until we stood before the ocean, where churning waves crashed against the rocky shoreline. With a casual shrug, he shed his gear and set it on a cluster of weathered rocks scattered across the golden sand.

He quirked a brow at me. "What? We used to do this all the time!"

"Yeah, *used to*."

"Back when you *used to* spend time with me!"

I glared up at him. "I've been busy."

"Get over yourself and get in the water, Princess."

I bent down to unlace my boots. "Explain how this is going to help, exactly."

The smile he gave me made my heart beat a little faster. He pulled off his own boots, dropping them in the damp sand. "Your life magic is rooted in water, so…" He gestured toward the expansive body of water before us, as if the rest was self-explanatory.

I snorted, straightening up and tugging off my leather vest, leaving only a thin camisole behind. "You're being far too literal, Ashford. When I was learning how to wield my flames, I didn't take a dive into a pit of fire."

"No," he replied, "but you never struggled to summon your flames. If anything, you've always struggled to contain them."

Fair point. Maybe that was my problem. I saw this part of my soul as something foreign. Maybe it was time I truly embraced it.

Kellen pulled his shirt over his head before he jogged to the shoreline. He didn't hesitate to dive in, vanishing beneath the waves. He emerged a few feet away, slicking his hair back out of his face. "Are you going to stand there all day?"

Never one to be outdone, I unbuttoned my pants and slid them off. Cool ocean air hit my skin, an unintentional moan slipping past my lips. Gods, that felt too good.

Kellen's crimson eyes fell on my body from across the water, and I flushed beneath his gaze. Slipping beneath the waves forced another audible groan from my lips. The cool water felt incredible after a day of training, all the tension leaving my body as I slipped my head beneath the surface. Why had we ever stopped coming here?

Flying down to this small stretch of beach after training had become a ritual for us when we were younger. We'd train all morning, eat lunch, and swim in the ocean before we had to be back inside for our afternoon classes. As we got older, our schedules filled up to a point of bursting, and when Kellen had graduated from his secondary schooling years before me, things changed.

I dipped my chin into the cool water, feeling salt coat my lips as I swam toward Kellen. The small leather slip holding my braid in place fell away, sending my white hair drifting with the waves. "What now?"

"Now, you simply float."

"That was your grand plan? To float in the ocean?"

"My grand plan was to get you wet and naked, the rest is up to you."

I scowled, splashing water in his face. He laughed, floating on his back and swimming several paces away. Leaving me alone in the waves, with only my thoughts as a distraction now.

I floated on my back, squinting against the golden sun, watching the white clouds pass over the sky like puffs of cotton. My body relaxed fully in a way I hadn't expected, feeling the ocean waves gently roll through me.

Drawing in a breath of air, I slipped beneath the surface. The immediate loss of sound, of the crashing waves on the shore and the birds racing along the shoreline, was soothing. My mind went quiet, filled only with the lull of the ocean. I kept my eyes open, the salt a welcome sting as I looked around the blurry, underwater world. The sand was nearly golden and pure, rolling gently in the ocean waves. Small silver fish swam past me in a school, arcing through the waves, the sheen off their bodies blending in with the silver light of the ocean.

I could almost feel it down here, the way my flames receded in my core. Subdued by the water. And there, left in its wake, was a small drop of water. I played with it beneath the waves, feeling it flow between my fingers. I loved this little piece of magic more than

I cared to admit, even if it was weaker than it was supposed to be.

I rolled it over my knuckles like a golden wave before my lungs ached for air. I pushed off the ocean floor back to the surface, breaking through with a gasp. The moment the air hit my lungs, the playful drop of magic vanished, lost to the ocean.

Kellen was seated on the shore, reclining in the wet sand where the ocean foam brushed against his legs. I climbed out of the water, my body feeling uncomfortably heavy after floating for so long. I lay down in the surf beside him, our legs nearly touching as we sat in a comfortable silence.

"I've missed this," he said after a while.

I heard what lingered between his words—*I've missed you.* "I've been—"

"Busy, I know."

I glanced at him sidelong, his eyes fixed on the ocean. "I'm sorry if I've been a shit friend lately."

I felt a small brush against my mental shields, Kellen's presence lingering beyond the walls of my mind. I ignored it, feeling his disappointment as he retreated back into his own head.

I couldn't let him in, not if this conversation was heading where I feared it was.

His features softened as he met my gaze. "You're not a shit friend, Aria. You've been absent, and I've started to wonder if I've done something wrong."

You stopped looking at me like a friend, and you've started looking at me like I'm so much more. "You haven't done anything wrong, truly."

"So why have you pulled away?" His eyes searched mine.

Because I'm afraid I'll start looking at you differently, too. "There's been a lot on my mind, with the life magic being weak and now my father looking to accelerate his plans."

"Why don't you talk to me anymore? Like you used to?"

If I open up, I might fall. If I fall, I lose control. I can't afford to lose any more control. "I'm just tired, Kellen. I promise."

He looked away again, his fingers absently running through the sand between us. I wasn't sure if he saw all I was desperate to leave unsaid in my gaze, but he let me hide behind the weak explanation. "I'm here for whatever you need, Aria. If you need to talk, to fight, or blow off some steam, I'll always be here for you."

I leaned my head on his shoulder, wishing it could be easier. In another life, one where I had the freedom to make my own choices, I might've been free to fall in love with Kellen. But in the fallen court, love was control. Relinquishing your heart was giving up your power. And, as a woman, your freedom.

So I reeled in the warmth in my chest, clamping down on the desire to feel something more than friendship for him. It was safer not to fall. To lock my heart away meant safety in a world that was anything but.

"Do you ever think," Kellen asked slowly, "about our future?"

I stilled. "What do you mean?"

"About our parents' expectations of us, who we'll... who they'll expect us to marry?"

My blood chilled, but I lifted my head from his shoulder as casually as I could. "Nope."

He raised a brow. "You never think about it?"

I always think about it. "I have years before that's a reality."

"What makes you so sure?" he asked cautiously.

"Orella still hasn't been propositioned, Kellen, and she's been courting on and off for years. I've got time." I tried to sound calm, but there was a small tremor working its way through my hands. I checked my mental shields, and sure enough, they were still in place. Gods, it was like he'd been reading my damned mind.

A pained look shot across his face. "Aria—"

I rose to my feet swiftly, a sheet of sand sliding off my bare legs and catching in the breeze. "I've got to get back." I didn't want to hear anything else he might have to say.

"Wait—" He stumbled in the sand as he rose, but I was already tugging on my training gear.

Leather scraped against my damp, gritty skin, and it was by sheer panic and will alone that my pants slid on at all. I rapidly tugged my top on, summoning my wings in a flash of silver. "Thanks for the lesson!"

Kellen looked dumbstruck, his mouth gaping open as if he were about to shout whatever it was he needed to say at me. "Aria—"

But I had already launched into the sky, leaving him as little more than a black speck on the white sand far below.

Chapter Five

After all of my bitching and moaning about the heat, Corvinna moved our sessions to one of the indoor training rooms within the castle the following afternoon. The witch had never been eager to test out my magic inside of a building, which may or may not have been entirely my fault. When I was young and still inexperienced, I had a burst of irritation during one of my lessons and set fire to an entire room in the castle in an instant.

The witch had put out the flames immediately, but I still incinerated everything she had brought with her... including, but not limited to, ancient tomes from the conquered witch kingdom.

She hadn't spoken to me for a month until my father tracked her down in the city and they brawled like they always did. When the witch had returned, I'd burst into tears and thrown myself at her feet, apologizing for the fire, for my powers, for my very existence. She had merely told me apologizing was for the weak and she'd beat me if she ever caught me doing it again. And we had proceeded on with our lessons as usual, as if nothing had ever happened.

Except for the location, of course. We never held lessons indoors, and she rarely brought anything of value to those lessons. Even all these years later.

As I stood in the training room, I distinctly noted that she hadn't brought her usual leather bag, showing up with nothing on her but the witch mirror we intended to use.

I raised an eyebrow at her as she rose from propping the mirror up against the wall. "Really?"

Corvinna scowled. "Yes, really. Those were ancient treasures, Aria."

"That was ten years ago!"

"Yes, and your emotions are as fickle and all-consuming as they were when you were a child. You only shove them down further than you did before."

I cringed at her painfully accurate assessment. Shoving off the wall I had been leaning against, I paced over to the witch mirror. "So, same thing with the amulet? I funnel my magic into this and hope it'll trap it so you can... what? Fuck around with it and try to fix me?"

Corvinna gave me a deadpan stare. "No, you're going to trap a kernel of your magic in this so I can examine it outside of your body, which will allow me to see if there is anything I can create for you to amplify the magic temporarily when you go to break the curse."

I shrugged. "Same thing."

The witch rolled her eyes, but a smile tugged at the corners of her lips. "If we can amplify your magic the day you go to break the curse, you'll have a much better chance of walking away with your life."

I looked away from the mirror to find that she was no longer standing beside me. No, she stood on the other side of the room, a faint, iridescent shield over her body.

I threw my hands up in the air. "Okay, that's excessive."

"This is my favorite dress."

I looked at the dress, a near replica of everything in her wardrobe: flowy, made mostly of silver, with violet stars falling down the skirt. A low cut, corset top with simple, thin straps. The colors played beautifully off her silver eyes and dark complexion, I'd give her that. But it didn't look especially different from any of the ethereal dresses she owned.

"Fine. But let it be known, I am offended."

"All the more reason for the shield."

I paced away, putting five feet between me and the enchanted object. It had a small, simple gold frame encircling an oval, dark mirror. I reached into my core, drawing up the same image I always dwelled upon when I pulled at the magic: the image of the sacrificial dove from my tenth birthday.

The meek magic rose from my core, drifting above the sea of fire. It reached my fingertips eagerly, and I spun it through the air in a small whip. The magic immediately recognized the witch mirror, recoiling from the cursed object, but it didn't have a chance to dissipate. The mirror glowed, omitting a black light from the frame, before it sucked the small tendril of magic into the glass. The life magic swirled gold within its frame, glimmering against the glass as if searching for a way out.

I smiled and glanced at Corvinna. My joy over our success began to wane as I noticed her brows furrow while she watched the magic struggle against its new prison.

"What's wrong?" I asked, my gaze darting back to the mirror.

"Your magic is just… it's so alive."

"Is that a bad thing?"

Her silver eyes snapped away from the mirror, searching my face. "Is it the same with the fire?"

I thought about it, drawing a few small flames to my fingertips. I rolled the flames across my knuckles, watching them eagerly bend to my will. "Not exactly. They feel alive, but in the way a limb or an organ lives on inside my body."

The witch nodded. "That's normal. It's a part of you. But the life magic seems like a different entity."

"How is that possible?"

Corvinna held my gaze for a moment, searching for something. Whatever she found, set her lips into a thin line. She didn't reply, instead walking over and scooping up the mirror before carrying it back toward the door. She reached into the hall, retrieving her leather bag. "I'm not entirely sure, but… it could be a good thing in the end."

"How?"

She tucked the mirror away, clasping the bag shut as she threw it over her shoulder. "It could mean the magic doesn't truly belong to you. Perhaps giving it up to end the curse won't be as painful. It also means that if I can find someone else who has it, I can take it from them and give it to you. If your body already houses foreign magic, adding to it won't be any great burden. And you have proven you can at least wield it, however poorly."

I froze, my eyes locking on Corvinna. "Someone like…" I couldn't bring myself to finish the sentence, my mother's face flashing in my mind. Corvinna had sealed off my mother's magic upon her capture. But, somewhere deep inside of her, she had a kernel of the life magic I inherited, a gift from her archangel father.

The witch's gaze hardened, and when she didn't immediately deny it, I closed the distance between us. "Tell me you aren't actually considering this."

"I don't like to lie to you, Aria."

I clenched my jaw. "It's not up for debate."

"I'm not entirely sure that's up to you."

"Why don't you give it a shot and see how far you get?" I said softly, feeling flames prickle beneath my skin.

The witch sighed. "She would most likely live through the extraction—"

"I don't care," I cut her off through gritted teeth. I wouldn't take anything else from my mother. I shoved away the all-too familiar prickle of guilt and sorrow that rose to the surface when I thought of all she had endured, all my father had stripped away from her, so I could be born.

"Aria, please be reasonable."

The flames flared in the hearth, violet fire blazing. The witch didn't so much as flinch, not as her shadows dove for the sudden blast of magic, smothering it immediately.

I gritted my teeth. "I am being reasonable. You will not touch my mother, nor will you tell my father there's a way her magic could help." I took another step closer, lifting my chin to hold her gaze. "Or I will no longer be complicit in these plans. Tell me how fucking easy it's going to be to break the curse, to give you and my father exactly what you want when I'm no longer a willing participant."

I expected the witch to react to the threat, for her eyes to flare and her shadows to thicken. Instead, she merely smirked and crossed her arms. "There's that fire of yours. I always knew you had it in you."

"Corvinna, I'm not—"

She waved me off. "I know, you're deadly serious. I, however, was not."

I blinked, confusion lining my face.

"I don't plan to use your mother at all. There is one other person on this continent that might help us."

I raised a brow. "Who?"

Feral rage contorted the witch's face for a flash, so brief I would have thought I'd imagined it if she said any other name. "An Alvar. The witches felt the shift in power twenty-four years ago, when Casen Alexandret Alvar was born."

"The Alvars are human."

She laughed bitterly, brushing her lavender hair from her face. "Hardly. They are half-human and have only ever bred with other half-humans or, if we trace their lineage far enough back, with fallen. There's more fallen blood in their veins than any other 'human' family on this continent."

"How does that help us?" I sighed, perching on the edge of the couch.

The witch grinned wickedly. "I cursed the Alvars, and it would appear the fates have impeccable timing because the clock on their curse began to tick with the most recent Alvar heir. Casen's mother had a drop of angel blood in her veins, and thus he was born with enough life magic in his veins to aid in breaking the curse."

"Life magic?" I started. How was that possible? As far as I knew, life magic was rare   among the angels. And how would it pass through such diluted bloodlines?

My father had to seize it directly from the source, from my mother's archangel heritage.

"Yes. And before you ask how, I regret to inform you I don't know the precise details of how Lilian Alvar possessed the bloodlines for such a gift."

"Could we… if we needed to steal it, would that be a possibility?" I barely knew this man, yet his family was an enemy of my people. I couldn't let my compassionate heart feel   a trace of sympathy for him.

Corvinna gave me a smile that held an inkling of pride in it. "If Casen Alvar ever comes within ten miles of you, I'd be the first in line to rip his heart from his chest and bleed his magic into your veins, my phoenix."

Corvinna canceled our lessons after extracting the sliver of life magic, stating there was little else she could do for me until she figured out how to adequately amplify my abilities.

If she could figure it out.

Lucky for me, she failed to inform my father of the sudden vacancies in my schedule. So, I rose before the sun, dressing quickly and slipping out a window overlooking the roaring sea. I folded my wings tightly, feeling my body drop for a few breathless moments before I spread them wide and glided along the water.

Sea spray misted against my cheeks and bare arms, gooseflesh trailing down my arms in its wake. The sun was peeking above the horizon now. Its rays clawed across the sky, setting the night dark waters alight with beams of glimmering gold.

I soared high above the castle, gazing down at my quiet, fog-covered home below.

Home.

It was odd, being raised in a place that had never truly felt like home. I read in a book once that home had less to do with where you were and more to do with the people you were with. As I circled the mammoth structure, all dark spires and stained-glass windows, perched far above the slowly-waking city, a prickle of sorrow washed over me as I flew toward the edge of Calasera.

I wondered what kind of person that made me, to grow up with such opulent excess, every physical need met and every comfort provided for, only to feel nothing but pain when I looked upon it. To linger so heavily upon what my life was lacking instead of all that it had provided me with.

I wondered if I was naïve to believe that I'd take a home in the slums over the castle behind me if only it meant the inside of that home was warmer. If there was love there, living beyond the decaying frame and tattered exterior. It probably made me a petulant child for believing I'd give up all my wealth just to be loved.

I shook off the thought with a pang of guilt as I landed behind the small white house   sat squatly on the corner of Clarenmour avenue. This small cafe, with its chipped white paint and sagging front porch, precariously toed the line of the middle-class markets and the slums. I walked up the creaking steps, not bothering to tug my hood up.

It had only opened ten minutes prior, and I doubted anyone would be inside. A small bell tinkled overhead as I walked through the door. Beyond the foyer, the space was painted a deep gray, bordering on black. The walls were lined with eclectic, albeit dark, paintings. The owner, Lucinda, had a story for every painting and knick-knack lining the walls, from her decades of travel before she settled in Calasera to be close to her mother.

I walked past the small tables, glancing behind the glass case at the abundance of pastries and breakfast delicacies, overflowing on their golden trays. Stairs creaked at the back of the shop, and I looked up to find Lucinda racing down the steps. Her wild, white curls were piled high on her head, a scarf serving as a headband keeping the stray curls carefully tucked off her sweat-slick face.

Her down-turned crimson eyes creased at the corners when she smiled at me. "Your Royal Highness, it's a pleasure to see you this morning." She bowed low at the waist.

"Lucinda," I hissed, glancing out the windows at the dimly lit street. "Please stop bowing to me every time I come in here. It's been five years now."

Lucinda rose, a goofy smile twisting her lips as she skipped behind the bar, bouncing on the balls of her feet. "Fine, fine, next time I'll avoid such civilities. I'll simply treat you as any other customer and blandly take your order."

I knew it was a lie. I had begged her to stop bowing nearly every time I came in, but she conveniently seemed to forget by the next visit. "I'll have—"

"One vanilla cinnamon milk tea, one extra-large black coffee, two pumpkin pastries, and two sausage rolls?" Lucinda prattled off, not waiting for me to reply as she punched the buttons on the front of her gold register.

My eyes widened with delight. "You have the pumpkin pastries back?"

Lucinda gave me a grin. "Baked the first batch half an hour ago."

She wound up the arm on the side of the register, and the drawer popped out with a pleasant ring. Lucinda bustled off to collect the food and start the drinks, not bothering to tell me what I owed. I suspected she'd let me eat here for free, not batting a pale eyelash if I simply stopped paying one day.

I reached over the counter and dumped a bag of golden coins

into the waiting drawer, leaving far more than what she had added up on the register. I always did, trying my best to preserve this perfect little shop. Business was good here, but Lucinda kept her prices dangerously low in order to cater to both the residents in the slums and the middle-class neighborhoods.

Lucinda placed the rolls and pastries in a cloth bag, filling our drinks into the ceramic travel cups I had brought with me. She handed me the bag, the travel cups safely tucked away inside. "Tell Rhea I said hi."

Rhea shoved half the sausage roll in her mouth, her golden eyes rolling back in her head as she let out a low moan.

I sipped my tea with raised brows, eyeing her as we walked down her street. "You act like you haven't eaten in weeks."

Rhea shot me a glare before she washed the sausage roll down with her coffee. "I didn't have time for a second breakfast before we left."

I snorted, offering her the rest of my roll. "You poor baby."

"Yes, pity me. Give me all the treats to ease my pains."

We rounded the corner, the large, dilapidated building in the center of the slums coming into view. It used to be an indoor market, but it had been out of use for decades now. As poverty grew in Calasera, the outskirts of the city decayed beneath its pressure, surrounding this small collection of now rotting, abandoned buildings.

The residents of the slums turned the warehouses into large housing units, where the homeless could rest at night. But the one we walked toward now had been converted in recent years to a sanatorium, of sorts. Illness was rare among immortals, but only when they took proper care of their bodies. There came a point, however, when starvation drained your strength enough to leave you vulnerable to the common illnesses festering in the squalor of the impoverished and neglected portions of the city.

The healthy fallen were at no risk of contracting such illnesses, but those who lived day to day, scraping together whatever meager means they could to feed themselves and their families, were susceptible. It was a problem my father ignored entirely. It didn't threaten his perfect world, or the fallen living in the upper echelons of society, so it simply wasn't an issue he cared to correct.

Rhea hoisted her heavy bag onto both shoulders, her smile fading as we approached the open doors. "There was another outbreak of plague in the outer housing districts."

I cringed, taking the steps two at a time. "Do you know how many people were affected?"

"Not a clue. I heard about it yesterday and stayed up late last night preparing more tinctures to bring over."

I glanced at the bag, filled to the brim with the small glass jars of elven medicine   Rhea had been making since we first met. It was one of the small things she still clung to from her childhood in Casserine, the only nod to her half-elven heritage. I was smart enough to never bring it up, to avoid shadowing her eyes with memories.

Those tinctures and herbs were one of the few things that soothed the outbreaks,   healing the less severe cases altogether.

We walked through the double doors and into the large room, freezing the moment we stepped out of the sun. The warehouse reeked of astringent and death. Row after row of listless patients lined walls. My father had forbidden any of the crown's healers from aiding the homeless, believing, like every fallen king before him, that only the strongest in our society deserved to survive. Still, the nature of a healer railed against such blatant suffering. Whatever healers were brave enough to go against my father's decrees raced through the room now, moving from patient to patient as they offered whatever aid they could.

Some carried tonics and medications, others healed with the small magic they had in their veins, drawing the infection from the blood of the sick. Still more offered only comfort care, easing the pain as the plague stole the lives of the fallen that were already too far gone.

The life magic in my veins prickled beneath my skin, rising to the surface in the face of all this death. Healer magic worked by mending and soothing, but mine worked to cure. To chase away death and heal as if you had never been afflicted.

I didn't have much of it to offer, and it always burned out far too quickly, but when Rhea mentioned how badly healers were needed three years ago... I hadn't hesitated to help. My father would beat me within an inch of my life if he knew, but it was a beating I was always happy to risk. Besides, I kept my face concealed, so no one here knew their princess was defying the decree of their king.

I wasn't trying to make a statement on my father's laws, no matter what I might feel about them. I just wanted to help. To feel like this magic was worth more than the sacrifice it was created for.

A short healer named Coralyn bustled up to us, greeting Rhea with a warm smile before she turned her eyes toward me. I remained tucked away inside my hood, cowl wrapped around my face. It wasn't uncommon for healers and those offering illegal aid to conceal their features, so her gaze didn't bother searching for mine.

"The sickest are lying in the back," the healer said to me softly. I followed her eyes, my heart faltering in my chest. The back of the warehouse held mostly children, cradled in their mothers' arms. Their small coughs echoed across the cavernous room, sending bolts of dread pounding through my chest.

The mothers all turned their heads up to me, tensing as I approached. I silently cursed the hood and cowl, wishing desperately I could peel it back and help ease their fears. Offer a warm smile and a comforting word, instead of this.

The children were fever-stricken, listless in their mothers' arms. I sat gently at the edge of their circle, giving enough space to allow them to relax their tensed arms.

"I'm here to help. I'm a healer, but I don't wish to reveal my face to anyone here as a precaution. Will you allow me to heal your child?" I kept my voice soft, soothing, giving them the space to come to me.

After a tense moment, all eyes locked on me, a young mother stepped forward. Her black eyes were lined with silver, her hair unbound and greasy. As if she had been awake, cradling the small girl in her arms since the moment the child had fallen ill.

Warily, she kneeled before me, relaxing her grip on the girl only enough to allow me to lay my hands on her. She couldn't have been older than four, her round cheeks flushed with fever. Her eyes were closed, moving rapidly behind her eyelids as she dreamed. It was her breathing that terrified me most, shallow and wet, a rasp escaping her slightly parted, chapped lips.

I placed my hand across the child's forehead. The magic warmed in my veins, so easy to grasp now that a child teetering on the edge of death sat before me. It didn't waste a second, the familiar glimmer of gold illuminating my fingertips. The mother flinched, as the child filled with a soft, violet light, lighting up the tracing of her veins. Her lungs illuminated in her chest, glowing through her dark skin. All at once, the light faded. The child's entire body relaxed, the ragged edge to her breathing gone. I held my breath as she blinked open two wide, crimson eyes, confusion twisting her cherubic features.

"Mama?" the girl said softly, sitting up gingerly. The mother's face shattered, a sob wracking through her as she swept the child up in her arms.

I went to move away, my gaze lifting to the next child in line, but the mother's hand darted out, gripping my wrist in her shaking, sweat slick palm. "Thank you, thank you so much. I thought she was—" Her words choked off into another sob as she released my hands, clinging to her child.

My throat felt thick, eyes stinging as I nodded curtly. Shame stabbed through me like a hot knife, and I looked away quickly. She shouldn't be thanking me at all. It was my father's fault these people had no aid, no resources. It was his policies that made their lives nearly unbearable. And I stood by his side in court every damned day, my silence on behalf of our people deafening. I was as bad as the rest of my family and the aristocracy, sneering down on those had fallen into poverty. I was wholly unworthy of her gratitude.

I was here to atone for their blood on my hands, to beg for forgiveness by offering the aid they'd been so vehemently denied.

I cleared my throat and looked at the other mothers. Their eyes were filled with an earth-shattering hope as they held my gaze.

"Who's next?"

Chapter Six

My magic lasted long enough to heal twenty-three of the sick
fallen, covering nearly all the patients in critical condition. Every
single child walked out the front doors with their mothers. Watching
them leave, healthy and whole to see another day, soothed something
deep within me. It was better than bloodying myself in training or
drinking on Rhea's couch on the days where my head was too loud,
and I couldn't reel in my emotions like I needed to.

This tired my body down to my marrow, draining me to the point
where my thoughts were blissfully slow, and I couldn't feel that
gnawing ache in my chest as strongly. It gave me a spark of purpose
that was dangerous, but goddess I loved it.

The reality that this would not be the last time these people were
on death's door, starving and giving into mortal illnesses, dimmed
the small spark of joy not long after I finished healing. In the silent
moments after the magic had left my veins fully, remembering   my
family was solely responsible for their wellbeing, and was failing
miserably, was enough to extinguish the fragile joy all together.

When Rhea had handed out all her tinctures, and the frenzy in
the sanitarium had calmed, we dragged ourselves back to her house.
She supported my weight through the winding alley, eyes darting

over me nervously. "You shouldn't drain yourself this much."

"It's fine," I murmured, my tongue feeling thick and heavy in my mouth.

She pursed her lips but didn't argue further. Legs weak and heartbeat racing, I forced myself up the three cracked steps and into her home before collapsing on the couch. My head pulsed in time with my pounding heart, my limbs too weak to settle myself comfortably against the cushions.

I stared up at her ceiling for a few bleary seconds, aware of Rhea mumbling something about cooking dinner. Before I could think of a response, sleep came for me hard and fast, dragging me down into a dreamless dark.

I woke slowly, eyes blinking furiously as I tried to fend off another wave of sleep. Confusion muddled my brain as I stared up at a cracked ceiling, lit with a beam of light cutting through the curtains beside me. I sat up, eyes darting around the room. Slowly, the events of the day before spilled back to me, and I buried my head in my hands with a groan.

After scrubbing at my eyes, I looked around Rhea's living room, jolting at the sleeping black wolf on the opposite couch. I groaned, rising stiffly as I crept over to her kitchen. I raided the plate of biscuits left out on the counter and downed a full glass of water, glancing at the wooden clock on the wall.

Two in the morning.

Fuck me.

I crept back into the living room and gave Rhea a murmured goodbye, lightly kissing the top of her fuzzy head. She let out a huff, her paws stretching out lightly, golden eyes blinking up at me blearily before closing again. Out in the garden, I drew in a steady breath of floral scented air. Jasmine ran wild in her backyard, wholly untended and beautiful, in the way all wild things were. I drew my wings to the surface, tucked my bag tightly under my arm, and launched into the night sky.

I watched as the world shrank away, the cool air a welcome sensation as it washed over my skin, chasing away the last traces of sleep. I flew until Calasera was little more than a glittering sea of lights far beneath me. Until all the world's problems seemed so small

I could finally allow myself to breathe.

Flying always had a way of putting everything into perspective. It cleared my head of all the rambling thoughts threatening to pull me under, allowing me to center myself in my body.

The fatigue I felt was bone deep, my mind still groggy and muscles aching. Magic consumed energy first, and when it was close to burnout, it began to eat away at the wielder's body. I had never neared burnout with my fire, the well of power too deep and my control too great to ever let it get to that point. But this life magic, this small, precious little drop of hope, fizzled out far too quickly, the last dregs of magic sucking at whatever energy it could find in my muscles and bones to keep it from extinguishing completely.

Burnout came in phases, and tonight, I was teetering dangerously close to the first one. It was a fine balance, like walking the edge of a wineglass. One wrong move, and I'd be crashing into the waiting arms of burnout at the bottom.

I couldn't bring myself to regret it, though. Not with the faces of the smiling children I'd helped tonight still blazing brightly in my mind's eye.

Goddess, I was so eager to collapse in bed now. I blinked my eyes clear as I flew above the castle, circling slowly until I found the window to the west tower still open.

I landed on the sill, tucking my wings in tight as I deftly slipped inside. With half a thought, my wings vanished, and I steadied myself against the sudden shift in my balance before I dragged my feet down the hall. I didn't realize I was swaying until two broad hands grasped my shoulders. A familiar, spiced scent washed over me.

"Whoa there, Princess, I've got you," Kellen breathed in my ear.

I didn't have the energy to protest, not as my legs gave out fully and I collapsed into his chest. I sighed deeply, the relief of no longer holding up my body sending a shiver down my spine.

Kellen held me against his chest for a moment, brushing my hair away from my face. He pulled back slowly, and I whimpered, squeezing my eyes shut against my shaking muscles.

The world spun as he swooped me into his arms. "What happened, Aria?"

I didn't answer as I nestled against his chest, his large frame cradling me as he walked down the hall. I closed my eyes, head lolling as I fought to stay awake. Until I got to bed, anyway. "Had a fun night out."

A soft chuckle rumbled against my cheek. "No, you most certainly did not. I've seen you drunk, and it's a lot more fun than this."

I scrunched my nose. "I haven't been drunk since—"

"Benedict's birthday. Trust me, I remember."

I cracked an eye open, glancing up at Kellen. His crimson eyes were on me, a slash of a grin across his sharp features. "Oh, really?"

His grin softened, and he looked forward as we rounded another corner and up the spiral staircase leading to my chambers. I closed my eyes against the slowly spinning ceiling, my stomach churning.

"You wore that soft gold dress, the backless one with the slit up one side, and drank so much wine you were dancing barefoot on the lawn by midnight. You made us both miss the toast, and your father tripled our training for a month." A soft laugh skittered over my arms.

I barely remembered the night. I only recalled the pounding headache the next day, waking in my bed with no memory of how I got there. The mud caking the hem had nearly ruined the gown. Only the training session the following morning, hung over and heaving every half-hour, was seared into my mind.

"And you what, watched over me and carried me back to my bed that night too?"

A pause. "Always, Aria. It's my job."

I wasn't sure why warmth bloomed in my chest. I almost hated myself for it, for allowing my body to go slack in his arms. For feeling... safe, if only for a moment. "I wouldn't say it's your job."

Kellen fell silent.

We turned another corner, and I heard the distinct shifting of armor.

"Mind grabbing the door?" Kellen murmured.

The shuffle of footsteps filled the hall, followed by the creak of hinges. We passed through the door, and I shut my heavy eyes once more, sensing his path as he navigated between the furniture in the antechamber of my room. He climbed the three steps to the sitting room before turning left into my bedchamber.

Kellen laid me gently on my bed, my head resting against the pillows. I moaned, my aching body relaxing into the soft plush of the feather mattress. After a moment, the bed sank beside me. I groaned, prying my eyes open to meet his. "Thank you for your help, but if you're looking to collect payment, I'm afraid you'll have to cash in another night."

Another full smile lit up his face. "I'll remind you of that tomorrow."

I threw a pillow at him, fighting my smile as he caught it, tossing it back with a laugh before he bent down to tug off my shoes. His fingers deftly unlaced my boots, his smile fading slightly. "What were you doing tonight?"

"I told you—"

He shook his head, cutting me off with a look. Tugging hard on my boot, he slipped my foot out and tossed it to the floor. "You don't need to lie to me, Aria."

I chewed on my lip, my eyes staring hard out the window beside my bed. I could see the dark city line from my room, dotted with glimmering lights, like fallen stars settling in the valley. "It would be best if you didn't know, Kellen."

He tugged off my other boot before he pulled me up to sitting. I pouted, but he stood and turned his back to me. "Your leathers will not be comfortable to sleep in. Tell me when you're under the covers."

I groaned but made quick work of peeling the clothes from my body, leaving me in only a thin camisole and undergarments. I slipped under the covers, clearing my throat for Kellen to turn back around.

To my surprise, he swung into bed to sit beside me. "Roll over."

I protested, but he held up a comb, raising a brow. I stared at the jeweled comb, a flush spreading through my body as he waited patiently for me to obey. The gesture was so soft, intimate in a way we never had been before. Slowly, I sank beneath the duvet, rolling on my side and fanning my hair out behind me.

"Were you safe?" he asked as the comb teased apart the knots riddling the ends of my hair. I closed my eyes, a shiver racing down my spine as he slowly worked up the length of tangled hair. For a hulking brute of a man, his hands were gentle. Almost reverent.

"Yes, I was safe."

He made a small noise in the back of his throat as he tugged at a knot near the ends before combing the full length of my hair, the teeth of the comb wringing a small, soft sigh from my throat.

"You shouldn't come so close to draining yourself, Aria," he said softly.

I stiffened, turning to face him, but he gently pushed my head back down.

"I'm going to guess you were using your life magic, since I doubt you could drain you fire magic in one night. So... whatever you did that you've deemed worth sneaking around to do, be more careful. You can't allow yourself to reach burnout, not when every-thing is riding on that small bit of magic."

I clenched my jaw but nodded. How could I forget when every-one here spent all of their time reminding me that my choices were hardly my own to make?

I felt him set the comb down, his fingers deftly braiding my hair back and tying it off with a ribbon. "Why did you run away from me on the beach?" he asked suddenly.

My heart skipped a beat in my chest, and I squeezed my eyes closed, keeping my breathing even. Kellen waited for a few moments longer before I felt the mattress shift. His footsteps rounded the bed, and suddenly his scent enveloped me.

Softly, he leaned over and pressed a kiss to my forehead, tucking a stray hair behind my ear. "I love you, Aria." He left quietly, the door clicking softly behind him.

I waited several beats to release my breath slowly. Rolling on my back, my eyes settled on the moonlight, glimmering across the golden filigree painted between the sunken panels of the ceiling.

My body begged for sleep, but my mind spiraled as I twisted the tassel of my comforter around my finger. Kellen's words played through head, the longing in his eyes clouding my mind and twisting my chest into an indecipherable bundle of emotions. I cared for him.

I truly did.

My life was better with him in it. He'd shield me from the cruel-ties of this court and maybe give me a life I could sink into, one day. Eventually, in a hopefully distant future, our parents might come to a courtship agreement anyway. It was out of my control, so maybe this was for the best.

But I couldn't help the small yearning in my heart for more.

Was that crazy? Maybe. Selfish? Definitely.

But... I couldn't help it. If I survived this war, I couldn't see a future with him painted in anything but shades of gray.

I wondered what it felt like to be in love. Was this it? This small warmth I felt for Kellen, the flushing of my skin in his presence?

It felt nice.

But was it love?

I rolled over on my side, abandoning the thread I had pulled at, and stared out my window.

I knew nothing of love or happiness if I were being completely honest. My understanding of such things came from the books on my nightstand, and maybe that was unrealistic. Maybe feeling safe with Kellen was what love was.

Maybe love wasn't the all-consuming, burn-the-world-down emotion that lived on the pages of my favorite stories.

But... I guess I had at least hoped I'd finally find my place, my home, when I also found love.

I stared out at the night sky, the three waxing moons and the spattering of silver lights bright enough to penetrate the city's glow. And I hoped then that settling like this wouldn't be so bad. He was my closest friend next to Rhea, so maybe being shackled to a friend wasn't such a bad fate after all.

The thought should have been comforting, but it didn't stop the well of tears in my throat.

It didn't stop the careful way I cradled the desire for something more in my chest.

I was on my way to breakfast the following morning, my body feeling stronger after sleeping in later than I was normally permitted. It would appear by the absence in my schedule that my father was still unaware Corvinna had temporarily paused our training sessions.

I rounded another corner, my mind set on heading into town for breakfast, only to come to an abrupt stop. My mother stood before my father's study, her eyes glazed and unfocused. I started, eyes widening as I took her in. She stood in a white dressing gown, her hair unbound and feet bare. She looked half-wild, like she had been pacing and pulling her hair in this hall for hours.

Her pale, delicate fist hovered above his wooden door.

Frozen like a statue, the only sign of life in the shallow breaths fluttering in her chest.

"Mama?" I whispered hoarsely.

She started, her fist falling quickly to her side as she cast those wide, dark blue eyes over me. My mother opened her mouth, then closed it quickly, bunching her fingers in the fabric of her gown so hard her knuckles turned white. "I was—" she started, but her words failed again. She shook her head, dragging her eyes back to the door.

I took a few careful steps toward her. "Here, I'll help you back to your room."

She stumbled back, as if I had struck her. "Don't."

"Mama—"

"Don't patronize me, Aria Iveliesse. Don't you fucking dare patronize me, just like everyone else in this castle."

I drew in a sharp breath, glancing around the empty halls. I needed to get her back to her room before this episode turned into something more. "Mother, I need you to go back to your chambers."

She bared her teeth at me, her frail arms shaking now. "I need to talk to him. I need him to understand, to admit I did it. I did what I was supposed to, and it's been decades. He needs to let me go, *I can't be here anymore.*" She was screaming now. She took another step toward the study, determination setting the sharp angle of her jaw.

Panic clawed up my throat as I closed the distance between us, gripping her shaking arms. "Shh, it's okay, I get it. Let's go back so we can talk—"

"I don't want to talk." She shoved me away, and I let her. I watched as she paced before his door like a caged animal, ripping at her hair. "I can't talk about it anymore, Aria. I don't want you to condescend to me, or to have Amabel slip another sleeping tonic in my tea. I don't want to be dressed in golden gowns and paraded with the other women, sedated and locked away. I need to talk to him, to make him see I can't *fucking breathe.*"

The study door creaked open, my father stepping into the hall with raised brows. My heart thudded irregularly in my throat, my limbs tingling against the effort it took to restrain myself. If I intervened now, if I stepped between them, my father would see it as defiance. She was my mother, but she was also his consort.

Not of her own freewill, but that didn't matter here.

Under fallen law, he owned her.

I clenched my hands shut so tightly my nails bit into my palms.

"Parisa, this is a surprise," he said softly, looking down at her near feral form.

He towered over her, his broad size dwarfing my frail mother.

My pulse quickened as she took two sharp steps toward him, squaring her shoulders and looking up to hold his gaze. "I have done all you asked of me. I… I want to go home."

"Do you, now?"

My mother flinched at the booming tenor of his voice, the cold amusement that limned the edges. "Yes. I have fulfilled my purpose. You don't need me anymore."

"Mother," I warned softly. It was foolish to remind him of how useless she was to him now. It didn't make her worthy of freedom in his eyes, it made her dispensable.

My father glanced at me, his face carefully blank. "You understand our daughter cannot leave with you, right?"

"Yes."

Something in my chest cracked, a part of my heart that was still young and small and forever broken.

"You would abandon your daughter for your own selfish desire?"

My mother's gaze hardened. "I have been selfless for too long. I have given you—" She stumbled over her words, her voice now thick with unshed tears. "I have given you *everything*, and I think it is time you set me free."

Silence.

It was an outright demand now, and my father did not take kindly to demands. He took two powerful strides toward her, and I allowed my eyes to flutter shut briefly. My heart thudded against my ribs, a tremor coursing up my spine. I couldn't move, though. I couldn't put myself between them.

He gripped my mother's pointed chin, forcing her to crane her neck to meet his gaze. She trembled, but her eyes… they were clear. A stormy, ocean blue, brighter than I had seen them in years.

"Parisa Aldine, you have served me well. You gave me Aria, the salvation of the fallen people. You spent decades here in a near perfect example of submission. You have never fought against me like this before." He leaned in close now, merely a breath between them. His voice was low, cold. "So let me remind you of your place. I don't give a fuck if you carried a thousand more blessed children in your womb and reared them all within this castle. I don't care if you spend ten thousand more years in Calasera, serving me silently. You will never leave this castle alive because you belong to me."

"I belong to no one." The words were soft, but not weak. I

flinched at her defiance, waiting for the blade at his side to be un-sheathed.

Preparing myself to watch her blood spill, her body to fall limp before me.

I needed to move, to intervene. I would stand by with everything except her death. I wouldn't let him kill her.

But my father only smiled. "Oh, Parisa. I stole you from your home as easily as one might pluck a ripe, delicious apple from a tree. I claimed you, body, mind, and soul. Every inch of you belongs to me. Every breath you take is mine. And when death comes for you finally, it will be my hand that delivers it to you."

He shoved her away, and her small, frail body collapsed. He stalked down the hall, his cloak trailing him like a shadow. "I will see you in my office tomorrow after breakfast, Aria."

I waited to hear his footsteps fade down the corridor.

As if released from a spell, I collapsed to the ground beside my mother. Her eyes were vacant once more, unshed tears lining them silver. I said nothing as I helped her to her feet, slipping my arm around her too-small waist and guiding her back to her chambers.

Chapter Seven

"She's lucky he didn't kill her there," Corvinna said, her lips twitching into a frown. We sat in my bathing chamber, the tub filling slowly from the golden faucet above it. The castle was one of the few buildings with running water in Calasera, this luxury only afforded to the royals and the aristocracy. Corvinna had announced this morning, rather abruptly and before the sun had graced the sky, our training would resume today.

I didn't have the energy to ask after her experiments with the witch mirror and   trapped sliver of magic within it; if it was producing adequate results, she wouldn't be here right now.

I watched the water fill the stone basin, the tub the size of a small swimming pool, extending to the edge of a circular window overlooking the city. "It would have been too merciful to kill her."

The words were out of my mouth before I could think twice. I didn't mean that, not really. At least, I didn't want to. I wanted to believe there was a way back to happiness for my mother. Or back to sanity, at the very least.

I rose, slipping my tunic and trousers off. I slowly undid my hair from its tousled braid, tugging it loose until it hung in waves around my waist.

"Alright, Princess, get in," Corvinna said as she pulled herself up on the shelf of the bathing pool. She tucked her legs against her chest, resting her chin on her knees. It was odd, seeing her perched like that. She looked more like a young girl than the all-powerful High Witch. As if she had been born a few decades before, not centuries ago when the witch kingdom still stood.

I always marveled when this side of her personality slipped through. I wondered who she was before the dark war, before she inherited her title and the fractured remains of the witch kingdom with it.

I slipped into the tub, my body instantly relaxing into the warm, lapping water. I sniffed, throwing a sly grin at Corvinna. "Did you put bath oils in this?"

A smile tugged at her lips, again making her look so young. "I figured it would help you relax. Ashford had the right idea taking you to the ocean, but he is not the correct person to train you. There was little chance you'd be able to do anything of value with him there."

I floated to the center of the pool, sinking until the water lapped against my chin. "How old are you?"

Corvinna arched a lavender brow. "I believe after a few centuries of life, that is a rude question to ask."

I rolled my eyes, paddling onto my back and staring up at the cathedral ceiling above. It was garish; the ceiling painted with flora and fauna of crimsons and greens, inlaid with gold. The Elway sigil adorned the center of the design. Even in my private chambers, I couldn't escape the flag hanging over my head like an executioner's blade.

"Why did you come to Calasera?" My next question was softer this time. In all the years the witch had trained me, I had learned little more than superficial facts about her, never anything deeper. When I was young, she scared me. Her raw magic, her unusual mannerisms and the ancient wisdom in her swirling, silver eyes. By the end of our first year together, the fear had waned into bald curiosity.

Now, she brushed me off when I alluded to wanting to know more about her. But, like a petulant child, it never stopped me from circling back and trying again another day.

She was quiet for so long that I was sure she would not respond. I almost jolted when she finally broke the silence. "Because sometimes, when you've lost everything, you'll sink to the lowest depths and ally yourself with an enemy in order to get it all back."

I opened my mouth to respond, but she cut me off. "Enough about me, Aria. My story is an ancient pain I'd rather not reopen. Find the thread of life magic, and let's see what you can do with it."

Wordlessly, I slipped beneath the surface, still staring up at the crimson ceiling. It almost looked like blood beneath the water, rippling and blending into a smattering of red.

I closed my eyes, sinking to the bottom of the tub and slipping into that weightless place that made it so easy to find the bottom of my power.

I found the small thread of gold, wrapped around my flaming soul as if holding on for dear life. I approached slowly, extending my hands toward it.

I am you, and you are me. We are the same. Come to me.

The magic unfurled itself, drifting out toward my outstretched fingers. The contact sent electricity racing through my veins. My eyes flew open, and I sat up in the tub, drawing air into lungs I hadn't realized were screaming for relief.

I gasped down the air in breathy gulps, smoothing my wet locks of hair out of my face. "How long was I under?" I gasped, glancing over at Corvinna. She was lounging on the lip of the tub, no sign she had moved to check on me.

"Close to five minutes."

I gaped up at her.

She waved a sharp nailed hand dismissively. "Oh, please. If you allowed yourself to drown, you would've been too weak to break the curse, anyway."

I glared at her, but my gaze quickly tugged down to my hands. They glimmered faintly gold. I kept my hands submerged, my heart thudding irregularly as I felt the power rise to the tips of my fingers. It was so different from the fire I wielded—cool, buzzing, calm.

Corvinna didn't speak as she drew a blade from her side, gripping it in her left hand and slicing it without hesitation. Blood ran a red river over her palm, and she held it over the tub. I went to raise my hands from the water, but as they neared the surface, I could feel my flames rising to consume this gentle, delicate river of magic that flowed through me.

I clenched my teeth as I tried and failed to control it. I had so much control when someone was going to die, when sick children needed me or a helpless creature drew its last breaths. But when it wasn't dire, when my heartbeat didn't pound adrenaline through my veins and my heedless empathy didn't seize control of my actions, I had no power to command this magic. It was infuriating.

"Put your hand under the water."

Corvinna pursed her lips but obeyed, her hand slipping beneath the surface of the bath. Blood eddied with water, floating above her hand in crimson plumes. I ran my fingers over Corvinna's wound, watching as a thread of glimmering gold seeped into the cut. Slower than it should, her skin stitched itself back together, leaving only a trail of crimson in its wake.

The witch drew her hand from the water, examining the now smooth skin before fixing her silver eyes on me. "How do you feel? Do you feel the same drain, as if it stole from your life force again?"

I shook my head. "I feel energized."

"Can you do it outside of the tub now?"

I chewed on my lower lip, pulling my hands from the water. The river of power immediately banked, draining from my fingertips and racing toward my core, toward the parts of my body still submerged. I cringed. "Any chance I can do this spell in a bathtub?"

The high witch leveled me a flat look.

With a groan, I sank beneath the water.

Showered and changed an hour later, I reclined in a chair to my father's left, ignoring Perceval's brooding, hulking form sitting across me. From what I gathered, Orella kicked his ass again in training, and he was not pleased about it. I didn't know why it bothered him so much; Orella had far fewer responsibilities than he did as the heir, and she filled her time with more training.

She was the best out of all of us, and I was more than happy to let her kick my own ass in training if it meant I'd learn from it.

When her mother wasn't parading her around court, seeking an advantageous match to marry her off, Orella was training. It honestly put the guards here in the castle to shame, how intensely she honed her body and skills. Perceval should feel little more than pity for Orella; for all her talent and discipline, the moment our father agreed on a betrothal, it would have been for nothing. She'd marry, inherit a monstrous estate in the mountains or perhaps her new husband would whisk her away to a barony or dukedom within the fallen territories, and her sole purpose would become producing a horde of children, hosting galas and leading female-based organizations within the aristocracy.

She had maybe another year free to kick his ass before she became just another wife, living her life for the man who claimed her hand.

Nevertheless, Perceval sat sulking across the table, an edge gleaming in his dark red eyes. And I had absolutely no desire to be the one to step on his toes in this meeting, earning his wrath for the rest of the afternoon. An angry Perceval was a nuisance at best and a backstabbing asshole at worst.

Kellen walked into the room, and I quickly straightened, now avoiding eye contact with two people in this room. I struggled to push down the flush creeping across my skin as memories of the night before rushed back. Of his kindness, the gentle kiss on my forehead, and the soft, sweet concern in his eyes.

Of the words he uttered when he thought I was no longer listening.

I cringed when he sat down beside me. In my peripheral, I watched as he set two mugs down on the table, sliding one in front of me. My eyes widened in surprise as I peeked inside, the scent of my favorite vanilla cinnamon milk tea wafting up with the steam.

I shot a look up at Kellen, eyebrows raised.

"I figured you'd need it after last night."

I smiled tentatively, sipping from the tea and letting out a soft moan as the warm spices rolled over my tongue. This was exactly what I needed, the sweetness of the drink ebbing away at my sour mood. "What do you want?"

Kellen rolled his eyes, sipping his own drink and smirking at me. "Just say thank you."

I set my cup down and gave him a saccharine smile. "Thank you."

Voice filled the room as the rest of the council flooded in, murmuring softly among each other. My father was the last one in, strolling to his seat at the head of the table, set between Perceval and I. He glanced pointedly at the two of us, and we both straightened in our chairs.

"Thank you all for gathering on such short notice," my father began, taking a seat in his chair and looking down the long table. The Fallen council comprised thirteen elders of the court, all titles inherited since the beginning of the Fallen monarchy. Nine out of thirteen of these council members had been in their positions during the dark war, back when Amaros Thain held the throne.

The council members dipped their chins, waiting for my father to proceed.

"It would appear we need to accelerate our plans. I've repositioned our troops, as you all know, to be prepared to storm Aeredale's capital in two months' time."

"What has prompted this drastic shift in the timeline, Your Royal Highness?" a man near the end of the table asked first. His eyes were the darkest black, his pupils barely discernible before they bled away into the bright whites surrounding his irises. His waxy white skin and bleached hair gave him an unearthly appearance. Turiel Malika, the eldest on the council.

Perceval claimed he was born when the goddess herself still walked this plain. I thought it was bullshit, but something deep in his gaze always left a shadow of doubt, that perhaps it might be true.

My father glanced up at Turiel with a tolerant smile. "If you wish to discuss the logistics of our timeline, I would be more than happy to do so in the privacy of my office after this meeting. For now, I merely need to inform you all that Aria," at the mention of my name, I stiffened, "will need a bit of a boost to fulfill her role in breaking the curse."

The council glanced among themselves before a male with black hair and blood-red eyes spoke up. "A *boost* to her magic?"

The doors opened once more. Corvinna strode in, her lavender robes billowing out behind her. Her eyes darted around the table as she took her place beside my father. Why was she...

My thoughts trailed off into panic. Everything capable of boosting my magic was well within her control, through spells or brews or witch tools that were beyond my comprehension. Everything except stealing more life magic.

She told my father.

Panic cut through me, cold and sharp, as I tried to meet the witch's gaze. She didn't even deign to acknowledge me as she clasped her hands together, smiling tightly at the expectant council.

"Princess Aria's life magic is not as strong as we had hoped it would be by now. If we had decades longer, perhaps she could have stepped into her magic and broken this curse with little effort. Because of the... *complications* that have arisen, forcing us to move our troops into position faster than we wished, King Elway and I," she gestured between them as if they were allies, presenting the facade of a united front, "have determined we need to find a means to bolster her magic in a less conventional way." I would have snorted at the hypocrisy in that gesture if it weren't for the death grip her words had on my heart. If she mentioned my mother, if she alluded to stealing her powers, I would burn everyone in this chamber to ash.

"And I assume," Turiel interjected, snowy eyebrows raised, "that you have a way to ensure our one and only hope at breaking the curse does not fail?"

Corvinna gave the council a bloodthirsty smile. "I have the best way to ensure she doesn't fail. Casen Alexandret Alvar was born with a small drop of life magic in his veins."

The room fell silent, and I exhaled slowly, releasing a quiet, measured breath.

Casen Alvar, not my mother, was the one we were here to debate. Thank the goddess it was some aristocratic asshole in Landora that would bleed for this, not my innocent mother. I still sat on edge, aware everyone in this room knew of my mother's powers, the magic she passed on to me. She wasn't entirely out of the woods, yet.

"How?" Adimus, a thin, ash blonde female, breathed.

My father's lips thinned. "It would appear that Dominic Alvar stepped outside of the laws of the Original Families and the System to fuck a low-born woman with a surprising blend of angel blood in her veins. The goddess only knows what he was thinking, but he brought into existence a child capable of foiling all of his plans. Something we can now take advantage of."

"How long have you known?" Turiel asked Corvinna sharply.

The witch merely shrugged, picking at her sharp nails. "I've known since the boy was born."

"And you didn't think to share this with the council?" Adimus asked incredulously.

"It was witch knowledge, and I held on to it until it served me to share with the fallen council."

Adimus slammed a fist on the table. "We are supposed to be allies—"

"I'd watch your tongue, Adimus Rahtiel, lest I pull it from your throat." Her words were soft, laced with hoarfrost and death.

He, wisely, did not finish his sentence.

"What do you plan to do?" Turiel asked, sizing up the witch and leaning back in his chair.

Corvinna glanced at my father, who replied, "Abduct him. We've had our Dwellers pressing in on their borders for years now, it wouldn't be hard to stage a raid on one of their outer farming towns beyond their wall. The Alvar boy is currently being mentored by General Ezra Briggs, and if we can lure them out to the border, we can imprison him and bring him back to Calasera."

"After," Corvinna interjected, "I'd have the life magic in his veins siphoned off and given to Aria, to ensure she will have enough to end the curse."

"Can the Alvar boy break the curse alone?" Turiel said.

Corvinna scoffed. "The curse calls for a child of Light and Dark to end the curse, a daughter of the fallen and the angels. Casen's blood is far too diluted for that, and even if it weren't, his life magic is too weak. He should only have enough to boost Aria's magic so she can survive breaking the curse."

"And we're sure Aria will absorb his magic?"

Corvinna finally glanced at me. She tucked a lavender braid behind her ear before she met Turiel's gaze again. "Yes. It is often easier to absorb magic from your own lineage, but life magic is unique. When Kahlios fell, his life magic split up and divided among a few angel bloodlines, but it has always been fragmented pieces of a whole. This magic longs to be put back together, restored to it's full, god-like strength. Like calls to like, and their kernels of magic will be drawn toward each other, creating possibly one of the strongest bonds in all the realms. His magic will be eager to be absorbed into Aria's veins, to join its other piece."

"Will he have to die for this?" my father asked Corvinna. His eyes were narrowed, his fingers tapping a steady rhythm on the table.

Corvinna considered. "It's hard to say. I'll have to see how attached the magic is to his soul to determine for certain."

My father interjected, "Did he inherit magic from his father as well?"

All eyes locked on Corvinna, varying degrees of understanding and anticipation dawning on the council.

"You mean the magic the Alvars stole from me?" Corvinna said with quiet menace. "Yes. He possesses the magic to wield shadows."

My father smirked. "He'll make a good pet once you're through with him."

Turiel nodded thoughtfully, glancing around at the other council members.

They discussed the logistics of the Dweller raid and how they would get Casen to Calasera without intervention. The rest of the meeting became a monotone background noise in my head as I watched Corvinna, her silver eyes never once meeting my burning gaze.

"What the fuck was that?"

The witch spun around, a placating smile already pinching her features. Fire licked at my fingertips as I reached her, smoke curling behind my teeth. The witch's gaze darted over my face and, in a flash of dizzying darkness, transported us to my bedchamber.

The room swam in my vision, the ceiling rotating around me as I stumbled to keep my balance. Fuck, I hated when she travelled without warning.

Blinking furiously to clear my vision, I pulled myself up to my feet, still glaring at the now smirking witch. "Why didn't you talk to me before announcing your plan in front of the entire elder's council?"

Her silver eyes narrowed. "I don't need to run my plans by anyone, girl."

I snarled, pacing toward her again, only to slam into an iridescent ward around her body. I slammed my fists against it, screaming in frustration. "Don't give me that bullshit, Corvinna. You knew I didn't want my father to know, to get the idea—"

"I protected your mother."

"You gave him one more reason to consider killing her!"

The witch leveled an exasperated look at me. "Put the flames away, Aria. I would never go to him if I didn't have a protective measure in place for your mother. After all these years, do you truly not trust me?"

My anger shriveled to ash in my chest. I collapsed on the couch, looking up at the witch in defeat. "What did you tell him to convince him abducting Casen would be the better alternative to using my mother's power?"

"I told him you'd never forgive him."

I snorted. "I highly doubt that was enough to convince him of anything."

Corvinna dipped her chin, taking a seat on the couch across from me. "And you would be right, but when I told him how you'd probably turn on him if he were to kill your mother and drain her magic, he conceded."

I flinched. "You did not say that."

"I did, and I stand by it. Your father has always sought the path of least resistance, and this was no exception. If he can please you enough to keep you docile, he will. It's worked for twenty years, why not give in one more time? Not to mention this plan comes with the potential to seize Casen Alvar through the dwellers, without any penalty on the fallen, and your father would love nothing more than to sink his claws into an Alvar descendant."

I glowered at the witch. "I am not docile."

Corvinna rolled her eyes, crossing her legs beneath her. "If you say so. Regardless, your father is more than happy to abduct Casen Alvar if it means ensuring your success."

I cringed. "Would it be kinder for him to die when you drained him of his magic?"

The witch's gaze sharpened. "You shouldn't pity an him, Aria. And if you're going to, then spare me from hearing it. Either way, he will die eventually, and I'd be more than happy to be the one to rip his heart from his chest if it'll make you feel less dirty stealing from him."

I twisted the rings around my index finger thoughtfully. "What exactly did Alexandret Alvar do to you to make you hate his descendants this much?" I knew the Witch Kingdom fell as a result of his betrayal, but... why was her hatred so focused on the Alvars as opposed to the entire human race that contributed to her loss?

The bloodthirsty smile on Corvinna's face faltered, a darkness creeping over her features I rarely saw. She didn't reply, simply gazing into the low burning fire in the hearth beside us.

I let it go, curling up on the couch, fatigue washing through me all at once. I glanced at the clock, cringing when it read half-past four.

It was the last day of the week. The Ashfords were hosting a dinner after sunset in honor of my birthday next week.

"Fine, I trust you." I yawned, curling up on the couch.

Corvinna quirked a brow. "Just like that?"

"Don't get me wrong, I'm still pissed."

"Figures."

"But I trust you."

Something flickered across her face, gone so fast I couldn't identify it.

"So make it up to me by waking me up in half-an hour and scrounging up some tea for me, will you?" I said between another yawn.

Corvinna scowled. "Oh, fuck off. I don't have to make anything up to you."

Still, half an hour later, I awoke to a grumpy witch holding a mug of piping hot tea.

Chapter Eight

The Ashford's estate was a towering building, half carved into the side of the eastern mountains, and looming far above the city. We took a carriage from the castle, for appearances more than anything. It was ridiculous that winged creatures allowed themselves to be bedecked in such finery, their hair fashioned into elaborate hairstyles and limb weighted down with jewels, making it nearly impossible to fly.

But here I was, wings tucked beneath my skin, riding in a carriage drawn by black horses through the mountains, gazing out the windows at the shadowed landscape beyond. My father sat beside Perceval, both males quietly conversing about the meeting from earlier today. Orella perched on the cushioned bench beside me, shoulder to shoulder, huffing occasionally to make her displeasure at the lack of conversation known.

I didn't care how bored she was, my throat closed up every time I opened my mouth to speak.

So I stared at the changing landscape, watching the violet lights of the city change to the dark, moonlit paths of the forests. The black treeline blurred by as we rode up the precarious mountain paths, snaking our way to the estate. I tried and failed to summon the will to survive this dinner, to push through the tedious conversation and expensive dishes that were always too small to leave you satisfied.

Maybe, if I were lucky, I'd be able to exit soon after dessert to 'retire early' and instead fly over to Lucinda's before she closed for the night. My mouth watered at the thought of a pumpkin pastry and a warm tea to wash it down.

"I don't understand why we were all made to come tonight," Orella murmured beside me.

I glanced at her. "What, did you have plans tonight?"

She didn't respond.

I twisted in my seat, my grin growing. "Or did you have a date?"

She straightened in her seat. "I am an Elway princess, Aria. I do not have *dates*."

"My apologies, did you have a tryst with another palace guard tonight?" I snorted.

Orella's eyes widened comically, darting toward Father and Perceval, still lost in their whispered conversation. "Do you want him to flay the skin from my body?" she hissed.

I laughed again, shaking my head. "So long as you don't bear an illegitimate heir, I doubt he'd care. You're over a century old, the thought you'd be a virginal bride is a bit... reaching, wouldn't you agree?"

Orella slapped my arm and Perceval's eyes darted over to us. His pale brows narrowed slightly, but my father murmured something in his ear and his attention was dragged back into their conversation.

I choked down my laughter while Orella looking pointedly out the carriage window for the remainder of the drive.

The manor came into view ten minutes later, the towering elm trees parting to reveal a sweeping drive leading up to the dark estate, windows lit with flickering orange light. And there, leaning against the railing with his arms crossed, gaze searing down the drive, was Kellen.

"Speaking of fuck buddies," Orella whispered.

I flushed, elbowing her in the ribs as the carriage lurched to a stop.

Kellen took the steps two at a time, reaching the carriage door in a few long strides. He pulled it open, bowing with a grin on his face as he held up a hand to help me out. I beat the butterflies in my gut into submission as I ignored his hand and helped myself down.

"What are you doing?" I said, stepping aside to let Orella, Perceval, and my father file out.

"Being chivalrous, Princess."

"Don't, it doesn't suit you."

Kellen laughed, nodding to my father in greeting. "Your Majesty, I hope the trip up the mountain was a smooth one?"

I expected my father to merely nod, to continue on with his conversation and ignore Kellen entirely. Instead, he *smiled* at Kellen. "Indeed it was. Thank you for the invitation."

I gaped as my father, Perceval, and Orella filed up the stairs into the well-lit foyer. "You invited us?"

Kellen's smile faltered a bit. "Sort of. Aria—"

"Kellen!" a shrill voice called from inside the house. A slight woman with perfectly coiffed hair and a sleek blue gown stepped outside. "Inside, please. You wouldn't want to keep the king waiting."

Duchess Ashford smiled down at me, and I nodded my head in greeting. I turned back to Kellen, my smile faltering as I took in his stiff spine, his jaw clenched tight. His eyes were still fixed on his mother, some silent exchange passing between them.

He broke contact with her, nodding his head once and guiding me up the stairs.

"Are you excited for your twenty-first birthday, Aria?" the duchess asked in between delicate bites of boar.

I chewed my food, trying to hide my grimace. I honestly hadn't given my birthday much thought, forgetting about it entirely until the fall chill had swept through the valley and Rhea had mentioned it casually over drinks last week. "Yes, I'm sure the gala my father has planned will be beautiful."

The duchess smiled at me, her eyes flicking between Kellen and I for the thousandth time, setting my nerves on edge. "We'll be in attendance, of course. We received your mother's invitation last month."

I sipped my wine to conceal my discomfort.

Last month, my mother spent twenty-two days catatonic in bed. Those invitations were sent out by Amabel, the preparations for the gala my father insisted I have coordinated by a team of already over-burdened ladies' maids in my mother's stead. I spent twenty-two late nights spoon feeding my mother broth, rotating her in bed, and cleansing her skin and hair with a towel until the episode finally broke.

As a result, I didn't even know where the damned party was being held. And I truly couldn't care less.

But galas and social events lived at the center of a fallen duchess's life, so I engaged in conversation with her about colors, themes, appetizers, and the tedious particulars of an exclusive guest list, until my father finally interjected.

By that point, our dishes were being cleared away by near-silent servants, the conversation dwindling as fast as the wine in the crystal decanters. He raised his glass, his eyes scanning the Ashfords with a twist of a smile on his lips. "A toast to my lifelong friends and my greatest supporters during these tumultuous few centuries in power. I thank you for your continued support at court."

Everyone raised their drinks, murmuring the sentiment as glass clinked together around the table.

Duke Ashford threw back the remains of the amber liquid in his glass, setting it down and eyeing my father. "It is our continued pleasure to support you, my King. We do, however, wish to discuss the terms of a strengthened alliance between our families this evening."

Strengthened alliance?

I glanced at Kellen beside me, but his eyes were locked on his father, the muscles in his jaw working.

"Barrett," my father smiled, his eyes finding mine, "it's as if you read my mind."

They all laughed, even Kellen, and my gaze snapped to his again. My heartbeat accelerated in my chest, my palms slicking with sweat. No, they couldn't be talking about—

Kellen rose from his seat, bowing before my father. "Your Majesty, I would be honored if we could take this conversation to the drawing room."

My throat went dry. I cleared it as best I could before I asked. "What conversation?"

Kellen stilled for such a brief moment, I'd thought I'd imagined it.

My father quirked a brow. "The arrangements for your engagement, Aria.'"

Chapter nine

E*ngagement?*

"Don't you mean courtship?" Orella piped in beside me.

Father waved her off, rounding the table to stand beside Kellen. "What the Ashfords have offered in exchange for Aria's hand negates the need for such formalities. Please, enjoy your wine and conversation, ladies. We will be back shortly."

I watched with wide, stricken eyes as all the men, save Benedict, left the room. Silence descended upon the dining room, thick and heavy, as I tried and failed to grasp on to the threads of my composure.

I could feel Orella's gaze burning into the side of my head, but I couldn't bring myself to meet it. To face the pity and concern etched on her face.

Reida, a near silent guest until now, quickly engaged the duchess in conversation in my stead, drawing her attention away from where I sat, frozen.

This wasn't supposed to happen this soon.

Orella hadn't even accepted a *courtship* yet.

I had a war to concern myself with, a curse to break and my life to preserve in the process. The Ashfords spent half the year in

Illenora, several days' flight from Calasera. And I had a mother who would likely throw herself from the cliffside into the sea the moment I wasn't here, riding Amabel's ass the make sure she was never left alone.

A mother who couldn't feed herself when the darkness inside of her swallowed her whole. A mother who would rot in bed if I wasn't here to intervene, to brush her knotted hair and cleanse her skin, to read her books and bring her vanilla cinnamon milk tea to remind her she was still alive.

I still needed her, even after a decade of this fucked up role reversal where I took care of her.

And... there was still that small spark of hope for a better life in my chest. The small desire for love and freedom and *more*.

It felt as though I were breathing through a reed, my body slipping beneath the crushing black of a lake. My legs began to tingle, losing feeling as the world narrowed down to this one moment. To me, staring at my half-empty wineglass, while a group of fallen men determined how they would further shackle me.

How they would drain me of my life magic, bleeding it into the soil for their vengeance. And how they would then chain me to another male, no longer my father's responsibility. I would become nothing, wasting away in a manor that's far too large and far too quiet to ever feel like the home I had always craved. Breeding my magic into small bodies, weighted with the expectations of my father's crown.

And that would be the end of my life.

Bleak, empty, leeched of all the hopes I might've once had for something better.

"Aria, would you accompany me to the powder room?" Orella said casually, taking a small sip of her wine and rising elegantly from the table.

The duchess's eyes flicked away from Reida up to one of the servants stoically standing in the shadows. "Matilda will lead you down the hall."

I blinked furiously to clear the tears threatening to push through, rising and giving the duchess the best smile I could muster before I followed Orella and Matilda down the hall.

Matilda left us in a large, cream-colored room attached to a bathing chamber. The moment the door was shut, she spun on me. "Get it together."

I blinked, my mouth gaping. "What?"

She crossed her arms, an impervious expression crossing her face. "I said you need to get it together, Aria. Before Father comes back."

"He announced—"

"I know what he announced, and I understand how you might feel about it, truly I do, but you need to pull it together. Now, before Kellen returns and asks to see you outside to propose."

All the rich food I had consumed twisted in my gut. "Fuck, I'm going to be sick."

Orella crossed the distance between us, gripping my cheeks in her cold hands. "No, you're not. You're going to take a moment to reel all those extreme emotions in, you're going to walk back into that room like the princess you are, and you aren't going to give father something to beat you over tonight."

My mouth watered, but I swallowed quickly. "I need to talk to Kellen."

Maybe... maybe there was a way to stop this. Or slow it down, for a few years at least. Or maybe he had an explanation, for why he hid this from me. Goddess, on the beach, and then again in my room...

I had thought he was trying to share his feelings, and in a way, he was. But *this*?

Orella gave me a pitying smile. "No, honey, you don't. He isn't your friend, not anymore. After tonight, he'll be your betrothed. You'll need to be more careful around him, toeing the same line you walk with Father and Perceval."

"But—"

"No, Aria. Trust me on this. I've lived this life for over a century longer than you. You don't get to have any feelings about this. This isn't about your heart, Aria. It's a business transaction. It's not personal, and just because it came sooner than you expected, it doesn't change the reality." She straightened, releasing her grip on my face. "Now, wipe that expression off your face, smooth out your hair, and meet me in the hall when you've gained control."

Her nimble fingers tucked a stray lock of hair behind my ear before she left, the door clicking softly behind her.

I perched on the edge of the vanity, fingers digging into wood. I tried and failed to reel in my emotions, to shrink them down to manageable pieces, small enough to shove into their respective boxes. It was no use; they were too strong, sweeping me away in a blaze I couldn't control.

Smoke curled behind my teeth, my veins igniting with anger.

Orella was wrong.

Kellen was a lot of things, but he was still my friend. Even if things had been shifting between us, a tension radiating through our friendship that hadn't existed before. Even if he looked at me differently, whispering that he loved me when he thought I wasn't listening.

He was still Kellen.

I couldn't put enough distance between us to see him as anything but the boy I'd sharpened myself against for ten years now. The boy who jumped off of cliffs into the icy ocean with me, caring for me in all the small ways he always had.

I pushed myself firmly off the vanity, pacing back to the dining room, my jaw set in determination as I channeled the unruly emotions swirling in my chest.

Orella and I returned to the dining room just as the door opposite of us opened, the men shuffling in. My father smiled broadly, clapping Kellen on the shoulder with a nod of his head. Like they had settled on an advantageous business transaction. Nausea lurched in my stomach, but I swallowed it thickly as I stared Kellen down.

Forcing him to meet my gaze.

He finally did, his smile dimming as his red eyes held on to mine. "May I see you outside, Aria?"

I lowered my mental shields, still holding his gaze. *Is that a request or a command?*

Kellen flinched, but I slammed my walls down before he could respond.

"Of course," I replied demurely, dipping my chin and earning a look of approval from Orella. He rounded the dining room to where I stood, my heart thudding irregularly in my chest with every step he took.

Kellen led me back down the hall I had returned from, taking a left instead of a right to lead me onto the terrace. I paced toward the balcony, eyes fixed on the lights dotting the slope of the mountains.

Kellen rested his forearms on the balcony, sighing wearily.

I closed my eyes briefly against the flash of anger in my chest, fighting for control over my tongue.

I lost that battle quickly. "What in all the seven hells do you have to feel exasperated over?"

Kellen glanced down at me. "I didn't want to do it like this, Aria."

I laughed bitterly. "Oh, my apologies. I'm so sorry this isn't panning out the way you envisioned."

"I tried to tell you—"

I pushed away from the balcony. "Don't you dare do that."

"What?"

"*Blame* me for being blindsided."

He threw his hands up. "You always knew this would happen, Aria."

I tasted ash on my tongue as I whirled on him. "No, I always knew it *might* happen, just like I always knew it *might* not, or that I *might* be bound to someone else, or I might die in this asinine war my father is trying to wage. I knew it was only one of about a dozen shitty outcomes for my future, but I had hoped that, while I was still so vital to my father's vendetta, this would be a problem I wouldn't have to face for years."

Kellen glared down at me. "So I'm just a problem you had to figure out how to deal with in the future?"

"You were my *best friend*!" I hated myself for the way my voice cracked, the trembling in my hands. Goddess, I longed to be in control of my emotions. To only feel the razor edge of anger at being taken for a fool, not this mess of bleeding pain in my chest. It was a weakness, to feel this deeply.

One I had never quite managed to cut out.

I swallowed around the unshed tears in my throat. "You were my best friend, and yet here I am. Blindsided and betrothed to you, watching you step into an office with my father and join his side against me."

"I'm on your side, Aria."

"Stop fucking kidding yourself, Kellen. You went behind my back and made a deal for my hand with my father to further your own ambitions. You're not on my side, you're on his. You now stand in line as the third male that controls my life, right behind my father and Perceval."

Kellen's eyes went cold. "Do you have any idea who your father was going to accept a courtship to?"

I shook my head curtly.

"Marckus Dalias."

My blood ran cold. "How do you know?"

"Because," Kellen said harshly as he took two short steps toward me, "he was bragging about it after the guards' meeting the other week. Baron Dalias met with your father last month and paid a steep price for a courtship with you, following the war."

Marckus Dalias was known for frequenting brothels in the city and leaving a bloody mess in his wake. He's banned from more than one establishment by the madams that run them, but the closer you get to the slums, the less protections are afforded to the women who work in those places. Desperation often makes one willing to endure a beating at a noble's hand, especially when he's carrying a heavy bag of gold.

I swallowed thickly. "You could have warned me—"

"I wouldn't be able to live with myself if something happened to you, Aria. Not at the hands of Marckus fucking Dalias."

"So what? You walked in my father's office and offered him a higher price?"

"Yes."

I stepped forward, eyes narrowing. "How much?"

He blinked. "What?"

"How much was I worth?"

"I didn't pay for you, Aria," he said softly.

"Then what could you have possibly offered him that would have made him throw away every other courtship? To skip straight to an engagement without a second thought?"

"It doesn't matter."

I threw up my hands. "Seriously?"

Kellen threw me an incredulous look. "I did it to protect you."

"I don't need your protecting!"

"Yes, you do!" he yelled, sending a jolt through me.

Kellen had never so much as raised his voice at me. I watched with wide eyes as he took a step away, pinching the bridge of his nose and squeezing his eyes shut tight.

"I'm sorry," he apologized softly, taking a step toward me.

I took a step back, keeping distance between us. "I don't need your protection, Kellen."

I was so sick of everyone making decisions for me, moving me around like a damn chess piece. Of deciding what I need, where I go and who I'll be. I was so painfully accustomed to it when it came to my father, but Kellen... I hadn't expected this from him. I couldn't help but look at him differently now, that small desire I'd been avoiding for him souring in my stomach.

"On the beach, I was trying to find the words to tell you," he said softly.

I threw my hands in the air. "I thought you were going to tell me you loved me."

Kellen froze. "You ran away."

I couldn't look at him now, at the bald hurt on his face, so I looked past him. At the stars dotting the black sky, the sparse clouds drifting across the three, yellow moons above. The burning desire to draw my wings to the surface, to toss these damned heels from my feet and fly into the night, raced down my spine. Gods, how easy it was to dream when the bars to my cage were invisible.

Even if I could feel them tightening around me now.

"Aria," he said softly, drawing my eyes up to his. "I could make you happy, if you let me."

As if I were choosing to be unhappy. As if any of this was my choice.

All the energy to fight him leeched from my veins, leaving my body feeling far too heavy. I tried and failed to shore up my defenses, to grip the frayed edges of my composure and hold on to the rage, but there was nothing there. Only a dark numbness, the desire to lie down and let it all roll over me.

Kellen's eyes raked over the stoop in my shoulders, the heaviness to my eyes, and I saw his misunderstanding dawn on his face. He closed the distance between us, and I was too drained to maintain it.

He cupped my cheek, and when I didn't pull away, he saw it as a small victory. I sank into his touch like the defeat it was.

"Let me protect you from this. If it's going to be anyone, I'm your best choice. I won't hurt you, you know that."

Did I? I wasn't so sure anymore.

Kellen reached into the inner pocket of his cloak, withdrawing a small, velvet box. My eyes fixed blankly on the box as he opened it, revealing a beautiful ring. Inlaid in its center, set between two small diamonds, was a large, dark green emerald.

My hand felt as though it was no longer attached to my body as he raised it delicately, sliding the band over my left ring finger.

I tore my eyes away to hold his, and I wondered how he saw me in this moment. We were so close, his head bent low over mine. I could see myself reflected in his eyes in the torchlight. Pale, wide-eyed, lips slightly ajar.

He smiled gently down at me, cupping my cheek once more, and my stomach twisted. Gods, how could he say he loved me when he couldn't even see me? How could he smile at me while I was drifting outside of my own body?

Gently, Kellen pressed his lips to mine, and though I'd thought about kissing him before, it felt wrong.

It felt more like he was claiming me in a way that had less to do with love and more to do with conquest.

He drew away, grinning now. "This is a good thing, Aria. Please, I'll prove it to you. I'm on your side, from now until forever. Whatever you need, whatever you want once this war is over, it's yours."

Freedom. I wanted agency over my own life. I wanted to exist in a body that wasn't controlled by the desires of others.

"I want you to put me before my father," I rasped.

Kellen's eyes darkened. "Always."

"Promise?"

He dipped his chin eagerly. "Anything, Aria. I will do anything to earn back your trust."

I clung to that one, small promise like a lifeline.

Maybe, in time, I could learn to love him. If I didn't have a choice in this, I'd have to make the best of it. My father would have only handed me off to a male he believed would control me as well as he always had, but maybe he was wrong for once.

Maybe happiness was a choice after all.

"Rhea?" I hissed into the darkness, hours later.

I stood on her threshold, eyes slowly adjusting to her dimly lit home. A gasp, followed by a loud thump answered. Rhea's head popped up in the stream of lamplight beaming in from the street outside her house. Golden eyes, dazed and bleary, met mine.

"Aria?" she said, voice groggy.

She rose to her full height, and I blinked. "You're naked."

Rhea looked down, wincing as she scooped up a blanket off the floor. "Yes. But you don't get to complain, showing up at my house at... what time is it?" She squinted at her clock hanging beside the fireplace.

"One," I said, flopping down on her couch and sending a spiral of flames into her fireplace. Violet light filled the apartment.

Two empty wine glasses sat on the low coffee table, two dishes still sitting on the kitchen counter, and a trail of clothes littered the normally tidy stairs...

"Oh my goddess," I gasped, looking up the stairs and back at Rhea, "did you have a date?!"

Rhea grinned, scooping up her shirt off the stairs and dropping the blanket to slip it on over her head. "Mhm."

I choked on a laugh. "Is said date still here?"

Rhea gave me a lopsided grin as she collapsed back on the couch, tugging the blanket up to her chin. "Yeah, she's been asleep for a few hours now."

"Does she know about your aversion to sharing a bed?"

Rhea winced. "Nope. I was planning on sneaking back into bed before she woke up."

"Do I know her?"

Her golden eyes darted away from me, hands running through her wild curls as she tried to tame them. She mumbled a name I could barely make out.

I raised a brow. "Repeat that?"

Rhea cleared her throat. "Lucinda."

I gasped, throwing the pillow in my lap across the coffee table at her. "Rhea! You better be nice to her, I can't find us a new cafe!" Not one with pastries or coffee and tea anywhere near as good as Lucinda's.

"It's casual, and she knows it! I promise, I would never put your tea and pastries at risk." She held her hand over her heart in a solemn swear. Rhea's eyes lowered to my dress with an assessing look. "Didn't you have your birthday dinner tonight?"

I didn't answer right away, looking down at the tassels on the blanket beside me. Rhea leaned forward, her golden eyes going wide.

"What the fuck is on your finger?"

I grimaced, holding up my hand. She nearly climbed on top of the busted coffee table to get a better look, pulling my hand up to her face. She let out a low whistle, her eyebrows raised, as she sat back down on the couch. "Kellen Ashford?"

"Yeah."

"And you said yes?"

I quirked a brow. "They don't normally let you take the ring if you don't accept." Not that I had a choice in it.

Rhea's eyes searched mine. "Without a courtship?"

"Apparently, the Ashfords paid a high price." I tried to brush it off, but my words fell flat.

"You aren't exactly exuding 'blushing bride.' How are you feeling?"

I didn't honestly know anymore. Everything was so muddled now, the outrage and sorrow blending with confusion after I spoke to Kellen. I sighed, setting aside the blanket and scanning the living room. My eyes found a corked bottle of wine abandoned on the floor. I swooped it up, uncorked it, and took a long swig. "I feel fine."

Rhea snorted, wiggling her fingers across the table. I passed her the bottle, watching her take a long drink. "A truth for a truth?"

I smiled softly. Rhea had asked me that same question years ago when our friendship was still new and any amount of vulnerability was scathing. She had asked for a truth for her own raw truth, making the sharing of information less painful than it would be if it was done alone.

"You first," I countered.

Rhea drew in a sharp breath, her gaze flitting to the stairs briefly. "Feeling anyone breathe in my bed beside me makes me think of my mom. We shared a bed, back in our little cottage in Casserine. And it makes me remember how it felt to wake and find… to find her not breathing. To realize how silent my world became in the absence of that small, soft noise I had barely acknowledged before. Whenever someone falls asleep beside me, it's all I can hear, the breathing and then the absence of my mother's, and I feel like the walls are closing in on me until I can't handle it."

I watched with silver-lined eyes as Rhea took a deep drink from the wine. She rarely spoke of Casserine. She never spoke of her mother. All I knew was that she loved Casserine, loved her home

among the elves. Even as a half-fallen, they accepted her. Until her
mother died, and she felt as if the island had died along with her.
Then, she fled. That's how she ended up in Calasera, searching for
a father she never found, only to end up alone and begging on the
streets at age twelve.

Rhea handed me the wine.

This game only worked if the other let the truth hang in the air.
No sympathy, no belaboring the point. A simple exchange of one fact
for another.

I drank deeply, feeling the sweet red wine dry my tongue.

"I might die to achieve my father's goals. And everyone's acting
like they can fix my lacking abilities and set forth plans for my future
as if dying is some far-off improbability. But…" I swallowed thickly. "I feel like I'm staring down a path I've never wanted. Kellen is
kind, and a part of me loves him, but there's a part of me that's so
painfully loud. And that part of me desperately wants to be free. I
don't want to be a duke's wife, standing a pace behind him at all the
galas. I don't want to run his house or bear him heirs. I don't want to
fulfill my one, singular purpose in life only to come back to this city
as someone's wife and little else."

I turned to meet Rhea's gaze, bright in the dim lighting. Luminous like an animal. "I used to hope I would live to find more. To
find a life I actually wanted. Now… I'm beginning to hope I will die
giving up my life magic. It would be easier to die swiftly, when the
alternative is rotting away in a cage of my father's making."

I saw it on Rhea's face, the desire to say more. But she merely
got up, walked into the kitchen, and returned a moment later with
another bottle of wine.

We didn't speak after that, sitting in each other's words, drinking
until the pain ebbed and our truth lost its razor-sharp, cutting edge.
Sitting with each other's pain, knowing there was little the other
could do to take it away. We've always known that the best thing we
could do for each other was to bear the weight of the words we had
shared, hoping it might feel a touch lighter to not be alone with them.

Chapter Ten

I drew in a steadying breath as I watched my mother staring out the window beside her bed. She hadn't moved when I opened the door, and I doubted she knew I was here. I couldn't bring myself to eat breakfast before walking over, and I was sorely regretting that decision now. Nothing but black tea sat in my stomach, churning with apprehension and anxiety.

Not that I'd been able to eat much these past few days, not when my stomach churned every time I glanced down at the glittering new ring perched on my left hand.

My mother had been more and more distant these past few months, drawing so deeply inside of herself I could hardly imagine following. I wished I knew where she went when she stared out at the city far below with that hollow look in her eyes. I wished she would let me in, only a little, to all the torment raging in her mind.

No one had told me the full story of how my father had taken my mother. What little I knew I had gleaned during her lapses in sanity these past ten years, when violence had preceded the silent melancholy I had become accustomed to now. She used to shatter vases, picture frames, chairs, anything she could get her hands on. All while screaming nearly incomprehensible pieces of her past.

From what I had stitched together, he lured her into a false sense of security on the border of the Veil, gaining her trust enough for her to step beyond the safety of angel territory, and the rest is too brutal for me to linger on for long. My mother had been kind, soft, and loving in my early years. I grieved what little I recalled of that version of her. I often found myself here, rooted in place behind her, wishing she would turn around with clear eyes and a warm smile.

I cleared my throat softly, my mother flinching at the sound. She always flinched, like a wounded, caged animal expecting the next blow.

She turned around slowly, the corners of her lips twitching into what was supposed to be a smile. "Ah, there's the almost birthday girl. I was wondering if you forgot about me."

I grimaced. "I've been busy, preparing for—"

She waved me off before patting the bench beside her. "Please, don't discuss all the preparations you've been making for your father's plans. I'd rather not know any more about his ministrations than I must."

I nodded, turning my gaze out the window. It was almost cruel, the view my mother had. From the vantage point in the tower, the city below was a glimmering, beautiful cityscape frame in by the eastern mountains. Dark, with buildings towering to impossible heights, wrapped in twisting metal and cathedral windows. All stained glass, spires, and golden domes kissed by the sun. The gold bedecking the city looked near molten in the sunlight, but it was truly beautiful at night. When the blue and violet flames lit the streetlamps and the moon silvered the golden roofs, the entire city bowing to the endless starry night reflected in the Delanora river before it poured out into the Paramana sea.

It was beautiful from up here, every small crack and flaw in Calasera concealed by the distance of the tower. And yet, this is the only way my mother had seen the city—from far, far away. She was always looking down on the world, from windows and towers, in paintings and dreams.

My mother ran her fingers through my hair, and I leaned gently into the touch. She did my hair for years until her bad days finally began to outweigh her good ones. I missed it, this casual touch, this small moment of being cared for. I closed my eyes as she split my knotted hair gently, brushing it through with the small, silver brush on the bench beside her.

"Mama?" I whispered softly.

"Hm?"

"Do you remember your twenty-first birthday?"

Her fingers halted briefly before she began weaving an intricate braid through my hair. "That was a long time ago, but I still remember."

"What happened?"

I could almost hear the smile in her voice. I longed to turn around and see it, however fleeting. "My parents threw me a party covering the entire capital. Every angel had their gaze set toward the castle courtyard, high above the city, waiting to watch another Archangel step into power."

I knew so little of angel heritage, of the other blood running through my veins. "Angels settle into their magic on their twenty-first birthdays?"

"Archangel heirs do, yes. There are only seven chairs among the Archangels, sharing the power in Estrellania. When an Archangel has a child, their settling will determine if they are destined to inherit the title of Archangel once their parent has stepped down."

I furrowed my brow. "Archangels step down?"

My mother laughed lightly. "Yes, they do not wish to hold power forever. Immortality… it changes a mind, and not always for the better. It is best to keep a healthy rotation every few centuries. The council will often put it to a vote when it becomes apparent an Archangel is reaching an age where it would be best to replace them with their heir."

My father would only yield the throne to Perceval in death. Someone would have to cut his head clean from his shoulders to end his reign. He'd allow centuries to go by, perched on his black marble throne, allowing his brain to rot away beneath the bane of immortality and still he'd relish his position as ruler of all he could grasp in his greedy hands.

I couldn't fathom a kingdom where they considered such a noble way of leading.

As if she heard my thoughts, my mother added softly, "Don't allow that fact alone to convince you of their character. The angels are… they are a prideful people, with little interest in those beyond their borders. They have slaughtered and enslaved and abused their way across this continent the same way the Fallen did before the dark war."

My mother finished the first braid, laying it thickly on my back before she reached for the second. I used that moment to glance back at her. A bitter edge now tugged her lips down, the small bit of levity gone from her features. "Are you concerned for tonight?"

She finished the braid, and I hesitated, twisting the small fray of the teal blanket on the bench. I wasn't sure how to answer. "Perhaps a bit," I said distantly, twirling the end of my braid as I stared back out the window.

My mother watched me for a moment longer before she turned her gaze back down on the world. "I am sorry I have been…" she trailed off, clearing her throat. "I haven't been a mother to you, Aria. You deserved so much more than I ever could have given you here."

My eyes fluttered shut at the hitch in her breath, the stinging behind my eyes sudden and unwelcome. "Mother—"

She held up her hand to stop me. "Don't make excuses for me, please. I know what your childhood has been, taking care of me while trying to bend yourself into whatever shape your father needed you to be." She turned to face me fully, cupping my cheek in her hand. "You grew up so fast," she murmured.

A tear escaped my eye, rolling down my cheek. She brushed it away and gave me a shaky smile. "I wanted to say sorry, for whatever pain I may have caused you."

"I never blamed you."

The sadness in my mother's eyes was oceans deep. "That almost makes it worse."

I didn't respond, instead leaning my head against my mother's shoulder as we lapsed into silence. This lucidity, this small glimmer of clarity, was rare from her. I couldn't bring myself to move from it, to speak another word, lest it slipped through my fingers again.

Chapter Eleven

I awoke the morning of my twenty-first birthday to a small black cat with golden eyes perched on my nightstand, a purr rumbling out of her chest. I flew out of bed, smothering a small scream in my throat. Rhea merely cocked her head to the side, casually licking her paws, ever the convincing cat.

"Are you insane?" I hissed, stalking across the room to lock my bedroom door.

She loosed a few short meows before batting a small box off the nightstand. I lurched, catching it in my hands and glowering down at her. She only blinked slowly, her feline face smug. I peered down at the box, the wooden exterior wrapped with a simple, green bow. "I told you no gifts."

Rhea came to perch beside me on the bed, rubbing against my arm as if urging me to open it. I sighed, scratching behind her ears before pulling the bow off, letting it fall in a pile to the floor. Cracking open the lid, a small, golden ring inlaid with a red gem glimmered back at me. Tucked beneath the stunning ring was a small piece of paper, which I quickly unfolded.

Happy Birthday! I wrote this because I can't explain the ring when I'm sitting next to you as a cat, but consider this our wedding

ring, in case you ever forget who your real soulmate is. It's from Cas-
serine. So it's a little piece of me to always carry with you.
   Love you, babe, don't ever forget it.
   P.S. I'm scheduled to be the bane of your father's existence
during your party, so I hope you can forgive me for not attending as
your strange animal companion for the evening.

I swallowed against the prick of tears in my eyes as I picked up
the band, fitting it snuggly on my right ring finger. I swooped Rhea
up in her cat form, mushing her against my cheek. "I love you more.
Be safe tonight, alright?" I wouldn't waste my breath begging Rhea
to let go of her band of thieves, to take up Lucinda on her offer to
work at the coffeehouse and to accept a supplemental income from
me. I had begged her for years to no avail, and I wouldn't spoil the
moment now with anything but a prayer to the goddess she would be
safe.

A knock on the door sent Rhea scurrying out of my arms, a moment before Kellen's muffled voice called my name. I raced over to
the door, tugging my robe tightly over my chest as I went. I opened
it to find Kellen smiling down at me, holding what smelled like a
cinnamon latte and a small gift bag. He grinned, and I waited for my
heart to skip a beat at the appearance of the dimple in his left cheek,
but... nothing. I pasted my lips into a smile, opening the door to let
him through.

He leaned down and gave me a quick kiss on my head before
walking in, setting the bag and drink down on the coffee table before
the hearth. He opened his mouth to speak but faltered, his eyebrows
narrowing as he stared at Rhea, perched on a chair with her golden
eyes fixed on him.

"I didn't know you had a cat," he said, turning back around to
face me.

"I don't. She's... lost." I inwardly cringed.

"Lost?"

"Yes, she sort of wandered in here. It's fine, I'll find her owner
tomorrow!" I waved him off.

He shrugged, reaching down to pet Rhea. To my horror, she flat-
tened her ears, hissing and swatting her claws at his extended hand.
Kellen jerked back, eyebrows raised as the cat resumed her casual
grooming, golden eyes gleaming mischievously.

"Anyway," he said, laughing softly and shaking his head. He

turned back to me, holding out the bag. "I wanted to wish you a happy birthday before anyone else."

Rhea chattered happily behind him, a self-satisfied look on her face.

"Thank you," I said to Kellen, reaching inside the bag to find two leather bound books resting at the bottom. I pulled the first out carefully, reading over the title in a small, scrawling script.

Poetry and Prose was scrawled across the cover, the pages weathered and yellowed with age. My heart tightened as I flipped through it absently. The second book had a black cover with the title written in sloping, silver script: *The Starlight Queen.*

"I noticed you haven't been reading much lately, so I thought I'd pick out a couple books for you to get back into," he said, rubbing his neck as he peered down at me.

My face softened. "Thank you, Kellen. It's perfect."

He noticed I hadn't been reading. Something in that small observation chipped away at the last traces of anger.

He smiled, clearing his throat. "Yes, well, with that I have a meeting to get to. I'll see you tonight?"

I set the books down and pressed up on my toes, brushing my lips gently against his. "Pick me up at seven? We can walk over together."

Surprise flickered over his face before he smiled against my lips, deepening the kiss. He pulled back only a bit, long enough to run his fingers across my cheek. "Sounds like a deal, Princess."

With a glance at the cat gawking on the couch beside me, he was gone.

Rhea watched me with wide eyes, her fuzzy head cocked to the side.

"What?" I narrowed my eyes.

She merely resumed licking her paw, looking up at me innocently.

I rolled my eyes and fell back on my bed. "I'm trying, Rhea. It's the least I can do."

This room was a near replica of my birthday from eleven years ago.

The same gold decor adorned the ballroom, painting the otherwise black and red space with notes of luxury. The aristocracy was in full attendance this evening, with those residing outside of Calasera having arrived at court throughout the week. It was a sea of blood red, with each guest boasting black wings adorned with jewels so large they could pay to feed an entire neighborhood in the slums for a decade. The only difference between my birthday as a child and now was I no longer had the comfortable space of standing beside my father on a dais all evening.

Now, I had to mingle among the many guests. I kept a demure smile pressed to my lips for so long my cheeks ached. I had said 'thank you' so many times my tongue was thick with the lie, and I had held my hand up to show off the engagement ring to so many women now my hand felt awkward and detached from my body.

The droning conversation blended with the lilting orchestra, the clinking of glasses, and the superficial laughter. It all merged into a low hum that pressed uncomfortably against my mind. How I loathed crowds and gatherings, especially when I was supposed to be at the center of it all.

"Aria?"

I jolted, tearing my eyes away from where they had fallen on the golden clock resting on the fireplace mantel. Kellen was standing beside me, speaking to two other couples whose names I had missed in the introduction, and I desperately hoped I wouldn't need to recall.

They all stared at me expectantly.

I cleared my throat, plastering a serene smile on my face as I dipped my head apologetically. "I'm sorry, I seem to have missed your question."

They chuckled softly, the dark-skinned man to the right leaning in closer to speak above the din. "I imagine, if I were you, I would also find it hard to focus. I merely asked if you and Lord Ashford planned on residing in Calasera, or if you'd acquaint yourself with Ilenora after the wedding?"

"And I told Lorien that it would be entirely up to my beautiful bride," Kellen added with a sweet smile.

My chest tightened. Goddess, he was too kind. And I was hopelessly ungrateful for… for wishing for more.

"I'd like to stay in Calasera for a time, once the war is over."

I cringed the moment the words left my mouth. The two couples shifted awkwardly, exchanging tight smiles and glancing between each other. I always forget how 'unbecoming' it was to mention the upcoming conflict among the aristocracy, outside of council chambers and war rooms. War was a messy, bloody business that these people liked to keep locked far away from their embroidered gowns and fine china.

Despite the fact that all the men in the aristocracy were conscripted to serve a mandatory decade in the fallen army. That was always for show, none of them actually expected to bleed for their country unless they hailed from a family that took pride in their warrior bloodlines, like the Ashfords.

What a privileged, polished life they lived, burying their heads in the clouds while the rest of the world was about to dissolve into chaos.

The delicate fallen woman standing slightly behind her husband cocked her head to the side. Her ash blonde hair swayed with the movement as she gave me an assessing look through strange, nearly golden irises. Such an unusual color for a fallen. "Do you fear it?"

I blinked at the baldness of her question, the open curiosity in her stare. "The war, or the magic that will help to facilitate it?"

She smiled softly. "The war, though I am also curious about how you feel about the magic you wield."

I opened my mouth to reply, my eyebrows quirking at the question, but the man cleared his throat. "That is hardly an appropriate question, Teryani. I apologize, Princess."

The woman bowed slightly, allowing herself to be whisked away by her husband, his grip a bit too tight on her arm for my liking.

"You wish to remain in Calasera?" Kellen turned to me as the other couple wandered off, leaving us alone on the edge of the ballroom.

I tore my eyes away from where Teryani had vanished in the crowd, looking up at Kellen. "Is that okay?"

"I'm surprised you aren't eager for a change in scenery, that's all. I won't mind staying for a few years after the wedding."

The wedding.

My throat dried out, and I tried desperately to clear it. "I… excuse me, I need to get a drink."

I walked away briskly before Kellen could respond, feeling the weight of his gaze as I wove through the crowds. I darted over to the small side table with flutes of sparkling wine resting upon it. Scooping up a glass, I swallowed the contents in one deep gulp, ignoring the guests lingering nearby and their curious stares.

Fuck, I needed to get a grip.

Talk of 'our wedding' and 'our future' and 'our home' made me feel like I was drowning. The engagement was new, so naturally this is where all the conversations would lead in a room full of people who solely cared about status and marriage and heirs.

If I was going to accept my future with grace and dignity, I needed to learn how to shove down this frantic, bleating desire to run any time the conversation drifted to questions of my future.

My eyes flicked over to the clock again. Gods, how much longer was I required to stay at my own party?

Would it be considered rude to turn in early? The image of my two new books, stacked neatly on my nightstand, flashed in my mind. I could be in bed, in a loose gown, with a mug of tea staying up all night to bury myself in someone else's world.

I groaned, reaching for another glass to dull my senses further. Drinking myself into a haze might be the easiest way to cope tonight.

"Enjoying the party?"

I jumped, swearing under my breath as the wine sloshed in the flute. I set the glass down, whirling around to glare up at Perceval. "I was until you showed up."

He laughed, reaching past me for a drink. "Why aren't you with your husband-to-be?" His gaze darted past us to Kellen, who looked trapped in another conversation, his body angled toward me. Like he had been following behind, only to find another couple in his path, filled with pleasantries and prying questions about our future.

I cringed, picking up the glass. "Why do you care?"

"I don't. I only thought I'd make polite conversation."

I peered around him, searching for Benedict or Orella or Reida. Literally anyone else to speak to. "I'm surprised you're here."

Perceval snorted, taking another sip. "Trust me, I'd much rather be off with Benedict right now. That bastard is going to have a more entertaining night than either of us."

I glanced up at him, curiosity getting the better of me. "Where is he?"

"Father didn't tell you?" A goading question.

"I don't have time for this," I said curtly, setting down my second empty glass and turning around. I spotted Orella in the corner, speaking to a fallen male I was positive she had no interest in, bore-dom dripping from her face.

I took three steps toward her when Perceval spoke again. "Father finally received some accurate intelligence on the band of thieves you've been hunting for him. He's going to intercept their leader to-night, at one of the manor houses along the river. His source, whoev-er that might be, tipped him off this morning."

I froze, my blood running cold. I forced myself to turn around casually, letting nothing but mild curiosity show on my face. It was a thin veneer, barely masking the terror racing beneath the surface. "Oh? What house?"

Perceval glanced around the room before stepping closer. "The Cliftons. You know, the gaudy black manor along the river? We used to go there for formal dinners all the time."

"Why aren't you with them?"

He glowered. "Because I'm supposed to show my support as the heir, Aria. Politics and all that shit. Goddess, you'd think it's your first day here in court."

His words didn't register as I glanced back at Kellen, his eyes still on me despite the conversation he was clearly trying to escape. I murmured a quick excuse to Perceval before slipping out through the terrace doors.

My wings were out, and I was flying into the city in a matter of seconds.

Chapter Twelve

I flew high above the city, ducking between clouds to stay hidden. Wind tore at my tedious updo, tugging strands of hair haphazardly over my face. I impatiently ripped the pins out, letting them fall to the ground far below.

I used the short flight across the city to reel in my chaotic thoughts, to slow my breathing and steady my heartbeat. I pulled the fear in, forcing my mind to clear. I was almost certain Benedict was already there, along with whatever team of guards my father had sent with him.

Which meant I didn't know what I would find once I arrived.

They could be lying in wait to capture Rhea, or I could step into an all-out fight.

If it was the former, I'd have to snag Rhea and force her to save herself. There was no way I'd get everyone from her band out, and frankly I didn't give a shit about the rest of them. I couldn't, not now. She was the only one I was worried about. Still, I knew it would be hard to convince her to leave them.

If it was the latter... I shook away the thought. No one could see me. I couldn't dwell on what would happen if someone recognized me, if my father learned I had abandoned my party to save the leader thieves' guild that I was supposed to be hunting for months now.

I banked over the river, Cliffton Manor coming into view. The large estate was a darker shadow against the night sky, its black spires and slanted roof nearly impossible to see at night, if not for the spots of blue lamps dotting the lawn. I landed softly on the roof, straining to hear.

There was no sound but the gently flowing river and the rustling of leaves as a crisp breeze blew through the surrounding trees. I paced the roof until I found a slant leading down to a cracked window.

This was so, so stupid.

Benedict could be inside the room, lying in wait for the thieves.

I sighed and slipped through, anyway. A lie formed on my tongue, a small excuse that I prayed to the goddess Benedict would accept, but when I landed on the soft carpet... I released a breath. It was empty. A cracked door on the other end of the room allowed a sliver of lamplight to cut through.

I was in a bedchamber, bedecked in deep purple and gold. I crept around the room, trying and failing to form a plan when I heard a crash downstairs, followed by several shouts.

Fuck plans.

I slid my dagger from the sheath on my thigh, ripping through my dress in two quick motions to free my legs. I kicked off the pointy heels pinching my feet before scanning the room frantically. I whipped open the closet, pulling an oversized cloak from a hanger. I tugged it on sloppily as I flipped through the clothes. I tugged a black silk scarf off a hanger and hastily tied it around my face before I pulled the deep hood over my head.

This could work. I only needed to get Rhea out safely.

I followed the commotion down the long hall and out onto a balcony overlooking the foyer. There, Benedict stood with a smug grin as five of his guards overpowered the three masked, hooded thieves. Sacks of loot sat abandoned on the floor, overflowing with precious jewelry, candelabras, a set of golden cutlery spilling out onto the wood floor.

Benedict's eyes flicked up to me, his smirk twisting with displeasure. "There's one more, up there by the banister," he said flippantly, crossing his arms and waving off one of his guards.

Not bothering to lift a finger of his own, I noted with rising annoyance. I'm sure he'd be touting a different story entirely when he got back to the castle this evening.

My eyes scanned the chaos below, and quickly they fell to a tall, lean figure, holding their own against two towering brutes.

That had to be Rhea.

She was lithe, skillful, and more than capable of cutting them down on her own.

I glanced at the guard barreling up the stairs, sliding my hand to the dagger in the sheath on my thigh. Freeing it, I waited two more breaths for the guard to crest the top of the stairs before I sent the blade hurtling for his throat. The blade struck true, sinking into the hilt and sending blood spraying up the walls. He took one stunned, stumbling step before he collapsed, blood oozing into the carpet. I tugged the sword free of his limp hand before I hurtled over the banister in one smooth motion, planting myself firmly between Rhea and the two other guards.

I couldn't out right use my magic, but I had learned a few tricks to take down an opponent in a more… *discreet* way.

Rhea's eyes flared as she glanced at me. The distraction cost her, the guard's sword slicing across her forearm. Rhea growled low in her throat, the sound more animal than anything, before she launched back into battle, pushing the guard back until he slammed into a wall. I engaged the one on the left, and soon our swords were clashing as we parried and deflected, falling into a rhythmic dance. It felt good, if I could set aside the terror and stress of the situation for a moment, to use my body after hours at the gala.

To feel the weight of a blade in my hand, a burn in my muscles.

The guard's sword slipped on my own, his body weight lurching him forward clumsily. I used that as my opening, lowering my blade and tugging him in by the front of his tunic. I parted my lips, blowing a small tendril of fire out and willing it down his throat. The guard stumbled back, the whites of his eyes stark against the dimly lit corridor. He dropped his sword, every muscle in his body spasming as he clawed desperately at his throat, before he collapsed to his knees.

The guard opened his mouth to speak, but only blood poured out. The poor bastard was dead before he fell over, his insides now little more than hot liquid pooling out of every orifice of his body.

The guard still fighting Rhea stumbled, his eyes flicking briefly down at his comrade. The split second of a distraction was all it took for Rhea to slice her sword through his side. He fell to his knees, hands clasping the gushing wound. I didn't pause for a moment, seizing Rhea's wrist in a firm grip and barreling down the hallway behind us.

"Stop them!" Benedict shouted from behind.

Oh, how very noble of you to join in.

I rolled my eyes as we careened down hall after hall, nearly slamming into the walls as we sprinted to put distance between ourselves and the guards hot on our heels. Finally, we turned a sharp corner to find a stained-glass window resting at the end. I let out a sigh of relief, picking up speed. "Grow wings," I yelled.

In a flash, Rhea turned into a raven, speeding ahead of me in a dart of midnight feathers. She flitted out the window before me, disappearing into the night sky. Just as the sounds pursuit almost caught up to me, shadows shrinking along the corridor walls, I launched my feet up on the windowsill.

I leaped out the window, wings unfurled enough to ease me to the ground. I slipped silently into the hedges lining the house, steadying my breathing and slowing my pounding heartbeat.

Two seconds later, the remaining three guards, followed closely by Benedict, launched out the window in a fruitless pursuit. Rhea was just another raven in the sky, indiscernible and lost to the wind.

And why would they ever search the ground, when they were pursuing what they assumed were two fallen fugitives?

I loosed a low, self-satisfied laugh, the adrenaline ebbing into giddy elation. Brushing my tangled hair from my face, I turned around to push through the hedges.

And ran face first into a solid, muscled chest.

Chapter Thirteen

My dagger was free and flying toward the figure in a blink, heartbeat pounding in my ears.

And just as fast, the figure blocked my attack, disarming me smoothly, and swiping my legs out from beneath me. I careened backwards; the figure swooping an arm beneath my lower back to break my fall. The familiar scent of leather and spices overwhelmed me, my eyes flaring as Kellen's face came into view, hovering over above my own.

"Couldn't leave all the excitement to your brother, Princess?" His joke fell flat as his eyes narrowed, searching my face.

I swallowed hard around the panic, the shock, and searched desperately for a lie.

If I laughed and agreed, blaming it on too many glasses of wine and the tedious conversation, he wouldn't believe it. It would take one conversation with Benedict to unravel the entire story.

I could lie and say I made it here just as they were leaving, effectively missing all the fun, but… I was still wearing the cloak and scarf from inside the manor. Not to mention all the blood on my bare feet and dress.

"Any chance you didn't see me jump out of that window?" I

asked in a small, joking voice.

Kellen gave me a deadpan look before pushing off of me, offering a hand to pull me up. "Not a chance in all the hells."

I opened my mouth to speak, but he cut me off as he glanced around the yard. "Not here."

My legs hung over the edge of the clock tower, hundreds of feet above the heart of Calasera. My wings draped behind me as I sat with my feet dangled over the edge, the weightless feeling of perching high above the world filled my body with a pleasant hum. Normally, I loved it up here. I would love it now, with the clear night sky and the distant sounds of the city below, if it weren't for Kellen's hulking form seated beside me. He stared straight ahead as he waited for me to fill the silence with answers I didn't want to give him.

I twisted the engagement ring around my finger as I searched for a way out of this. I owed it to Rhea to keep her secrets, to preserve her life here in Calasera. She risked so much more than I did in this friendship. It was a truth that always went unspoken, another strain of guilt I could never quite shake. My father would beat me within an inch of my life if he ever discovered the truth, but I would still keep my life.

She would lose everything.

But... Kellen was going to be a permanent part of my life now. How could I ever hide this from him? He would have to find out eventually, whether it be by my admission or by catching me sneaking around to see her. Unless I ended the friendship once we were married and it was no longer safe.

It was selfish, but I didn't think I could do that.

I didn't want this future with him, but if it was the only future I was given, then I should at least try to make the best of it.

Could I risk it?

Kellen's hand covered my own, halting the nervous twist of the ring around my finger. I jolted, looking up from my hand and straight into his eyes.

They were so open, so desperate to understand. "You can trust me, Aria. Please." The last word was a whispered plea as he leaned in close, our foreheads nearly brushing.

My heart beat quickened in my chest and I squeezed my eyes

shut.

Can I trust him? Do I have a choice but to try?

He promised to put me above my father. He promised to keep me safe. The boy I grew up dueling and jumping off cliffs into the ocean with. The one who knew which books I loved to read, and which tea to bring to a meeting to brighten my day. He was still the same person. And he cared for me.

"She's my friend," I breathed, choking as I let the small truth escape.

Kellen stilled. "The leader of the thieves' guild?"

I nodded.

"How?" he asked cautiously, and I opened my eyes to find he had put space between us again. His hand loosened on my own.

I chewed on my lip. "Does it matter?"

"How long?"

I pulled my hand from his. "Since we were children. Please tell me that you'll keep it a secret."

His gaze hardened then, and my breath caught in my lungs. "You've been hiding your friendship with a criminal since you were a *child*?"

"She hasn't always owned the guild—"

"And when she started it, the first thing you should have done was turn her in."

Ice raced through my veins. "Kellen, please don't tell him. Please don't make me do this, I can't lose her."

He stood up and ran his hands through his unbound hair. "Aria, she's stealing from your court. She's robbing the people who serve your family."

I stood to face him, crossing my arms over my chest. "My family is the reason she has to!"

"No one has to resort to crime."

"Oh, fuck off. You can't possibly understand what it's like out there without the support of your rich father."

Kellen threw his hands up. "And you can?!"

"Yes, because I've seen it! I actually give a shit enough to go help them—" I cut myself off, eyes flaring as I realized what I'd let slip.

Realization dawned on Kellen fast, his face slackening. "You've been draining your life magic for them."

"Kellen—"

He held up a hand. "What you're doing is illegal, Aria. Healers aren't supposed to aid those on the fringes of society. If you father finds out..." he trailed off, clenching his jaw. "How long have you been helping them?"

I ignored his question. "You don't find it fucked up that we leave them there to die?"

"What I think doesn't matter."

I barked a laugh. "Maybe it matters to me. Tell me you agree with my father's decrees, that it doesn't bother you in the slightest that our people are suffering, *starving to death*, while the aristocracy dines on seven course meals and sleeps soundly every night."

"*Enough.*"

I paced toward him until barely a breath rested between us. "Tell me you don't care."

He didn't reply.

I drew in a steadying breath. "Kellen, please. What I do is harmless, and she's my best friend. I can't betray her."

"And I can't betray my people by allowing her to continue to thieve her way through the city."

I held his gaze, rage burning through my chest now. "No, you'll just allow the people that remain out of sight to suffer. I didn't take you for a blind fool, but I guess I was mistaken."

"Enough."

I drew in a sharp breath as Kellen grasped my arms tightly, lowering his face until we were nearly eye level. "Why are you trying to get yourself hurt? Please, I am trying my best to protect you, but I can't protect you from yourself. Stop trying to antagonize him, Aria. This won't end well for anyone."

Is that what he thought of me? That I was little more than a petulant child, prodding at her father for attention or a reaction? That I stood here, begging him to keep my friends secret and to open his eyes to more than just the safe, privileged life he's led, solely to goad my father?

I pulled out of his grip, anger rising on a fiery wave. My mouth filled with ash as tears flooded my eyes. I wanted to tell him to fuck off, to raise my fists and fight him on this narrow ledge. To scream and rail against him and all that he stood for. Instead, I held his gaze and begged, "You can't tell him, Kellen. I can't lose her."

His eyes hardened, and he straightened up to his full height. "And I can't lose you."

"*Please.*" I lurched toward him, tears thickening my words. "Please, I know you think you'll be helping me or saving me from myself if you tell him, but you won't. It'll ruin everything, I can't lose her. He can't hurt her, Kellen, please just look at me."

But he turned away, just out of my reach. "I will not lie to my king, and I will not allow you to put yourself in harm's way like this again."

Tears fell down my cheeks now, flames biting at my fingertips. "I begged you to put me first."

Kellen glared down at me. "That is exactly what I'm doing."

"No, you're putting him first. You're on his side against me, telling me what I am and am not allowed to do. Controlling me as you see fit. I begged you to put me before him in this marriage, and the first chance you get, you turn on me." I closed the distance between us again, my heaving chest brushing his with every ragged breath. "Why don't you just beat me yourself? Raise your hand and mare my body the way you know he will when he hears of what I've done. You think this is some sort of childish rebellion? Learn from my father and beat it out of me until I've broken to your will. We both know it's only a matter of time until you treat me the same way he does."

Kellen raised his hand slowly and, goddess be damned, I flinched. His eyes softened as he brushed a knuckle down my face, wiping at the tears coursing down my cheeks. "Everything I do is to keep you safe, Aria. Even if it means protecting you from yourself. And I am bound by oath to protect our kingdom and answer to my king. I cannot let this continue."

I slapped his hand away. "He'll hurt me if he knows, Kellen, and you're still going to tell him. How is that keeping me safe?"

His gaze hardened, his hand lingering in the air for several painful heartbeats before he let it drop. "He won't kill you, Aria."

My heart cracked.

It wasn't untrue. My father wouldn't kill me. I was too valuable. And what I was doing was treasonous in Kellen's eyes, so it needed to be stopped through whatever means necessary.

I bit back on a sob and turned away from him. I was so stupid for hoping, for even a fleeting moment, that he could be different.

I stepped off the clock tower, allowing the free fall to wipe away the tears gathering in my eyes.

I walked down the hall to my room, barefoot and weary.

Rhea wasn't at her house. If she was smart, she'd be staying out of it until things cooled off. I had no way to reach Rhea, to warn her that Kellen might go to my father. That I'd be tortured for information the moment my father caught wind of our friendship, of my betrayal. I could only offer a prayer to the goddess that she was safe.

I had expected to find my father, flanked by his personal guard, waiting at the stairs to escort me to his office, but the castle was oddly empty. The gala had ended hours ago. I'm sure my father concocted a wide variety of excuses for my sudden absence, and I'm sure the gossip persisted through the night despite those excuses.

I round the corner, my steps faltering.

Corvinna stood before my bedchambers, her face twisted into a scowl.

I glanced briefly down at my ruined dress, splattered in dry blood, and my bare feet peeking out from beneath the ripped hem. I dragged my eyes back up to the witch's, offering a sheepish smile as I forced myself to walk toward her.

Her scowl only deepened.

She didn't speak, only reached behind her to hold the door open. I sighed, walking into the antechamber and glancing longingly at my bed through the cracked door. How I longed to curl up beneath the covers with a book and pretend all of my troubles were nonexistent.

The door clicked shut behind me. "Care to tell me where the fuck you went?"

I unclipped the stolen cloak, dropping it on the settee beside me as I contemplated the best course of action. If I concocted a story only to have Kellen swoop in with his account, she'd be pissed at me for lying.

If I gave her the truth, though… there was no telling how she would react. After all these years, the High Witch's motivations were still hazy, her cards held close to her chest. She hated my father, yet she stood at his side as a part of his inner circle. She disagreed with his course of action most of the time, yet she still supplied him the tools he needed to move forward.

The Witch Kingdom stood against the fallen until their human allies turned on them. It was an alliance built solely upon a common enemy.

I turned to face Corvinna, her eyebrows raised expectantly. "I just stepped out."

Lying it was, I guess. I couldn't bring myself to voice the truth, not when it threatened Rhea. I doubted the witch would care about a thief, even if that thief was a pain in my father's ass, but I wasn't entirely sure she would lie to him when confronted.

"You just stepped out?" Her voice was lethally quiet.

I nodded.

Her eyes roved down my dress, past the blood and tears, to my bare feet, before pointedly finding my gaze again. "Must have been some walk."

I reclined on the couch, biting my lip.

"How about I phrase this differently, and I offer you to opportunity to share the truth with me?" she said, stepping around casually to perch on the low couch. "Kellen Ashford is in your father's office now, spinning a tale that does not paint you in a good light."

My heart plummeted.

He actually did it. He actually went to my father.

Corvinna leaned forward, bracing her elbows on her knees. "So how about you tell me everything, so when we leave this room in five minutes to walk to your father's office, you have at least one ally by your side?"

Chapter Fourteen

My nails dug small, crescent shapes in the palm of my hand. We sat in my father's office for long, anxious minutes, marked by the ticking of the grandfather clock in the corner. Corvinna leaned against the wall, darkness brooding around her shoulders as she glared at my father's empty desk.

I told her everything, barring Rhea's actual name and her precise location. That information wasn't necessary to get the point across. The witch had listened, her expression carefully blank, before she escorted me here to wait for my father. Apparently, this meeting couldn't wait for morning.

Corvinna had said she would do her best to mitigate my punishment, but there was little else that could be done. My father would hunt for Rhea, but I had kept her identity, her home in the slums and her few acquaintances a secret. For now, she wouldn't be in any real danger from my mistake.

The door opened behind us, and though I flinched, I didn't turn to face my father. Heat crept up my neck as he walked leisurely behind me, each footstep measured and controlled. I slowed my breathing as he took his seat, keeping my eyes fixed on the edge of his desk. It was a fine desk, as all the things in this grand, drafty castle were. But this desk had actually seen some use over the hundreds of years it had sat in the center of this room.

Scuffed from quills or cups or blades, worn down as kings poured over battle plans and laws and tax proposals. My father had a habit of tapping one of the small daggers he kept on the desk against the edge, chipping the wood and leaving fine little slices along the side.

I watched him lean forward in my periphery, waiting for him to speak. "I'm going to give you one chance to tell me where you went tonight."

I peeled my eyes from the desk and leveled an even look at him. My father's eyes were the red of fresh blood, hot and churning. They nearly glowed now with barely controlled rage.

My lips curled in a cold smile. "Out."

I expected the slap that landed across my cheek, enough to brace for it. I allowed the shock of pain to flare before I seized control of it. I shoved the pain, the bite of tears in my throat, down deep until I couldn't feel it anymore.

His knuckles tightened on the desk. "Corvinna," he called without taking his gaze off of me.

The witch appeared like a wraith beside me, peeling from the shadows and solidifying, as if she had been little more than darkness in the corner a moment before.

My father's gaze darted up to her. "What did you find out?"

"Nothing. She said she merely stepped out for a stroll."

"I find it difficult to believe you don't know the truth," he growled.

Corvinna's lips twisted into a small, feral grin. "I'm sure you find many things difficult, King. I, unfortunately, am not responsible for any of them."

My father watched her for another moment before rage shattered his facade. He rose, flames licking up his arms, and hurled a dagger at the wall behind her head.

I gripped the chair to remain seated, to keep my spine straight and the gasp that had climbed up my throat from passing my lips.

Corvinna didn't flinch. The thickening shadows slowly rose to consume the dagger now imbedded in the wall. I watched as those shadows wrapped around the handle like incorporeal hands, plucking it from the wall and pointing the blade at my father. Gently, the shadows placed the dagger back on the desk.

The witch leaned in close, malice flickering in her silver eyes. "Aiming a dagger appears to be another thing you find *difficult.*"

Heat and darkness flared in the room until the witch broke his gaze and walked over to the low couch before the hearth. She lounged on it, flashing my father a wicked grin. "It's a good thing you have a back-up plan, isn't it, Adriel?"

The heat receded from the room, my father sitting heavily in his chair. He waved his hand at the cracked office door, and my heart seized in my chest.

The door opened fully, two sets of footsteps walking into the office. I looked back, my eyes crashing into Kellen's. His features were drawn, his gaze distant. And he wasn't meeting my eyes. He looked to my father instead, offering a small nod as he rounded the desk to stand just behind him.

And trailing after Kellen, hands tucked leisurely into his pockets, was Perceval. He stood to our father's right, inclining his head and giving me a smug smile. My mind reeled back to my party, realization sinking like a rock to the pit of my stomach.

He set me up.

Perceval's smile grew, reading the words I couldn't voice in my eyes.

My father clicked his tongue in disappointment. "I truly wish you had just told me the truth, Aria. I don't know where this behavior is coming from, not when you've always been so…"

Docile. Submissive. Flawlessly obedient.

"So loyal to the crown, to your duty as an Elway."

I clenched my jaw, refusing to take the bait. This had turned from a meeting to an interrogation, and I would sooner die than reveal anything about Rhea.

"Perceval informed me he was concerned for you, after you left the party early. Kellen overheard and offered to follow." My father leaned over his desk now, his gaze narrowing. "So imagine my surprise when he reported back that he found you outside the Clifton manor, right after Benedict informed me a fifth thief appeared halfway through the battle and derailed the entire operation."

I hated how my chest tightened as I glanced up at Kellen, my eyes meeting his for a brief second before I tore them away. I could feel my heart breaking in my chest, his betrayal slicing me to the bone. The last piece of our friendship crumbled between us, and I couldn't help but wonder if it was ever real at all. If any of it ever meant more to him than getting me here, in this position of power over me, standing in my father's favor.

If he ever cared about me, or just all the things my name and title could do for him. Gods, it was violating, analyzing the years of friendship and memories, the trust and simmering emotions I couldn't ever fully deny now churning in my stomach, making me sick. It was all a lie. It had to be, because if any of it were real, he'd never be able to turn on me like this.

Worst of all, I hated myself for leaning into the friendship he had offered. For actually believing it were true, and for mourning its loss now.

I had to force the pain down before it crashed upon me like a tidal wave, swallowing hard around the rising lump in my throat.

I looked back up at my father, steeling myself against the pain I knew was to come. "What do you expect me to say?"

His gaze narrowed. "I expect you to sit here and admit to everything you wouldn't tell Kellen when he found you. I expect the truth, Aria."

"I can't give you that."

"What do you mean you can't—"

"I mean," I leaned forward, my temper flaring, "that perhaps I'm not as docile or submissive as you believed me to be."

My father stood so fast I didn't see him move. He was in my face, pulling me up to stand by the length of my hair. I clenched my teeth against the pain as he leveled his gaze with mine, his eyes glowing like hot coals. "Watch your tongue or I'll cut it from your mouth. You don't need to speak to perform your duties."

"Actually," Corvinna drawled, "there is a spell she needs to speak, so I'd strongly advise against the removal of her tongue."

My father's jaw clenched, his hand flexing in my hair as he searched my gaze for several pounding heartbeats. He threw me back in my chair, my back ramming into the wooden arm as I collapsed. My father paced away, taking his seat behind the desk and adjusting his jacket lapels. "Kellen, if you would," he said casually, waving him forward.

Kellen?

My gaze shot toward him, taking in the tense line of his jaw, the hardness in his eyes.

And when he raised his gaze to mine, the world slowed.

Because of course my father would call Kellen into his office if he needed information. He didn't need to torture it out of me, not when Kellen could slip inside my mind and flip through the pages of my thoughts as easily as one perused a book. Anger dissolved to panic as I slowly began shaking my head.

A lie, I needed a lie that would put an end to this—

I had to block him out, to keep him out of my mind. I had been so, so stupid for forgetting how easily he could get information. But... he'd never been able to breech my mental walls. I checked that my shields were intact, the blazing wall of fire around my mind sealed tightly.

Kellen loomed over me now, a flicker of regret in his eyes as he drew me gently up to stand before him. The world seemed to fall away, my father forgotten in the background, as I stared into the eyes of my best friend, my almost lover, my betrothed.

"Please," I breathed, allowing all the pleading and pain to show in my gaze.

Something flickered in his eyes, but his jaw tensed and he didn't reply.

In a flash of silver, his magic struck my mind, and I was falling.

I had always known Kellen's magic was strong, unique. But I had thought my shields were strong enough to block him out, to keep my mind safe from someone like him. I realize now he had been holding back. Every small brush against the walls around my mind were out of consideration, not necessity. Or maybe he'd always been hiding his strength to lull me into the false sense of security, to ease me into our decade long friendship. Now, he sliced through that wall of flame, stepping straight into my mind.

I was powerless to stop him.

His presence was overwhelming. It was invasive when it wasn't something I welcomed, my mouth filling with a sour taste.

His mental fingers leafed through my memories, sliding through the hours before like turning back a clock. I couldn't do anything but watch over his shoulder, peering down at the events of the last few minutes. He watched the scene unfold from my perspective, all my thoughts and emotions layered over the images as if he were truly looking at it from my point of view.

Kellen lingered on the memory of my tears falling from the clock tower high above Calasera, lost to the breeze and stifled by the roar of the city below. On the way I had looked at him, like he was a stranger.

He gently turned over the memory, a small glimmer of sorrow ricochetting through my mind. When Kellen settled over the image of Rhea fighting alongside me in the manor, I felt his fear like it was my own. He sifted through the image slowly, rotating it around in the palm of his hand, examining it from every angle.

Looking for a way out of it, I realized. A lie, anything to give my father that wouldn't be so incriminating.

Lie. Don't tell him the truth, please. I promise I had a good reason; I promise this was worth it. Please trust me, Kellen, please.

Kellen stiffened, setting the memory down slowly.

He continued digging, a dull ache forming in my temple as he flew through my life. I watched in horror as flashes of Rhea's face filled my mind's eye, every one of her smiles and crude jokes, her echoing through my head like a ghost. Tears spilled down my cheeks when Kellen lingered on the image of Rhea's home, the chipped paint and uneven pavers, the overgrown garden and the worn couches in the cozy, dimly lit room.

Every bottle of wine, every tear and laugh shared. He rewound the clock; the years falling from our faces until he was staring at the two of us, locked in a brawl in an alley in the slums. Two twelve-year-old girls, so at odds, standing on opposite ends of life... and somehow, we had become everything to each other.

And he watched Rhea shift from a half-elven woman to a wolf, a cat, a bird. Always black, with those clever golden eyes.

Kellen watched our every interaction. Watched our friendship grow, felt every emotion coating the rich memories. I looked on through blurry eyes, noting with no small amount of pain that she was the only bright, golden memory in my murky mind. Everything else was dreary, dark, exhausting. But Rhea had become the sun at the center of my world.

If I hadn't been so utterly violated, I would have been grateful he witnessed it all. That he saw and felt all I had these past nine years.

There was no way he would give me up now. Surely this would

show him how it would cleave my soul in half to lose her, even if her occupation was a crime against the crown.

Kellen set my memories aside, turning to face me. A glimmer of silver in my raging, fiery mind.

My heart plummeted from my chest when I saw the said, apologetic look on his face.

"I'm sorry, Aria."

Chapter Fifteen

When I opened my eyes, the room was spinning. I nearly collapsed, but Kellen's arms were there to catch me. He eased me back into the chair, brushing absently at my hair, tucking it behind my ears. I would have slapped his hands away if I could only make the room slow down, if I could keep my stomach from lurching. Finally, my vision stabilized on my father.

He fixed his gaze on Kellen, thick brows raised expectantly.

Kellen's hand fell away from my cheek, and he straightened. I closed my eyes against the words I knew were coming. The pain they would bring.

"Aria left to help the leader of the thieves' guild escape because they're friends. They met nine years ago, when she snuck out to walk through the markets in the slums. Rhea is a shifter of elven and fallen origin, and she lives in a green house off one hundred and thirty-second street."

Each word, cold and clinical, sliced me open. Our friendship reduced to little more than a summary, Rhea's most damning truths spilled out before the one person who could order her to be executed for them. Her life here was over. If they didn't catch her, she would have to leave the city.

She would have to leave me.

Tears flowed freely down my cheeks now and I hated myself for it.

My father rose from his seat, dismissing Perceval with a flick of his wrist. He rounded his desk, shaking Kellen's hand. Like he had done some great fucking deed. Kellen dipped his chin like he was proud of the things he had said, of the way he had ripped into my mind and violated me, resurfacing with my whole, bloody heart clenched in his fist as an offering.

My father turned a disgusted sneer toward me, and in a flash, his hand lashed out and struck. I reeled to the side, pain lancing across my cheek. The taste of iron filled my mouth, but I forced myself to swallow it thickly. Slowly, I straightened in my chair, holding his burning gaze with my own defiance.

I left my emotions raw, a torrent of rage and fear and sorrow.

My father leaned down, bracing either hand on the side of the chair, trapping me in place. "I should beat you for associating with half-breed scum. For choosing that bitch over your own people, over your duties."

I couldn't suppress the laugh that slipped from my lips, short and cold. My mind was too hazy, my thoughts too distorted and cracking under the pressure. "She is helping my people better than you ever have." She kept so little of the riches she stole, spreading the wealth out among the thousands of needy hands in Calasera. Caring for those that my father refused to defend.

I barely felt the second strike, biting across the first.

I could have sworn Kellen flinched, and my resolve snapped. Smoke curled behind my teeth, and I locked my gaze on my father's. His grin was feral as his eyes flicked down to my hands, violet flames now spiraling around my fingertips.

"I think you have forgotten," he said softly, his hot breath rolling over my face, "who your master is, Aria Iveliesse Elway."

My father reached inside his jacket pocket, drawing out two clear, stone manacles.

Dread lurched in my chest. Mantrivar stone, mined from the eastern continent. Rare, its abilities to smother magic something we understood so little about.

"Oh, is this really necessary? Such dramatics, Adriel," Corvinna said, rising languidly from the couch.

My father whirled around, pinning her with his stare. "Did you know? All these years, did you know what she was doing?"

Corvinna halted, her face hardening. "You do not command me."

A muscle feathered in my father's cheek. "You may be right, that I do not control you. But it is well within my right to punish my daughter as I see fit."

I lurched forward, my flames springing to life in my palms, but two broad hands gripped my shoulders. I slammed back into my chair, twisting around with a growl to find Kellen standing stoically behind me. Violet flames lashed out at him, but he didn't so much as grimace at the pain as they burned his palms.

My father snapped the manacles around my wrists, and my magic stalled. Like a siphon, the manacles drained the magic from my veins, leaving their clear stones swirling with purple light. Every last bit of energy drained from my limbs. My muscles ached, my chest hollow and throbbing.

"Corvinna," my father breathed, his eyes still locked on mine. "Take her to the pit. A week in darkness will soften her resolve."

Bile crept up my throat, but I refused to give the fear any control.

My father turned to leave the office.

"I'll never forgive you if you kill her," I rasped. One last, futile attempt to stay his hand. There had never been love between us, that much I knew. I couldn't beg his heart to reconsider, not when I wasn't entirely sure he had one to begin with.

But we had always bartered in terms of power and compliance; the less I thrashed against my leash, the more privilege and leniency he gave me.

My father stilled, glancing over his shoulder as he recognized the real meaning underneath my words. If he moved against Rhea, I'd strike back one day. I'd hold on to this until I found the most opportune moment to fuck him over.

He walked out the door, calling casually over his shoulder, "It's a good thing I have never valued your forgiveness, Aria."

Chapter Sixteen

Kranziath was the only prison in all the fallen lands, carved into the heart of the eastern mountains.

The original fallen constructed the prison centuries ago, back when the gods still held power over Corvale and the fallen were little more than subservient beings beneath the Goddess Xerexes. At the heart of the prison lies The Pit, a round tunnel plunging into pure darkness, burrowed by some fearsome beast that no longer dwells on this plane.

Prison cells line the upper portion of The Pit, descending level after level into the gloom of the mountains, locking away the worst of Arkala's criminals. Little more than flickering torchlight chased away the shadows from the corners of their cells. There is only one way into those cells—flight. And all the prisoners in Kranziath have their wings cut off after their trials.

It was a cruel fate, one that drove the prisoners to madness.

Death would be favorable to a life in darkness, wingless and left to rot.

The lower half of The Pit, bisected by a hallway and a narrow path around, had a different use. Instead of building more cells into the belly of the prison, the ancient fallen left it empty, using the unnatural darkness as the perfect den of tortures. One my father employed far too often on his own children.

The only modifications made was a large metal grate half-way down, with one locked door to enter.

To keep winged creatures down in its belly, where the darkness could drive them to madness.

I stood with my toes resting at the edge of the pit, trying to quell the thrashing in my chest. To swallow the bile biting at the back of my throat. There was something so horribly unnatural about a creature with wings living in the belly of a mountain, so far away from the sky and the freedom of flight.

"I'll see if I can get you out sooner," Corvinna said softly.

I didn't allow hope to take root. My father wasn't one to go back on what he said. Giving in, even for his own children, was an intolerable sign of weakness. So seven full days in the pit it would be.

"Don't allow the darkness to taunt you," she continued, still not facing me. "The moment you listen to what it says, you'll lose your mind."

"I've been down there before—"

"Never for this long, Aria."

I grimaced, staring down at the bottomless dark. My father used to find it amusing to discipline us as children by sending us down there. It was only ever for a few hours at a time, never long enough to do anything more than scare us back into submission, and never for any real transgressions.

This was different. Those few hours alone at the bottom were terrifying. I'd had nightmares for years after.

Corvinna turned away, lingering for a moment as if she might say more. She didn't. The witch motioned, and two guards gripped my arms.

I fought the urge to lash out, swallowing around the instincts to shove them off. I was going down there regardless, and it would only hurt more to fight.

I closed my eyes as we descended, only one torch held by the guard on my left lighting the way. I swallowed another surge of bile as we passed through the open grate. Twenty feet further, and the ground came into view. The darkness beyond the torchlight was vile, writhing like disembodied shadows.

My legs nearly gave out when their iron grip released my arms.

Wordlessly, the guards launched back up through the grate. I watched with shallow breaths as the light drew away from me, tracking the small torchlight until the darkness consumed it whole.

The sound of the metal cell door slamming shut ricochetted through my bones, and it was only then that I allowed the tears to fall.

The pit was alive, in the way all the world's ancient darkness lived.

It moved and writhed, sentient and hungry as I sat in the center of the pit and tried to control the primal fear in my chest.

The original fallen, those whose births preceded the dark war by at least a century, believed true evil lived down here. Whether it was a creature that prowled the belly of the eastern mountains long before the fallen walked this realm, or something that slipped through when the Goddess Xerexes split the fabric of time to bring her people here. Whatever it might be, our legends say it's alive. In the fallen lands, there are creatures formed from shadows and mist, always lurking in the corners of your eyes, intangible and elusive. These creatures feed on suffering and pain, siphoning it to fuel their wickedness.

Whether these stories were true or merely folklore, I stared into the darkness and tried to control my breathing.

I sat up straight, closing my eyes and trying to find comfort in the black behind my eyelids. There was little change, but at least the shadows here didn't move and shift, stalking me like a mountain cat.

My father wanted me fragile and broken when I emerged.

So, I needed to calm my breathing and maintain my sanity. It would feel like an eternity before I saw light again, but I could find comfort in the darkness. I could meditate until I no longer noticed the shreds in my soul, the fear in my stomach, or the chill rippling through my veins.

I could sink into that place of calm that allowed my body to move and fight despite the primal fear that always surged before a battle.

He wanted me to break, but I couldn't afford to.

I couldn't afford to lose anything else down here.

The pit was a manifestation of madness itself.

It deteriorated your mind with its oppressive darkness and heavy silence until there was nothing separating you from the beasts that roamed the belly of the eastern mountains.

Discerning the passage of time was impossible, with meals dropped off inconsistently and rarely enough to never quite satiate the gnawing ache of hunger.

The longer I remained down here, the more I started to believe in the legends that claimed the pit housed an entity of shadow and mist. The darkness was unnatural. The silence was worse. It felt like a held breath that never released; the stillness balanced on the edge of a blade.

Waiting for one small push to descend into chaos.

As the hours or days or weeks trickled by, the darkness moved around me. Spirits' hands brushed across mine. Breezes that felt like the pacing of lost souls would stir beside me. An occasional dark mass would stalk my steps as I walked the length of the pit, somehow more tangible than the rest of the surrounding darkness. My eyes would play tricks, bending colors into the endless black as they tried and failed to see again.

Soon, even the softest of sounds was far too loud.

My breathing, the shuffling of my feet across the ground, the scratching of my nails against the stone walls, it all echoed painfully around me. As if captured by the entity that called this place home and replayed back over and over until it drove me to teeter along the edge of insanity. I tried to lay still, to press my back flat against the cold earth and not move at all, but somehow that was worse.

It felt like a weight draped over my body, as if the darkness sat upon my chest and restricted my breathing.

So I paced.

I counted steps, or breaths, or heartbeats. As if any of that would help me discern how long I remained trapped in purgatory. I ran my hands along the stones, searching for bricks jutting from the wall as if I could scale them back toward the daylight far above.

I was attempting to find a foot hold when something scuffed along the floor. I recoiled, a burst of panic shattering my delicate sense of calm. I stood frozen, hands pressed against my pounding chest as I waited for the sound to shatter the silence again, for this intangible beast to form into something real, something with teeth and claws and bloodlust.

Again, a scuffle sounded on the floor, and I nearly caved to the screaming fear in my gut. I couldn't tell if it was across the pit or right beside me, if I had seconds or minutes until a predator I couldn't see came for my throat—

"Aria," Rhea's voice came from the darkness before me, and I crumbled to the floor.

Relief crashed through my body like a tidal wave, an incoherent sob breaking my silence. "I thought you were... I thought he was going to kill you." My voice cracked on another sob, fresh tears coursing down my cheeks.

Fuck, I had been so sure I would never see her again.

I'd been so painfully convinced that I'd emerge from this goddess-damned pit to find her dead or... gone. Forced to leave because I fucked her entire life up.

There was a shuffling in the dark, and a breath coasted over my face. I felt her sit down beside me, our backs pressed to the curving stone wall. She laced her fingers through mine, her hands warm against my icy skin.

"You shouldn't be down here." The words were a weak protest, at best. I selfishly wished she'd stay here, by my side, until the light finally came for me.

Rhea scoffed. "Please, let's save your arguments for later. I think I've more than proven by now that I can take care of myself."

"How did you find me?"

She shifted, her feet shuffling against the dirt floor. "I came straight to the castle after you saved my ass at the manor. I was a fly on the wall for that entire meeting."

My throat thickened. "Oh."

"Where else would I go?"

Home. To pack and flee, to start a life I couldn't ruin for her.

Rhea tightened her grip on my hand. "I wouldn't leave you, Aria. If we ever leave this place, we'll do it together."

Tears pressed against my eyes, falling safely in the darkness. "I don't deserve you."

"Most don't," she joked, though her voice was softer than normal. "So, you're engaged to that asshole?"

A defensive reply climbed up my throat reflexively, but I swallowed it quickly. The Kellen I knew had deteriorated so rapidly that

I was still reeling. I twisted the engagement ring around my finger. "You can't stay here. You should go—"

Rhea's hand caught my own, stopping the nervous tick.

"Can you see?" I asked in surprise.

"Yes."

"Cat eyes?"

She snorted. "No, cats can't even see in total darkness. I stole this design from a creature that roams the belly of the eastern mountains, a *daemoaecum vermis.*"

A large worm-like creature with one pitch black eyeball in the center of its skull. I shuddered. "How did you get close enough to see one of those?"

A pause. "I didn't come straight to Calasera, you know."

I leaned my head on Rhea's shoulder, taking a shuddering breath and sinking into the comforting scent of her. "What'd you do?"

"I shifted into every creature I could when I left Casserine, trying to find my place in this world. I flew from the Elven lands after my mother passed, changing between the different birds I found, flying with their flocks for short times. I twisted myself into a wolf and tried to run with different packs, but I think I smelled too different for them; they never accepted me."

"And then you, what, shifted into the monsters in the mountains?"

"Mhm. I climbed the mountains as a hellhound, found a cave and wound my way through the belly. Observed the creatures dwelling there, their pale, slick skin, void of all color. Their large black eyes had never experienced a single ray of daylight. I lived among them until I decided slugs and fish and the stray animals that wandered too far into the mountains didn't satisfy me."

"You ate slugs?"

"Yes, they're quite abundant in the caves."

"That's disgusting, Rhea."

"Oh, shut up. You still think I'm hot." She planted a fat kiss on my face, and I reeled away, wiping at my cheek dramatically. "You should try to rest."

"Are you going to leave?"

She paused. "I can't stay down here the entire time, though I wish I could. The Guild scattered, and I need to get some things out before your dad ransacks everything I own. Besides, your father has

everyone on alert for a shifter, so if the Hellhounds catch my scent,
I'm fucked. I'll come as often as I can, though."

I nodded, shifting and laying my head in her lap. "Can you stay
until I fall asleep?"

Rhea stroked my hair, tucking it gently behind my ear. "I'm not
going anywhere right now. I'll wake you up if I hear anyone coming."

Sleep came for me swiftly, and I was grateful for its numbing
embrace.

I tried to sleep through the week, but the darkness had other
plans.

I wasn't sure if it was my own fear, or simply returning to
this place that did it, but my childhood nightmares returned with a
ferocity that stripped away any comfort sleep might have brought.
Nightmares of falling, plunging into a darkness I could never escape
from. Nightmares of my mother's screams morphing into something
inhuman, something other. Dreams I had no business seeing, of my
violent conception and the way my mother sobbed upon my birth.
Nightmares of my father, towering above me like I was still a small
child, flames in his palms and violence etched into the lines of his
face.

They all began the same, with darkness consuming everything
around me, rotting the floor beneath my feet until I slipped into its
depths and collapsed into a new hell. I think the worst part was the
isolation in those moments before I fell, my eyes desperately searching for someone to save me, to take my hand and keep me from
sinking.

No one ever came.

I simply fell, my hands reaching for help that would never come.

I only allowed myself to rest only when Rhea visited. Her presence chased away the nightmares, but she came too infrequently to
keep my mind intact.

When exhaustion stole the strength from my body, I sat with my
back pressed to the wall, staring with unblinking eyes. The longer I
stared, the more convinced I became it stared back.

That was when the whispers began.

Muttered words in a flowing, ancient language I had never encountered before.

The whispering of a long hem brushing across stone.

The murmuring of my thoughts, leaking out of my head and taking shape in the surrounding air.

The words were always too soft to discern, but I leaned forward and tried to follow their cadence, regardless. The shuffling of footsteps always seemed to walk toward me, slow and measured, but when they rested directly in front of where I sat, I'd reach my fingers out to touch whatever being approached only to close my fingers around nothing. I always tried to reel my own thoughts back into my head, but I couldn't control the taunting words spoken in my own voice, circling around and around in the air, spewing such vitriol that it was better to lie on the floor and cover my ears than intervene.

That was when the screaming began.

My throat burned raw, but it was my mother's screams I heard in the cacophony reverberating around me. Shrieks from her episodes in my childhood and her depressive moments into my adult years. The screams tore from her soul when her depression cracked into mania, and her violent fits shredded her mind.

Soon, I was curled into a ball, begging the screaming to stop. The shrieks turned to laughter, first bubbling in hysterics from my own lips and soon echoed by the demons lurking in the corners of the pit. They fed off my terror, swallowing it whole. Feeding on my fear and anguish.

When I was finally near breaking, when covering my ears or lulling myself into fitful sleep no longer brought the relief of sanity, a torchlight appeared in the center of the pit.

The flickering orange glow illuminated my father's face, looking down on me impassively.

And though I hated him more than I ever had before, I wept in relief at the sight. I allowed my body to go limp, like I was little more than a sleeping child, as he scooped me in his arms and flew me from this den of horrors.

Blood and dirt caked beneath my nails.

I stared at my broken, aching fingers as the maids silently stripped the clothes from my skin. They sloughed off stiffly, the dress I wore the night I entered the pit filthy and tattered.

My skin was raw and red beneath, the sight of it eliciting soft murmurs from the servants behind me. I gritted my teeth, raising my hand to dismiss them. "Leave me, I'll handle it myself."

A pause, then shuffling footsteps approached. "Your Highness—"

"*Leave,*" I snarled.

I still felt half-feral, madness lingering in my peripheral. I flinched from every shadow in the corners of the room, my body longing for sleep, but my mind quaking at the thought of another mind-shattering nightmare.

Of being chased from fitful dreams to find I was back in the pit, being stalked by creatures or ghosts or demons I couldn't see.

The servants left in a soft rustle of skirts, the door shutting gently behind me.

I had spent years picking up the pieces my father left me in alone. I was so painfully used to this that I didn't try to fight the process. I simply allowed myself these few moments of grief as I tended to the wounds he'd left, before beginning the long, tedious task of stitching myself together once more.

I looked at my reflection in the mirror, the haggard girl staring back a ghost of who I was only a week prior.

Deathly pale with dark smudges rimming my violet eyes. The hollows beneath my sharp cheekbones were sunken, gaunt like a skeleton.

I stepped into the awaiting bath, the water steaming.

Fire licked beneath the surface of my skin, but the mantrivar stone at my wrist siphoned it off, glowing a brighter shade of violet. Draining my energy with whatever magic was bold enough to rear its head when these manacles still remained in place.

I sank into the heat, allowing it to melt away the layer of grim on my skin as I rested my head against the lip of the tub. And I gave myself five minutes of weakness to cry. Tears slid hot trails down my cheeks, my mouth filling with a bitter taste. I choked on a sob, swallowing the sound as it threatened to cleave my chest in two.

I bit down on the flesh of my forearm, muffling a scream that rose from the barren depths of my being.

I shoved my head beneath the water until my lungs burned for air. Until the pain inside my chest and splitting through my mind turned to something primal, something physical.

I could handle physical pain. I knew what to do when my lungs screamed for air, when my body tip-toed closer to death. Seconds ticked by beneath the water, my back pressing flat to the bottom of the tub. I kept my eyes open the entire time, watching the lamplight bend in tub water around me, golden and warm. I didn't think I'd ever want to exist in darkness again. Every second that passed cleared my head further, until black dots chased at the edges of my vision and I was no longer feeling the pain inside my head, not as my body screamed for air. I burst through the water with a sharp gasp, raking the heavy wet locks of hair from my face.

I rested my hot cheek against the side of the tub until my breathing had evened out, and I no longer felt as though I were going to faint.

I reached for the bar of soap along the lip of the tub and rose from the water, my skin rippling as cold air blew over my wet body.

I scrubbed my raw skin hard, chaffing the jasmine scented soap against the aching flesh, sinking deeper into another level of pain. I scrubbed until I couldn't feel the darkness of the pit on my skin, couldn't smell the lingering traces of dank air and mildew.

I did my best to clean under the manacles, the skin beneath red and aching, chafed from the slide of stone against my wrist bones. I half succeeded, getting most of the dirt out before the raw skin beneath began to bleed.

I lathered my hair, raking through every knot before repeating again. I took a rough brush to my nails, relentlessly digging the dirt and grime and gore from beneath my nails.

When I was bright pink and clean, I withdrew from the bath.

I would not shed another tear.

I would not dwell on the pain any longer.

All that had occurred was neatly placed in a box, compartmentalized in the darkest corners of my mind where all the pain lived. Where it could no longer bring me to my knees.

I didn't bother with clothes, walking into my candlelit room to feel the chill breeze from the cracked window pebble my skin.

It reminded me that I was alive.

I turned every wall sconce and lamp on until my room was bathed in a warm, golden light. I cracked all the windows, breathing deeper as the sounds of the night, rustling trees and the calls of night birds, chased away the silence.

And when I took the sleeping tonic, left on my nightstand by one of the ladies' maids, I collapsed into my bed and sank deep into the welcome embrace of a dreamless sleep.

Chapter Seventeen

It felt as though I had been sleeping for only minutes, weightless in a dreamless sleep, before hands began pulling me back into my body. I groaned and fought, drawing my arms and legs tight to my chest.

Maybe they'd leave if I refused to move, if I allowed the drug induced sleep to claim me for another few days.

Goddess, that's what I needed. What my body craved, days and days of endless, dreamless slumber.

But the hands were persistent, a voice now accompanying those intrusive shakes. "Aria, *rise.*"

I grumbled a curse, my tongue feeling thick and rolling in my mouth.

Another irritating shake, then, "Aria, it's your mother."

It was as if someone dumped a pitcher of ice water over my head. I pried open my too-heavy eyes to find the blurred image of Amabel leaning over me.

"What did you say?" My words were slurred, my tongue impossibly thick and cumbersome.

"It's your mother. She's having another episode, and I fear the guards will finally alert your father."

I let Amabel drag me to my feet, shaking my head and digging my fists into my eyes to force myself awake. "What kind of episode?"

A pause. "The violent kind."

Shit.

I stumbled into the bathing room, turning on the sink clumsily and burying my head beneath the ice-cold water. It worked well enough, my eyes no longer fighting to close, my head clearing a bit.

I threw on a loose green dress, slipping my feet into my boots as I paced back out to Amabel. "Take me to the kitchens first, and then we'll go see my mother."

Not fifteen minutes later, I walked briskly behind Amabel, steaming hot tea sloshing precariously in a mug in my hands. The sounds of chaos cut through the silent, sleeping hall as we rapidly approached my mother's chambers. Shouts, the shattering of glass, inhuman screeching. I all but ran to my mother's door, brushing past the disgruntled guards looking on from the gaping doorframe.

I glared at their hands, twitching toward their sheathed blades. "At ease, this is my mother."

They hesitated, gazes flicking down to me before they relaxed their grips.

Inside my mother's chambers, three nursemaids cowered from her wrath. Curtains hung torn, light slicing through the room in broken beams. A coffee table lay overturned, the shattered glass from the hall now scattered across the floor in pieces. The remains of my mother's dinner were smeared into the plush rug beneath the ruined table.

And in the center of it all, eyes wide and vacant, hands ripping out chunks of golden hair, was my mother. Her screeching had stopped, simmering down into incoherent muttering.

"Leave us," I breathed, eyes locked on her.

She hadn't noticed me standing there yet.

Two out of the three handmaids left quickly, bowing in a hurry as they fled the scene. Amabel remained, her black eyes narrowed on me. "This is getting out of hand, Your Highness. I implore you to reconsider—"

"Now is not the time," I said cooly. "Leave us."

"Your Highness—"

"That was not a request, Amabel."

She hesitated for a brief moment before bowing shallowly, leaving the room in a rustle of heavy black skirts.

When the door closed softly behind us, my mother flinched as if someone had struck her. My heart ached as her wild, glazed eyes skimmed past me, unseeing. She was so lost in her grief, her memories gnawing on her bones and burrowing into her mind, that she couldn't see what was in front of her.

I flipped over the coffee table, placing the hot tea on the cleared surface. "Hey, Mama. I brought you some tea."

She muttered beneath her breath, her pace quickening as her agitation spiked. "I can't do this again, I can't lie down and take it—" she said between sobs, her shoulders heaving.

"You don't have to do anything, Mama. You're done now, remember?" I said softly as I bent down, gingerly scooping up the shattered glass and piling it into a nearby waste bin.

"It was all a lie, from the start. He never loved me, and I *left* with him. Why would I leave, *how could I leave?*" she moaned. She bit down on her knuckle as she paced, hard enough to draw blood.

I swallowed thickly as I scooped up the last bit of glass, careful to keep my movements smooth and slow. Like I was in the room with a wild animal, measuring each step I took to avoid triggering an attack. I walked toward her, counting each ginger footstep as I tried to control my breathing.

I stopped a pace away, gently reaching out and placing my hands around her wrists. "I brought you tea."

Her wild eyes flashed toward mine, scanning my face as her features contorted. "Did you drug it like that bitch Amabel does?"

"No, Mama, there's no medicine in it. Just vanilla cinnamon tea."

She paused, the haze clearing slightly from her eyes. "With milk?"

"And honey."

Her arms relaxed, and she allowed me to lower her hands to her sides. Her fingernails were torn, dried blood caking beneath them. I glanced behind her at the windowsill, bloody claw marks marring the surface.

My eyes darted back to my mother's face, and I gave her

another gentle smile. "Why don't you sit?"

I led her to the settee, lowering her until she rested against the cushions. Her hands were shaking now, so I picked up the teacup and brought it to her lips. She breathed a small sigh of relief when she drank her favorite tea, her eyes clearing a little more.

Her eyes snapped to mine as I lowered the mug. "Aria?"

"Yes?"

"Why can't I go home?"

Sadness ripped at my chest, screaming to be released. I ignored it. "You are home. Your home is here, with me. Don't you remember?"

Sorrow welled in her eyes, deeper and colder than the Paramana sea. "This isn't my home. This is my hell."

The last of the fight drained from my mother's body, and she slumped like a worn doll against the cushions. It was over.

Now I had to pick up the pieces of my mother that had shattered around the room.

I gathered a small bowl of water and a cloth, scooping up her favorite book and a soft bristled hairbrush as I walked back over to where she sat.

I cleaned up her fingernails gently, glancing at her vacant gaze every few seconds, waiting for the raw pain of her ruined nails to elicit any reaction.

She didn't move, didn't speak, hardly blinked. Her pale blue eyes fixed on the embers in the hearth beside us, the red glow reflected in her too-wide pupils.

"Your birthday is next month," I murmured softly. She wouldn't respond, but... talking made me feel more useful. I swirled the washcloth in the water, staining it a reddish brown. The water dripping from the rag back into the bowl was the only sound for several heartbeats.

"I was thinking about throwing you a small party," I said after a moment, sitting beside her on the couch now. I picked up the silver brush, gingerly combing through the knots at the end of her hair. "If you're feeling up to it? I know how you love to dance."

Loved to dance.

My mother used to dance with me when I was small, and she was still the center of my universe. She loved music more than anyone I had ever met, sinking into a melody the way I sank into my books. And she was breathtaking when she danced, a true talent. At least, she used to be.

Back before she finally let the darkness take her under, after my tenth birthday.

"I could have Reida play the piano for you, if you wished. It would only be a small gathering. I'll get you that spiced cake from town, the one with the buttercream frosting you love so much?" I prattled on to my nearly catatonic mother.

I guided the tea to her lips again, helping her draw in a sip. Sighing in relief when her mouth actually parted.

I set the mug aside before reaching down and guiding my mother to her bed. She drifted like a ghost, her bare feet shuffling across the floor. I slid her beneath the thick white comforter, gently guiding her head to the pillow and tucking her in. She stared unblinking at the ceiling, so still I'd think she was dead if it weren't for the steady rise and fall of her chest.

I went to work scrubbing the blood from her windowsill and picking up the last bits of glass and debris strewn around the floor. When everything was tidy, and all the sharp things in the room were passed off to the guards, I sent for Amabel.

She would be forced to sleep in my mother's chambers for the next few nights, until she was back in her right mind.

"Amabel's on her way, Mama. I'm going to step out front to wait for her." I leaned in close, brushing the hair from my mother's pale cheek. I turned to go, but she made a small, meek noise in the back of her throat.

"Did you need something?" I asked softly, turning back to face her.

My mother's blue eyes tore away from the ceiling, now locking with mine. "You should kill me."

A chill skittered down my spine, my stomach lurching. "Mama—"

"Your life would be so much better if I were dead."

I opened my mouth to deny it, to refute her claim, but... I couldn't bring myself to find the words. So I fled, walking briskly out into the hall. I nearly crashed into Amabel on my way out, ignoring her concerned look as I raced around the corner.

Ducking into a shadowy alcove, I pressed my back against the cool stone, my breathing coming in shallow pants.

Fuck, I... I can't do this anymore.

I had just been torn apart for over a week, my mind fracturing and my heart aching. I didn't know where Rhea was, my father was surely going to continue my torture in the morning, and I still had an engagement ring on my finger to that bastard I used to call a friend. I had to tend to my own wounds alone and stitch myself back together, only to be dragged from the sleep I so desperately needed to care for my mother.

For the one person who should be caring for me.

She should have been there when I came back out of the pit, helping me scrub my skin clean and comforting me when I cried. She should have been the one that brought me comfort and helped me piece myself back together again.

Instead, I couldn't take one night alone to care for myself.

Your life would be better if I were dead.

I choked on another sob, burying my face in my hands, as I tried and failed to deny her words. I didn't want her to die. Fuck, I'd spent the past eleven years trying to keep my father from killing her.

But I couldn't help but wonder if she would be better off dead. If maybe keeping her alive and trapped in that tower was a selfish thing to do. I didn't want her to die, but I wasn't doing anything to help her live, either. Just because I fought to keep her heart beating didn't mean that I fought for her life.

She had lost her life a long time ago.

Chapter Eighteen

Corvinna lounged on the low settee before the fire, examining her nails. I stood against the wall on the other side of the room, examining the witch.

"Are you going to fill this silence, or shall I try to fit in a small nap while you brood?" She yawned delicately.

Flames and vitriol rose to the tip of my tongue, but little more than a whisper of smoke filled my mouth before the manacles around my wrists ached. The cursed stone put a stop to the fire I longed to spew before so much as a spark could form.

The manacles couldn't slow the venom coating my words, though. "Why the fuck are you here?"

Corvinna arched a lavender brow. "Your father asked me to stay with you until he is back."

"Where did he go?"

Corvinna paused. "There was a small issue with one of the Dweller clans, so he went to see if he could resolve it."

I smothered my surprise at her straightforward reply. "Why don't you wait in the hall, then?"

"Because it could be hours before he gets back, Aria. What did I do to deserve your anger? If anything, you should be thanking me."

"For what? Lounging on the couch while my father dealt out his punishment? For escorting me to the pit? How about for showing up with no update on where Rhea is or what my father has done this past week?"

A knowing smile tugged at the corner of her lips. "Oh, I think you're the only one who knows where the shifter is, Aria, let's not play stupid here. Not when it's just the two of us."

I crossed my arms impassively, holding her gaze.

"How about you thank me for not turning you and your little thief of a friend over the moment I learned of your friendship years ago? Or for searching tirelessly for a solution to your magic that won't get you fucking killed the moment your father starts this war?"

The anger and utter helplessness pounding through my veins had swirled into such a thick poison that I didn't care I was fighting with the High Witch with no magic to defend myself. I wanted to rage against something, to feel anger in place of pain and weakness. "Should I also thank you for creating me? How about I kiss your ass for being the self-serving bitch you are, instructing my father to kidnap my mother and create me for his vengeance?"

Corvinna stilled. Darkness thickened in the room, threatening the integrity of the fire in the hearth.

I didn't back down. I took another step closer, raising a shaking finger at her. "Should I thank you for the leash and collar that came with my existence too, witch? If you think I should grovel for not handing over the *only* person who has ever looked at me like I'm worth more than my powers and my title and my so-called 'purpose,' then *you can go fuck yourself.*"

The only sound between us was my own heaving breaths and the crackling of a log in the hearth.

For a fraction of a second, I was certain she was going to strike me dead. I wondered, almost morbidly, if she would use her taloned fingers to carve out my heart, or if she'd simply let the writhing dark-ness consume me whole.

Corvinna rose, and my breath hitched.

But the darkness receded, and she spun on her heels and walked into the bathing chamber. I slowly lowered myself on the velvet chair, the weariness sinking its teeth into my bones. The only thing keeping me awake now was the anxiety pounding through my veins with every heartbeat. As if surviving a week in the pit had triggered this flood of adrenaline, the need to fight my way back to the light, and I didn't know how to turn it off.

Corvinna emerged with a shallow bowl and a rag.

She sat beside me and silently dabbed at my cheek. "All that screeching reopened your cut."

I blinked, registering the hot trickle of blood down my cheek. I noticed the bruising and the barely healed cut below my eye last night. One of my father's rings must have sliced into my skin when he struck me.

I was so unaccustomed to injuries that didn't heal, but with the mantrivar stone on my wrists, it stifled everything about my immortal existence. I healed at a rate even slower than a mortal, all of my energy siphoned off into the clear stone locked around my wrists.

"Why did you do it?" I asked softly when her dabbing had slowed and the blood no longer trickled down my cheek.

I watched Corvinna lower the rag before pulling out a small jar of a silver-tinged cream. "Why did I help your father create you?"

I nodded, wincing as she rubbed the cream into the slice along my cheek.

She sealed the jar up, but didn't move right away. I turned to face her, but her silver eyes were distant.

"I thought it was a necessary evil. I was angry, and I didn't care about the rest of the world at the time… I simply wanted everyone to hurt how I did."

"Do you ever regret it?"

She took a long moment to answer, her gaze unfocused, as if peering into the past.

When she finally looked up, her eyes were empty and dull. "All the time."

When pacing became too difficult, my legs heavy and aching, I resorted to tapping my fingers on the armrest. Hours passed, and I had quelled the anxiety enough to curl into a ball on the couch. Still, I didn't sleep.

Still, I waited.

Finally, when the sun had long since set and the moon was high into the sky, a knock sounded. I leaped to my feet, but Corvinna beat me to the door. She gave me a small warning look before she cracked it open.

"I came to check on her." The deep timber of Kellen's voice skittered over my skin.

My blood simmered once again, and it took every ounce of restraint to sit back on the edge of the couch instead of tearing the door away from Corvinna and screaming at him.

I spent the first half of the week in the pit, ruminating over everything Kellen did. Hours and hours spent breaking down each interaction between us over the entire lifetime of our friendship. Analyzing each word he spoke to me, each lie he spun about our future, and all the 'choices' I would have in it. Every small fluttering of attraction I felt stir in my chest, the hesitant warmth that had been growing since we were children.

And I shattered every one of those memories against the last.

Against his forced presence in my mind, the blank stare he gave me before he invaded my thoughts. It didn't matter if he believed what he had told me about our future together; that reality was little more than an illusion. The moment my father asked him to betray me, he did so unflinchingly.

Kellen might love me, but I would never matter to him more than his position in this court.

Corvinna gave him a deadpan stare. "How the fuck do you think she is, Ashford? Come back when you have news of the king's return."

She went to slam the door in his face, but he stuck out his foot, his boot propping it open. "I have news."

Corvinna didn't move her hand off the handle, her eyes glaring down at his foot like she was considering cutting it off. "Out with it," she said through clenched teeth.

"Let me in first."

"No."

I rose and pushed Corvinna aside, pulling the door open.

Kellen's face slackened when I stepped into view, concern furrowing his brow. "Aria, I'm—"

I held up a hand to stop him, stepping aside to let him in. "Say whatever it is you came to say and then take me to my father. You have five minutes."

Corvinna didn't move from her position by the door, holding it open as if she would throw him over the threshold the moment he finished speaking.

Honestly, I wouldn't stop her if she did.

"I went with Benedict and Perceval to Rhea's house. It was empty, Aria. They searched the entire neighborhood, and your father still has men out searching the city streets, but she hasn't been caught."

I kept my face neutral. "I appreciate you sharing this. You can leave now."

"Aria—" He reached for me, but I flinched away. He froze, brows furrowing. "Aria, please. I would never hurt you—"

"Too late for that."

"I didn't have a choice."

I barked out a laugh. "You could have lied!"

"It's not that simple. He could take everything away from me—"

I turned away, running my hands through my hair. "You handed over my best friend and turned me in to my father for what? Your fucking title? You're standing with my father, with this court? I never knew you were such an arrogant, vain asshole."

He lurched forward, gripping my arm and forcing me to face him. His crimson eyes flared brighter, the gold band around his pupils nearly glowing. "Make no mistake," he said in a low, pleading voice, "when I say 'everything,' Princess, I mean *you*. He could take *you* away."

"Hands off of her, Ashford," Corvinna growled.

Darkness spread across the floor, but Kellen ignored it. He brushed a stray lock of hair from my face, stepping in closer. "Please, I am sorry. That will never happen again, I promise."

I pulled away, jerking free of his grip to put precious inches between us. To clear my head of his presence, the scent and feel of him muddling my thoughts. "Don't make promises you can't keep, Kellen."

"There won't be another reason—"

"Oh, you think this will be the last time he uses you against me?"

He clenched his jaw. "Once we are married—"

"Once we are married, *nothing* changes. This will be my life, bound to a man that will always kneel before this crown, before my father, first." I took two dangerous steps closer, the anger knitting itself back together in my chest. "If you think this is the last time, you are sorely mistaken. Our union is nothing but another tool for him to wield against me, and the moment he needs to 'put me back in line,' he'll ask you to do what you did yesterday all over again."

"Then don't step out of line!" Kellen yelled, throwing his hands up in exasperation. "What the hell were you thinking, Aria? Befriending a thief, some half-breed shifter that was terrorizing the aristocracy for years? You chose *her* over your own people, your own family?"

"Careful, Ashford—" Corvinna started, but I cut her off.

"You saw what she meant to me, Kellen. You were in my head, holding my memories in the palm of your hand." I choked, trying to hold his gaze, to stare deep into his eyes and find a shred of my old friend still in there. "How could you give that to him? I asked you to put me before my father—"

"*I am putting you first*," he roared.

I faltered, shadows filling the space between us thickly, settling around Kellen's ankles in silent warning. He didn't so much as glance at them. "Every fucking decision I make is for your best interest."

I scoffed, but he took two brisk steps toward me, rage twisting his features almost beyond recognition. "It isn't my fault that you don't know what's best for you."

"What's best for me? You think getting my best friend killed is what's best for me?!"

"It is when you chose your friend poorly. If you would just listen to me—"

I closed the last few steps between us, shoving hard into his chest. "Why? So you can lecture me like my father? So you can stand here and tell me that, so long as I do what you want me to, everything will be okay?" Bile bit at the back of my throat.

This is what my life would be. There was nothing I could do to ever escape the chafe of this collar, to loosen the hands that gripped my chains so tightly. Every inch I gave, they only demanded more.

Kellen's jaw tightened. "Goddess, why do you want to make your life harder than it needs to be, Aria? Stay out of the slums, don't befriend criminals, and follow your commands. Play your part in this damned war and *come home to me*. Why is that so hard to do?!"

"So I can be your pretty little wife in her golden cage on the mountain, Kellen? Is that all you want from me, to shut up and follow my father's plans so I can return and resign from my duties?" I was in his face now, snarling up at him. If only my flames weren't so woefully inaccessible. "Has it ever occurred to you I might want more? That I might feel *suffocated* here, and that I might hate my purpose and simultaneously hate the thought of not having one outside of it? Did it ever occur to you I'm *drowning*?"

He brushed his fingers along the cut on my cheek, his gaze shuttering. "Did it ever occur to you I know that?" He stepped in closer, my breath hitching. "Did it ever occur to you," he continued, his breath now coasting over my mouth, "that all I want is for you to lose your usefulness to him so I can take you far, far away from here? So that maybe… maybe he can't reach us there. And maybe you'd have a shot at being happy."

I almost sank against him.

Almost.

But it wasn't enough. Not when my father's presence was always looming over us, ready to snap whatever small, fragile bubble we might attempt to build a life within. Not when Kellen so easily caved beneath his authority. And certainly not when he would always make decisions for me in the name of protecting me.

"You're not the hero in my story, Kellen. You're just another hand holding me under."

He recoiled like I'd slapped him.

I pulled away, wrapping my arms around my body to fend off the cold that had settled in the absence of his warmth. "Thank you for updating me. You can leave now, Corvinna will take me to see my father."

I didn't turn back to look at him. Instead, I stared out the window, weariness finally overtaking the adrenaline that had been rushing through my veins. I listened as the hinges squeaked, Corvinna no doubt holding the door open wider and gesturing for him to leave. After several long, painful seconds, I listened to the sound of his boots across the floor.

I only allowed one weak tear to roll down my chin when the door finally shut behind him.

Chapter Nineteen

"How was your week?" my father asked cooly, not looking up from the stack of parchment before him, quill poised in his left hand.

A thousand sarcastic, acid coated responses crept toward my tongue, but I swallowed them all. He wanted me broken, docile, silent.

If he caught the slightest bite to my words, if he thought there was a possibility I still wouldn't submit to him, he'd throw me back down there. Or he'd find more creative ways to shatter me again.

So I didn't reply, sliding into my seat and keeping my gaze blank, fixed in my lap.

I watched him raise his head in my periphery, examining me. After several heavy heartbeats, he placed his quill in the waiting inkwell, leaning back in his chair. He sipped his drink and tapped his fingers thoughtfully on the desk, each sound sending a shock through my core.

The pit did its job well; I felt broken.

Only, where my father hoped to break me in a way that would let him reshape me as he wished, I was the kind of broken that was sharp, lethal. Ready to cut across his skin and draw blood. "Look at me, Aria." His words were soft, but I flinched all the same.

I peeled my eyes from my hands, slowly dragging them up to hold his gaze. He looked well rested, not a hair out of place. Certainly not as if he had gotten in from a long trip to the southern elms.

My father searched my blank gaze, and whatever he found there curled a small smile onto his lips. "I hate to see you like this, Aria. You know that, don't you?"

A shiver traced down my spine, and I forced myself to nod. To bite my tongue until it bled.

He rose, his powerful body prowling around the desk to perch beside my chair. My heartbeat accelerated, every muscle tensing in my body as he raised his hand. I braced for the impact, squeezing my eyes shut, but his finger merely traced a gentle path down my cheek. "You know I only punish you because I love you. You are far too precious to waste half-measures on."

I counted the seconds until his cool finger left my cheek, until I heard his boots click on the floor as he retreated behind his desk once more. I exhaled slowly, controlling the release of air between my lips as I forced my eyes open. "I have learned my lesson. I am sorry, Father."

"Good. Now, we can put this all behind us."

I swallowed thickly, raising my manacled wrists. "How long will these remain in place?"

His gaze flicked down at the stone. "Until I am certain your actions match your words. I expect your presence in my dining room tomorrow evening. We have cause for celebration, tonight."

My brows furrowed. "Celebration?"

The smile that overtook my father's face settled a tight knot of unease in my chest. It was a rotten, vile grin, the kind I'd seen on his face far too many times, when someone lay dead at his feet, or he stood poised to checkmate an opponent. "Wear something nice. Tomorrow, we toast the goddess for our good fortune."

I waited in the hall for Corvinna to exit my father's office, back pressed against the wood paneled wall. He didn't catch Rhea, if what Kellen said was to be trusted. What else could we be celebrating? Did the witch have a breakthrough, and does she now have a way to amplify my powers to break the curse?

Maybe their ploy to capture Casen Alvar worked while I was locked away in darkness. It would make sense, considering he had just returned from visiting with the southern dwellers. Perhaps he had retrieved Casen Alvar after his capture? It had to be something big, for him to insist on making me wait for dinner tonight to announce it.

I straightened as Corvinna slipped out of the office, gesturing for me to walk with her. I shot her a sidelong look as we moved down the hall, out of earshot.

"Your father wishes for me to join the dinner tomorrow," she said, avoiding my look.

A knot twisted in my stomach. "Just us?"

"Kellen will be there as well."

I searched the witches face as we rounded a corner. "Surprise wedding?"

She barked a short laugh. "As if your father would miss the opportunity to preen before the aristocracy at a royal wedding."

"Then what's wrong, Corvinna?"

Corvinna twirled a small braid around her finger loosely. "You missed a lot this past week, and he would like to update you once he's rested from his trip."

"So this is just a normal dinner?"

We stopped in front of my door, and I turned to face the witch. Finally, she met my gaze, some unnamed emotion churning in her eyes. She nodded after a long pause. "I'll pick you up tomorrow at eight."

I watched the witch walk briskly down the hall, the knot in my chest unfurling and taking root. Corvinna had always straddled the line of ally and foe, and each time I thought I figured out which side she stood on, she would make another move that would lead me back to questioning her.

I've played this game with her for long enough now to recognize when her self-preservation in this court became the priority. Or when my father would make a move that forced her back to his side.

Regardless of what was being 'celebrated' at this dinner, I knew one thing for sure: I was going into this without a single ally by my side.

I wore a nice dress, as requested, but didn't bother to do anything to my hair. I left it damp and loose, drying in soft waves around my waist as I walked out into the crisp air on my father's private terrace.

His chambers overlooked the ocean, the waves crashing against the rocky cliff-side. The terrace was large, more of a courtyard, attached to the western wing. Kellen already sat beside my father, his eyes snapping up to meet mine as I entered. I had braced myself for this moment, steeling myself against his presence as I walked over.

I barely spared him a glance, my eyes moving past Kellen to my father, whose chin dipped in a silent greeting as I took my seat on his left. I scanned the table, noting the absence of settings for Orella, Perceval, Benedict, or Reida.

So it really was just the three of us, then.

The foreboding that had crept in yesterday tightened its grip around my lungs.

"I take it you are feeling better, after resting this afternoon?" my father said in way of greeting. His eyes flicked over the healing wound on my cheek, before darting down toward the stone manacles around my wrists.

I only needed to play nice for one meal. So, I picked up my wineglass and forced a small smile. "Yes, much better."

I sipped the wine as I eyed my father over the rim, waiting for him to make the first move.

His fingers tapped a steady rhythm on the table, muffled by the white cloth. So formal, so perfectly curated, even in the privacy of his own chambers with only three people to witness it. Servants filed in, the first line whisking away the barely touched appetizers, the second replacing the platters with silver trays of food.

Fish in light sauces, a small hog with an apple shoved in its gaping mouth, roasted veggies and mushrooms floating in a gray sauce. I eyed all the food, glancing inconspicuously between the three of us. "Are we expecting guests?"

My father smiled tolerantly as the servant, a mousy young fallen with ash blond hair and nearly black eyes, filled his plate with a sample of each dish. "No, but as I said before, we have a matter to celebrate."

The wine soured in my stomach.

I tried to ease it by tearing off a piece of bread. I glanced across the table to Corvinna, trying and failing to catch her gaze. She stared at the candelabra in the center of the table, the flicker of the flames reflecting in her irises, too lost in her own thoughts to acknowledge my stare.

When my father didn't elaborate, I swallowed my bread thickly and cleared my throat. "Do you mind if I ask what we're celebrating?"

My father sipped his wine and grinned back at me. "We are celebrating the victory of securing the life magic you need. Corvinna has already begun the spell work she needs in order to draw out the magic and stabilize it before transferring it to you." He waved off the details as if they were irrelevant. "She informed me a moment before you arrived it will take only a week before she is ready."

I raised my brows, once again failing to catch the witch's gaze. Why hadn't she said so earlier?

"So Casen Alvar is here in Calasera, in our prisons? Is that where you went, to retrieve him from the dwellers?"

Kellen shifted. It was a small movement, but my eyes snapped toward him. His gaze remained on his wineglass. The foreboding twisted into something like fear.

My father's smile was a slash of white teeth, more closely resembling a wild animal than a victorious man. "No, unfortunately that mission was a disaster. Well, I suppose not a complete disaster, the Dwellers killed Landora's General, Ezra Briggs, but the abduction of the Alvar boy proved futile."

My brows furrowed in confusion for one brief, blissful moment.

Then, the reality of what was occurring, of why Corvinna refused to meet my stare and why my father looked so horrendously victorious, crashed into me. The breath deflated from my lungs, my limbs tingling as my heart plunged to my stomach.

My father watched every ounce of confusion vanish from my face, watched the terror seize control of my composure, before he leaned back in his chair. He raised his wineglass in a toast. "It's a good thing we always had a back-up plan, isn't it, Aria?"

A back-up plan.

My mother.

I flew out of my seat, my body recognizing the threat, the need to fight, before my mind could fathom the reality I had stepped into. Guards shifted behind me, crossing swords with a clink of metal over the doors.

A horrible, painfully breathless feeling crept up my throat as I spun away from the guards to face my father again.

Only to find Corvinna finally, finally looking up at me.

In that moment, I hated her like I never had before.

My creator, my teacher, my friend.

She was only ever just the bitch who was in the background, pulling my puppet strings to make me dance how she needed me to. I was little more than a vessel to deliver her vengeance, a tool in her belt as much as I was a weapon in my father's.

My hand darted toward the steak knife on the table, and before I could consider the repercussions, I hurled it at her face.

Black, shadowy hands caught the blade a mere breath before it made contact. The witch's silver eyes didn't so much as widen in surprise. She merely looked at me with that empty, blank stare she had donned all night.

"You cannot do this to her," I rasped, facing my father.

My father sipped his wine slowly, mulling it over in his mouth before swallowing. "Now you're telling me what I can and cannot do?"

"I won't let you."

He set the wineglass down and spread his arms wide. "Then stop me, Aria. Please, by all means, if you cannot *let* me do this, stop me."

My chest cracked in half as my traitorous eyes fell to Kellen. Goddess, even after all of this, I still expected him to move, to speak, to *fight* for me.

His fist clenched tightly on the linen table, but he didn't move.

I told him you'd never forgive him.

Your father has always taken the path of least resistance.

That was what Corvinna had said after the meeting. She had said my father would not claim my mother's life if it meant having to fight me every step of the way to end the curse, to submit. That it wouldn't be worth it.

My father's last words before he left me to be thrown into the pit flitted up through my mind, twisting in my stomach like a knife. *It is a good thing I have never valued your forgiveness.*

"I will never stop fighting you," I said softly.

My father raised a brow. "Really?"

"If you kill my mother, if you bleed her magic into my veins, I will spend every day of the rest of my life railing against you." I slammed my hands on the dining room table, rattling the dishes and tipping over a glass of wine. "I will not break your curse, nor will I fight in your war. The moment I am free of these manacles, I will burn you and this entire goddess-damned city to ash. If you value my cooperation, if you value your *life*, you will leave my mother in peace."

"I think you will find you don't have as much control as you think you do, Aria," he said softly.

Rage blinded me. I whipped a steak knife from the table, taking two brisk steps toward my father, only for a slither of shadows to wrap around my torso like strong arms. My father watched in amusement as the witch's shadows turned to taloned hands, snatching the knife from my grasp and tossing it back onto the table.

It would appear she has finally settled into her role as my foe. Or perhaps she has always been my enemy, my father's right hand in every way, and I was too desperate for companionship to have recognized it sooner. I had been a lonely, weak child that was too desperate for a scrap of affection from someone who fit the shape of the parents I had been denied.

Goddess, I was so pathetic.

I had believed her when she promised my mother would be safe. It was a cruel lie, preying on my desperate need for any semblance of control.

My father's laugh made my stomach lurch. "You seem to have forgotten your place here, Aria. I may have been too lenient with you in recent years, and for that I am regretful." He rose, straightening his jacket smoothly. "You do not get to step outside of the rules I have laid out for you without punishment. I feel I've been fair, haven't I?" He slowly walked around the table, closing the distance between us.

I swallowed the burning in my throat, staring at him with all the anguish and rage that I could no longer conceal.

"I have given you your role, afforded you more freedoms than any other female in this court, and still you befriend a half-breed thief, terrorizing my loyal subjects. Now you stand before me and presume to tell me what I can and cannot do." He sneered down at me, stopping a pace away. "So let me remind you, Aria, that your freedoms were a kindness I will not willingly extend again. Your sole purpose has always been to break the curse, to be the sword I will wield when we reclaim Corvale for our people."

He was so close now, I could feel his hot breath brush my cheeks.

"And then," he said softly, gripping my chin and forcing me to hold his gaze. "You will yield your magic to the duke. He will take your position in my court, and you will fall back into place as little more than his bitch, used for breeding more powerful heirs into our bloodline." He released his grip on my chin, and I jerked back a step.

Kellen flinched, his jaw tensing, but still he remained seated. Still he kept his eyes adverted like the coward I now knew him to be.

My father turned to pace back toward the head of the table.

He took his seat, picking up his steak knife and cutting into his meal. "I never imagined you'd inherit such strength, far exceeding even Perceval's. I'd be a fool not to take advantage of it. You should be proud to do your part, Aria," he added between bites of meat. "You have secured a lasting memory as the princess who restored power to her people. Your sons will become some of the strongest leaders the Fallen have ever seen. You should be happy."

We lapsed into silence.

I took my seat, stared blankly at the spread before us, and watched my life play out before my eyes. My mother, killed for her power. My magic, handed over to a man that was too cowardly to defend me, even now. My children, raised to kill each other for a throne bathed in blood.

And my life, forever remembered as the martyr that sacrificed her power for her people and bred her magic into the royal family.

I was destined to become just another woman, bled dry by the ambitions of men.

Chapter Twenty

In the absence of fear, anger took hold.

I lay in bed, hardly sleeping despite the weight of the mantrivar stone draining my magic. I stared at the shadows dancing before the fireplace, allowing the anger to sharpen every edge of my resolve. To form me into the weapon I needed to become.

I rose before the sun, moving through the motions to get dressed as I replayed my father's words over and over in my head.

He was going to kill my mother.

He was going to drain her magic and pour it into my veins.

And he expected me to crumble beneath the weight of that revelation, to fall to pieces so he could reassemble me the way he wanted to. It was always a possibility he'd kill my mother. I lived in fear of that reality every day.

That fear was the reason I did my best to take the brunt of her growing insanity, forcing her to take her medications and drink her tonics. To sleep enough and eat enough so she didn't draw attention. To be the one that camped out in her rooms when she was catatonic, or to sneak into the kitchen for tea to soothe her when she was violent.

I bore the load of her illness to prevent my father from growing exasperated enough to kill her on a whim one day. Her life was a gift my father allowed her to keep every single day. I had always known it could come to this.

I had only expected him to hold it over me for longer.

It was the best leverage he had. The most effective thing he could use to tighten my leash, to remind me of my vulnerability in this court. How my entire existence was at his mercy.

I made one small decision, one fleeting act of defiance against him, and he set fire to the illusion of the life I had built. Suddenly, the freedoms I had enjoyed now felt as intangible as smoke. It had never been real. I had let myself be pacified enough to taste a semblance of contentment.

And the moment I did something he didn't approve of, something that made a fool of him… it all dissipated to reveal the extent of the cage I lived in. Goddess, I was never any different from my mother.

I held my gaze in the mirror, resolve hardening to stone within me.

He was going to kill my mother.

Unless I killed him first.

A small groan slipped past my lips as the manacles fell to the floor. The relief was immediate. Magic flooded my veins, pouring through my body with heat. It rushed to my head, my skin tingling as it settled close to the surface once more.

The witch tucked the manacles away in a box, distaste curling her lips as she discarded them on the nightstand. I watched silently as she drew the witch mirror I had trapped a glimmer of my magic in from her bag, setting it flat on the low coffee table. With a wave of her fingers, the thread of gold magic spun away from the frame, the glass rippling like disturbed water.

The magic lurched toward me, slipping back beneath my skin with little more than a warm tingle racing up my forearm. I flexed my hand, watching the golden glow meld with the violet magic in my veins before it vanished again.

"Anything else?" I cleared my throat.

Wordlessly, Corvinna reached in her bag and withdrew a palm-sized, obsidian crystal. "I used that strand of magic to create a conduit. Once you have more life magic, you'll have very little time to learn how to wield it. We'll be able to funnel the magic through this crystal during the spell to break the treaty's curse."

"You mean once you've killed my mother and stolen her magic, I won't have time to properly learn how to wield it?"

Corvinna's piercing gaze met mine for a few heartbeats before she lowered her chin. She offered no apology, nor did she try to justify her betrayal. Instead, she studied me with a cold, detached calculation. All the moments of kindness between us, every trace of the friendship we had slowly built over the years, vanished.

I wanted to set everything on fire. I wanted to watch the witch, my father, Kellen, and this entire fucking court burn to ashes.

Instead, I stepped forward and gently picked the conduit out of her hand. "Teach me how to use it."

I stared at the small white bird at the peak of the aviary.

It flapped against the glass dome ceiling, desperately searching for an escape that did not exist. I wondered if it was born in captivity, like me. Forever staring at the world beyond the glass, wondering if the blue skies outside the dome were kinder, sweeter.

Perhaps this one had been born in the wild before it was thrust into this prison. Like my mother, taking the endless possibilities of a free life for granted before my father clipped her wings and left her in a cage to rot.

I wondered if it was worse to have had freedom and to have lost it, or to have never had it at all.

I sent two narrow spirals of fire toward the bird, cringing as they pierced the creature's wings. I watched the bird plummet, a pained squawk cutting through the air as its small body fell. I caught the creature in my open palms, perching on the stone bench as I cooed softly, my heart clenching with guilt. The bird's chest rose and fell rapidly, its two black eyes staring up at me in terror.

"I'm sorry," I murmured, stroking the downy feathers. "I didn't have a choice."

Delicately, I extended the bird's right wing, examining the damaged muscles and burned skin. Bird wings were so fragile, it took just a few severing injuries to the major muscles and tendons and they would never fly again.

So similar to angel wings, like a perfect, miniature model.

I slipped the conduit from my dress pocket and unraveled the life magic in my core, willing it to trust me as I banked the fire in my veins. It came willingly, rising to greet the injured creature in my palms.

The stone warmed in my hand, and the life magic flowed through the stone. It made the magic more… malleable. Easier to control, to funnel it in a way I had never experienced before.

Violet flared from my fingertips, the bird letting out another desperate squeak as it mended the muscles around the bird's wings. It was shaky, delicate work, a bead of sweat forming on my forehead as I tried to control the flow of magic.

It couldn't heal too quickly, stitching together the wrong muscles or healing the skin and feathers before the damaged tendons were fully repaired.

But gradually, I felt it heed my command. The magic slowed its flow, working meticulously. I closed my eyes, visualizing my work, until the magic stalled, and I opened my eyes to find a whole, healed wing before me.

I didn't allow myself to celebrate, not as I slowly examined the healed flesh. I pressed the wing in delicately, and the bird let out another pained noise, its beak now open as its chest inflated and deflated rapidly.

The wing wouldn't close against its small body.

I grimaced, stroking the bird's head softly in a feeble apology. "I'll fix it, I promise," I murmured.

Cupping the bird in my hands, I sat down on the bench beside me. Out of the corner of my eye, a small dart of black fur caught my attention. My breath snagged in my throat, and I casually glanced around the aviary.

I was alone, save the guards Corvinna had left in her stead, standing dutifully outside the door.

I slowly released the breath I was holding, absently stroking the bird's head, keeping my gaze carefully averted from the small, black bird with golden eyes in the bush beside me.

"You shouldn't be here, but fuck am I glad that you are," I breathed.

I sent another burst of life magic through the bird, watching as the bird's breathing slowed, the pain ebbing. "Listen close, because

I have about a minute before those guards come in here to check on me." I swallowed the sob threatening to creep up my throat, ignoring the world shifting beneath my feet. "I have only a week to save my mother's life, and I'm going to need your help to do it."

Chapter Twenty-one

A week felt like merely a day when every minute that passed was a minute closer to my mother's death.

It was all just one long, painful day. I attended to my normal duties at court, training in my spare time, doing my best to avoid my father's scrutiny. I forced myself to grovel before him the day after the dinner, blaming my protest against his plans on the exhaustion, the stress of the day, my unruly emotions.

Anything but him. Anything but the fact that he announced his plans to kill my mother as casually as one announced a solution to a mildly irritating problem.

He had accepted my apologies, as I knew he would, but not without a punishment. He informed me, as I was leaving, that my mother had another bout of psychosis, and she would no longer be receiving visitors.

I had felt his eyes bore into the back of my head, waiting for me to turn around, to fight him again. But I had merely said it was for the best before departing. I couldn't give him any reason to doubt I was anything but sincere in my apology.

I took my lunch in the aviary each afternoon, much to Corvinna's dismay, who usually accompanied me. She hated birds, and I had never questioned her aversion to them. So, she stuck me with a guard outside the aviary doors and left me be during my lunch hour. This became the one moment in the day where I could let my mask fall and focus on something that didn't make me feel so utterly useless.

Each day, I sat in the center of the glass building, selecting a new bird to hone my skills on. I used a small, precise flame to burn through their wings, and then spent an hour meticulously stitching their delicate muscles back together. I felt wretched, inflicting pain on these small creatures only to experiment on their wounds, but it was a necessary evil. Each day, I gained more precision; the movements coming more naturally than the day before. Now, I only worried about speed.

Would I be fast enough when the wings I sought to heal were so much larger than the doves?

Today, though, I sat in the aviary and eyed the clock. I steadied my heartbeat, schooling my face into a calm, controlled mask. I recited the lines I had rehearsed the night before and sealed away my emotions brick by brick.

The aviary door opened behind me, his presence sending one last jolt of anxiety through my core before I shoved it down.

Kellen rounded the corner, hands loose at his sides, his face infuriatingly impassive.

He should be distressed, groveling. If he were the man I had thought him to be, he'd be begging for my forgiveness. Instead, he raised his brows and looked down on me in question. "I'm surprised you asked me to meet you."

And I'm surprised you're a cowardly piece of shit.

"I'm surprised you came."

Kellen loosed a sigh and sat beside me. "Of course I came, Aria. I'll always come."

Right.

I forced myself to look up at him. "I need to know a few things before I can move on. Before I can… forgive you." I choked on the words, clearing my throat quickly.

Kellen's face softened, a spark of hope glinting in his eyes. "Can you forgive me? I wasn't sure—"

"It depends on your answers."

His jaw snapped shut, and he nodded.

I turned to face him, discreetly putting distance between us. I couldn't stand it, sitting this close to him.

"Were you a part of the plan, the original meeting where my father and Corvinna decided to… to use my mother's magic?"

I watched his throat bob, his shoulders sag, and his chin lower in resignation. "If I say yes, will it be over? Will I have lost you forever?"

You lost me the moment you let me go on the clock tower.

I forced myself to grip his hands, to peer up into his face with a wavering smile. It felt foreign, like a puppet moving on strings. "No, Kellen. I don't think you'll ever lose me."

His gaze darted up to mine, searching. "Yes. I was a part of the meeting, and I tried to suggest alternative options. I need you to believe me when I say I tried. I begged the council to allow me to capture Casen Alvar instead of the Dwellers, but your father wouldn't allow us to waste any more time."

Of course he viewed saving my mother's life as a waste of time.

And of course Kellen was too weak to fight more, to try just a little harder.

"It's not your fault. You have as little control over this as I do."

Lies. He's a man in the fallen court. He always has control. If he stepped out of line, spoke out of turn in a council meeting, people would perceive it as merely a man engaging in politics. Perhaps view it as a power move, if things played out correctly. It was something that would gain him respect.

If I spoke out of turn or had the audacity to suggest alternative moves, my father would punish me. I was to be seen, never heard. My place in those rooms had always been symbolic.

Relief softened Kellen's features. "Thank you for understanding—"

I pulled away, rising and wrapping my arms around my body. I didn't have to fake the need for space, or the sudden chill that had swept through me.

"It doesn't absolve you from everything, Kellen, but it's a start. I… I want to believe   our future can actually be the things you've promised, but you've shattered my trust time and time again."

He rose swiftly, reaching for me, but I flinched away.

His hand hung in the air for one heavy moment before he slowly lowered it. "It can be, Aria. The moment your father has everything he wants, I'll take you far away from here. Illenora will provide you with the relief you need from this place."

"You heard what my father said last night..." I trail off, nausea churning my gut. The expectation that Kellen would take my place to the left of his throne, the expectation that we remain here and produce children with our powers mixed in their veins.

Kellen's resolve hardened, his expression determined. "Once we are married, things will be different."

Goddess, I think he actually believes that's true. It's more sad than anything, his denial. His belief that he can stay my father's hand, and that everything he's done truly has been for my benefit.

I turned and faced him, dropping my shields enough for him to see the anguish in my eyes. "Maybe. Either way... I have accepted my mother's fate, but I can't move past it without saying goodbye, Kellen."

I saw the understanding dawn on his features and immediately wage war with all the reasons he should deny me. All his oaths and commitments and ambitions. I didn't dare release a breath of relief while he held my gaze, determination setting his jaw. "I can fix that."

Three days before my mother's execution, I perfected it.

The flow of magic needed to heal the delicate tissues in their wings was a steady, precise stream I commanded. I looked down on the small bird in my hands, the same white bird I had first attempted to repair.

The little creature that flew against the glass day after day, relentless to break free.

With the last of the wounds healed, I stroked a soothing finger down its beak. I walked out of the aviary, bird clutched close in my hand, moving swiftly to an open window down the corridor. Gently, I placed the bird on the ledge and watched it perch, shaking out its ruffled feathers.

I watched the bird move forward, small hops toward the edge of the stone windowsill, as if waiting to feel its small body press against glass. I smiled the moment the bird felt the breeze pick up, freedom just one leap away.

The bird didn't hesitate to launch itself into the sky, flying free with no cage in sight. I crossed my arms on the windowsill and rested my chin atop them, watching the bird vanish into the sky. As the

outline of the small creature disappeared into the never-ending blue,
I felt a small flutter of hope and longing beat back to life in my chest.

Chapter Twenty-two

"I can give you thirty minutes before I'll come to get you," Kellen said softly.

His key turned in the lock, opening the door to the mother's bedchamber. Kellen had manipulated my mother's guard rotation, leaving a measly half an hour vacant. Just long enough for me to 'say goodbye.'

I nodded my thanks to Kellen before slipping into her room, closing the door softly behind me. Darkness filled her chambers. No fire burned in the hearth, not a single lamp illuminated on any of the end tables. The antechamber was in disarray, pillows thrown on the floor, furniture shoved haphazardly out of place. My father dismissed my mother's ladies earlier this week, leaving her alone in her misery. I heard whispers of her growing more and more violent, refusing her tonics and medications when the healers visited.

I'm sure they restrained her, forcing them down her throat all the same.

No one knew that offering her tea grounded her, or that simply continuing on as if she wasn't in the middle of an episode helped to reel her back into her body. She didn't need to be coerced, just gently cared for until her fractured mind could remember that she wasn't actively in danger. She just needed to be cared for until her memories let her go. But they never bothered to learn, always resorting to measures that made everything worse.

I picked my way through the mess to the dark, gaping maw of her bedchambers. Summoning a small flame to my palm, I peered into the shadows.

More disarray: clothes piled on the floor, books thrown around, even a wardrobe was tipped over. And there, stirring in the large bed in the center of the room, was the small frame of my mother.

"Mama," I whispered.

Her pale blue eyes settled on me, blinking slowly through the haze of whatever sedatives she was on currently.

Tears stung behind my eyes as I sent the flame in my hand to the hearth before her bed, then to spark the candles and lanterns in her room until a flickering, violet light filled the room.

I had only thirty minutes to do this.

I'd healed bird wings in less time this past week, but this would be more difficult. The damage was extensive, the delicate muscles connecting her wings to her back had been destroyed over and over again before they finally healed with salt shoved into the wounds to prevent her body from mending the scar tissue fully.

I hadn't seen her wings since I was a child. They caused her so much pain when they were out that she had simply stopped summoning them. She couldn't extend them fully, so they remained crumbled and bent behind her body, doing little to evoke anything but pity. And the goddess knew how much my mother hated to be pitied.

"I'm here to help you," I murmured, perching on the edge of her bed.

She blinked once at me, a slow, absent movement.

I reached for her hands, cringing when my fingers brushed her cold skin. "Mama, I need you to get up."

She opened her parched lips, but no words came out.

Desperation tightened in my throat as I glanced back toward the entrance. I could heal bird wings quickly, but I had no idea how long this would take me. I couldn't waste time.

I tore my gaze back to my mother. "I know it hurts, but I need you to trust me. Please, I'm trying to free you from this place, just like you've always wanted."

"You can't," she rasped.

I stood up, pouring a glass of water from the metal pitcher on her bedside table. I held the cup to her lips, easing the water into her mouth. Goddess, were they even feeding her? She looked so frail, her collarbones jutting up through her ashen skin. "I can and I will. Don't you want to see your home again?"

Her eyes struggled to stay open, to focus on my face. "I can't be freed, Aria."

"You can—"

"I'm too broken. At least I can help you in my death. Leave me before your father returns," she said softly, resting back against her pillows.

I slammed the cup down on the table, determination setting my jaw. "Get up."

She didn't move, so I reached down and hefted her to standing. Her weak legs nearly gave out before she straightened, pushing me feebly off her. "I can't be saved," she insisted.

A pleading childlike voice clawed up my throat. "Mother, please, we don't have time to argue. Can you show me your wings?"

She took another shaky step back. "I-I can't, Aria."

"I need you to so that I can heal them."

My mother's jaw went slack, her eyes darting over my face. "So you can what?"

"*Heal them*, Mama." I held out the hand that gripped the conduit, the stone warm in my palm. "This gives me enough control over the life magic to finally heal your wings."

My mother's eyes settled on the stone, disbelief still plain on her features.

"Please, before I run out of time. Can you show me your wings?" I asked again.

After another hesitant moment, she nodded weakly, her tongue darting out to lick her dry lips. She closed her eyes, drawing her wings to the surface. They unfurled behind her, my mother drawing in a sharp breath as they appeared. They were massive, white feathered and pearlescent. It would have been beautiful, if not for the scar tissue marring the muscles at the base of her wings. Or the missing patches of feathers, revealing blocky, mottled skin beneath.

Ruined. My father had completely ruined them.

I closed my eyes briefly, drawing in a breath and a bit of courage, before I gestured for her to sit on the edge of her mattress. "This may hurt at first. The magic will have to undo all the existing damage."

My mother drew in a shuddering breath, but she nodded. A small glimmer of hope sparked in her murky eyes, and the sight of it was enough to break my heart. If this failed...

I brushed the thought off quickly, reaching out and tracing my fingers over the first of the scars. The life magic stirred in my gut, rising to the surface. I spun it through my fingers, funneling it through the conduit, sharpening and honing my control.

My mother's face contorted with pain as the golden light seeped into her skin, her lips trembling as she closed her eyes against it. She bit her lip but didn't scream.

She didn't so much as cry.

I bit back tears as I thought of the hot blade he would have used to cause this damage, of the coarse salt he smeared into the wounds to prevent her immortal blood from healing fast enough. Repeatedly, he damaged them far beyond repair. He did everything he could to rip away her freedom, to shatter her will to fight back, all so he could bring me into this world.

It would have been less cruel to cut them off, but my father relished in this sort of misery. The torture, the agony, the chronic pain, he knew it was all a weapon to maintain control.

Slowly, bit by bit, the scar tissue dissolved, as if turning back the clock and racing toward the moment her wings were first cut into. With now open wounds peppering her wings, my mother's breathing had turned ragged. She dug her nails into her knees, bunching up the fabric of her dress.

And then, she relaxed.

The light filled each wound. Her skin stretched together, new flesh reaching across the expansive wounds until they were covered with pink, healed tissue. Feathers sprouted, her wings twitching against the burning itch of feather regrowth. And finally, the light faded, revealing a perfectly mended wing.

In the violet light of the room, each feather shimmered with a faint rainbow, as though kissed by sunlight. I traced my finger along the arch of her wing as she stretched it out, extending it farther than she ever had before.

A sob croaked from my mother, and I looked up to find her covering her mouth. Tears poured down her cheeks, her eyes now the bright blue of shallow waters. With a shaking hand, she brushed the feathers, another choke escaping her wobbling lips.

Tears turned my throat raw as I silently shifted to her other wing. "One more time, okay?" I breathed.

She sobbed into her palm, nodding vigorously.

This one healed faster, the magic funneling where I told it to, tearing into the scar tissue that almost perfectly mirrored the damage on her other wing.

When I finished, I slowly rose. My body was drained, leeched of all energy and shaking with the exertion. But my hands shook for a different reason as my mother slowly stood, stretching both of her wings out. I swallowed thickly as another sob escaped her lips, her wings tentatively curving around her body.

"Do they still hurt?" I rasped.

My mother wiped at her eyes with trembling hands. "There's no pain. It's as if it never happened." A beam of moonlight broke from between the clouds outside and spilled in through a crack in the curtains. It gilded each feather, reflecting a light in her eyes I hadn't seen in years.

I swiped at the tears coursing down my cheeks and gripped my mother's arms. "Are you ready to fly again?"

Chapter Twenty-Three

It was strange how witches' robes seemed to suit me far better than the heavy, brocade gowns of our royal house.

The ethereal silver robes, fitted over a simple white dress, matched the cool tones of my skin and violet eyes. I turned from my reflection after a lingering look to find Corvinna filling the doorway like a shadow. She didn't smile, her silver eyes peering through me.

"You look good."

The handmaids in the room gracefully bowed as they left, leaving us alone.

I stepped away from the mirror, my jaw tight. I wanted to say so much to her, but I couldn't risk it. Not now, not so close to the ceremony. So I watched as she silently walked into the room, her eyes scanning the space as if searching for someone.

"No small black cat today?"

I smiled sweetly. "I never had a cat."

Corvinna gave me a small, knowing smirk. "I'm sure we'll see your friend soon enough."

I didn't take the bait, allowed nothing to show on my face. "Are you here to escort me to the temple?"

The witch nodded but made no move to leave. "I doubt we'll see each other for a while after the ceremony."

My eyes narrowed slightly. "Planning a trip?"

"Something like that."

"Do you wish to have a sappy goodbye, witch?"

A ghost of a smile tugged at her lips. "I'd be an idiot to expect any form of sentimentality from you now."

I didn't bother to deny it.

"I'd also be an idiot if I didn't at least offer my condolences before this begins."

A flicker of rage burned in my gut. I tried to swallow it, to force the burning in my throat down before I spoke. "Your condolences are all you're here to offer?"

As if my mother were already dead. People offered 'condolences' when someone died of an illness or in battle, not as some sacrificial lamb on the altar of vengeance. Especially when Corvinna would be the one to ultimately claim her life.

The witch dipped her chin. "I hope you'll never have to understand why I've made the choices I have, my phoenix."

I swallowed the fire in my mouth.

Pacing toward the door, I tried to shove down the vitriol I longed to spew at her. I lost the battle as I lingered in the threshold glancing over my shoulder at her. "And I hope you'll never wake to find the morning where the weight of those choices crushes you alive."

Only the elder's council, my siblings, and Kellen lined the throne room.

Corvinna escorted me down the aisle toward my father. He stood with his arms clasped loosely behind his back, smug satisfaction settling around his mouth. He was always one to celebrate victories too soon, resting upon his success before the dust had settled. I ignored the burning gaze of the small crowd as I made my way to the front to stand beside my father.

Corvinna left my side the moment we reached the foot of the altar, floating up the stairs like a shadow until she reached the top. She turned, those ethereal silver eyes glowing with the magic coursing through her veins as she looked down at us. Any trace of emotion or the hint of remorse that I saw in her in my bed chambers was gone.

She smiled a cold, inhuman smile. "We have waited centuries to take back what belongs to us. I knelt before your king as the blood dried on the battlefield, my people fallen and broken by Alexandret Alvar's betrayal. My kingdom is gone, and what remains of yours is a sad representation of the power the once great fallen people held."

Ancient rage flickered in her eyes, the temperature in the room dropping to an icy chill. An anger that never died, never eased. Goddess, how it must burn to hold on to all that rage for centuries.

"This curse will stand until light and dark coexist in the same being, and water mingles in the veins of fire without extinguishing its flame," she recited the treaty again, her eyes drifting toward me. " I knew it would be a challenge to create the embodiment of a curse breaker, which is what made the treaty so 'clever' to begin with. Aria's life magic won't be enough to break the curse. If she tries, as she is now, she may die before she is successful and the plague will rot the earth, leaving nothing but a husk of dried land to stake our claim."

Corvinna turned behind her and gestured to a cracked door, leading to the servants' passageway. The door opened, and my heart dropped from my chest.

A guard led my mother to the altar, hands bound and eyes downcast. Corvinna turned her gaze back toward the stiff-backed council as my mother's soft, shuffling footsteps filled the silent temple.

"Today, we will give Aria the last dregs of magic she needs in order to become our salvation. Parisa Aldine is one of the last remaining creatures with life magic in her veins, and today I will bleed her magic directly into Aria's soul." Corvinna stepped aside, revealing my mother fully to the elder's council.

To my horror, they clapped.

The relief on their faces was palpable, their eyes settling on my mother like she was little more than a pawn on their chessboard. My heart clenched in a fist as I watched her stare at her feet, her thin lips pursed into a tight line. She said nothing, did nothing, just as she always had.

Corvinna led my mother to the altar, a lamb to the slaughter. My mother trudged up the steps without a fight, laying down on the white marble. She began to shake, her legs nearly giving out as she eased onto the cold stone. The sharp, trembling breath she drew in as the witch guided her onto her back echoed through the room, reverberating in my ears.

My mother lay prone, and the room held its collective breath as the High Witch brandished a dagger as dark as the night sky.

"You will watch," my father said softly beside me, not tearing his eyes from my mother's body. "You will keep your eyes trained on her until the life leaves her body and the goddess claims her soul. I want you to see every drop of blood drain from her veins and leech onto the floor, and know that all of this is your fault. That if you had obeyed, I would have allowed your betrothed to retrieve Casen Alvar in her place. Or, that if you had simply been better, been good enough, none of us would be here now."

I drew in a slow, steadying breath, forcing the rolling wave of anxiety to ease, loosening its grip on my chest as his words glanced off the shields I had in place around my heart. I let that chilling calm wash over me, spreading through my body with each inhale and exhale.

And I turned to face my father.

His gaze flicked down at me, brows raised.

"I want you to look me in my eyes and know that it is your fault, and your fault alone, that you have led your people to eternal damnation. That your time spent as their ruler was a waste, and it is because of your actions alone that our people will never return home."

His features twisted with rage. He opened his mouth to speak, flames sparking at his fingertips, but he was too slow. In one heartbeat, the glass windows in the temple shattered, and everything descended into chaos.

Chapter Twenty-four

A black wolf the size of a horse led the charge against the fallen who had gathered here today to watch my mother die.

Rhea ripped my father from my side, her powerful jaws closing around his torso as she dragged him across the temple. They exploded in a frenzy of burning orange flames and red blood, snarling clashing against my father's roar of fury. Through the windows, fallen men and women, clad in the black cloaks of Rhea's guild, poured into the temple. Magic thickened the air as they clashed with the elder's council. Guards burst in through the doors, blades drawn and magic sparking at their fingertips.

For a moment, I stood still in the center of the chaos, untouched by the battle, eyes fixed on Corvinna's blade hovering above my mother's throat.

Time seemed to still as our eyes locked, blazing silver crashing against violet, before everything came slamming back into me at full speed. I sprinted up the dais on a wave of violet flames, ready to combat Corvinna's shadows, already swirling around her feet.

"Lower the blade, witch," I called above the din.

Her gaze betrayed nothing. I watched her hesitation, the silent battle warring in her eyes. I prayed to the goddess she'd drop the blade and back away.

I saw her decision settle on her face barely a second before she moved.

I sent a spiral of flames toward her hand as it brought the blade down, blocking the blow. Darkness slammed into flames with a ferocity I had never seen before. All these years, she'd been holding back on me in training. She unleashed everything now. Each blow slammed against my body, shadowed hands reaching through the flames to claw at my skin with taloned fingers. I fortified the wall of fire, pushing the witch back until my mother was beside me. She rolled off the altar, sweat gleaming along her brow from the heat.

"We need to go," she said, her voice breathy and panicked.

"*You* need to go." I quickly fought off another blow of darkness.

There was only so long I could hold off the witch before my magic fatigued. I was no match for her, I would falter eventually, and she'd aim to incapacitate me. I never planned to leave with my mother.

I only needed to buy her enough time.

My mother's gaze hardened. "I'm not leaving without you."

Another blow from the witch's magic sent a bolt of pain slicing through my head. "Yes, you are," I said through gritted teeth.

My mother's wings unfurled behind her, but she shook her head. "What kind of a mother—"

"The kind that never wanted to be my mother in the first place."

The words were harsh, but true. I ignored the pain on my mother's face, turning my full attention back toward the witch. "Cut the bullshit heroics now and go. You can't fight, you can barely access your magic anymore, and you'll only get me killed faster if you stay."

A black wall of darkness encircled me, and I stretched the wall of flames around us. My body shook with lapsing control, the fire desperately fighting to escape and incinerate this entire godsdamned temple. It was always harder to hold the fire back, to keep it tamed and in control, when I used this much of it. I faced my mother, forcing a small smile for her benefit. "Take this as a gift and flee. Go home. You never wanted this, so I'm giving you your only chance to get out. Take it."

Her face broke, tears rolling in thick trails down her cheeks. I forced myself to turn away, to push back against the witch's assault as my mother's wings unfurled from behind her.

She hesitated for a second longer. "I will come back for you. I regret many things, but you were never one of them, Aria."

I swallowed around the lump in my throat, unable to reply.

A gust of wind told me she left, flying up to the ceiling of the temple before vanishing out one of the open windows.

The witch's attacks faltered, her attention diverted on my mother, and I took the opening. I rallied the flames to my open hands, dropping the walls. In a blast, I aimed all my raging, violet power toward her chest.

At the last second, Corvinna's eyes snapped back to mine, and she blocked the torrent of flames. I watched as they blasted against a shield of darkness, panting as the magic between us cleared.

"It seems you finally found your backbone, my pheonix," the witch said softly.

"Shut up," I snarled, sending another barrage of flames at her face.

The flames dissolved before they could heat the skin on her cheeks. She closed the distance between us in slow, measured strides. "Unfortunately, you've made your stand too late."

Another spiral of flames shot toward her, but they split apart, bending to the witch's will. She didn't miss a step.

"You are the only one that can reclaim our homeland, Aria. You need to break this curse, and you're throwing all of it away."

Another strike, another effortless block. She was no more than five feet away now.

"Your vendetta has never been my own," I said through gritted teeth.

"You could have saved your people—"

"*At what cost?*"

Corvinna stopped short.

I stood panting, sweat trickling down my temple as I fought to maintain control over the flames. "I would have doomed all of Corvale to bloodshed and tyranny, and you fucking know it. You wanted Corvale's soil soaked in blood, to look down on the ruins of all that Alexandret Alvar slaughtered to create, and to laugh on his grave. Stop trying to sell me the bit about making the world a better place, you can't hide your true motivations from me. You don't want a better world for the fallen, you only want to watch the humans bleed for what they did to you."

"Struggling to keep your power under control again, Aria?" she breathed, her eyes flickering down to the flames circling my feet.

I gritted my teeth and held her gaze.

"I used to wish for the world to burn up in your flames, for the humans to suffer and bleed as I had," she murmured in the space between us. A rare glimmer of hesitancy shone on her features.

I wanted to pry at it.

I wanted to pull at the thread, at whatever had made her reconsider her alliance, but I didn't get the chance.

Corvinna's eyes flicked up behind me, her mouth setting in a hard line.

All common sense fled my body in a rush, and I turned my back on the witch. Behind us, the battle raged on. Magic and steel flared through the air, the thieves from the guild holding their own against the elders and the guards. Swords crashed, screams of anger and pain echoed, blood flowed. My father had summoned his demons, and they slammed into the side of the mountain, screeching and snarling as they fell into the battle against the guild's surprising numbers.

Standing still in the middle of the chaos, a solitary figure in the center of battle in the courtyard, was my father.

And held against his chest, a blade to her throat, was my mother.

Chapter Twenty-five

I was running.

Blurs of white stone and green trees flew by as I sprinted through the open temple doors, barreling past the garden beds to reach my mother in time.

Bursting through those doors was like turning the volume up on the battle to a deafening pitch. I reeled, but didn't hesitate to draw the sword on my back. I ripped it free from its sheath, not pausing a moment as I launched into battle. The chaos had closed around my parents, and I couldn't see them through the haze of black demons and fallen clashing together.

It was all a blur of gold armor and black cloaks, feathers and scales.

I hacked my way through the demons without remorse, cutting down every guard as I pushed through to the center where I had seen my father. It pained me to recognize the faces of Rhea's guild, tearing into battle for me. For their names to rattle through my mind, filled with years of memories. Thieves, yes, but they were good people. They stole from those at the top, all over Arkala and into Veritas. And they took their fair share, lining their own pockets thickly, but they did so much for those in the slums that never had a chance of escaping.

I didn't see Rhea among the crowd.

I pushed through the battle, shoving all thoughts of Rhea and the thieves around me from my mind as I cut through one more fallen guard, his armor gleaming in the bright sunlight as he fell.

I looked up to find the crowd parting, the battle thinning in the center of the courtyard. And there he was, still holding a blade to my mother's throat. Time slowed to a crawl, the din of battle falling to the background. My pounding heartbeat filled my ears as I shoved the body of the guard off my blade, running toward my mother. I summoned fire in my veins, noting the distance between us with rising panic.

I looked at my mother like it was the last time, my eyes roving her white dress and her ocean blue eyes. The sorrow and defeat there cut through me, when hope had blazed a bright path across her face only a moment before.

I was so close now, my eyes locking on my father. On the cruel cut of his smile, his burning crimson eyes. His soft voice sliced through the battle like a killing blow.

"I believe you have forgotten your place again, little dove."

A scream clawed its way up my throat as I lurched toward him, violet flames spiraling from my fingertips, but it was a second too late.

My father dragged his blade across her throat.

A line of violent red appeared on her porcelain skin. I threw my body forward, ready to die for this. But I was being pulled backward, all my momentum caught around the middle. I looked down at my torso to find two powerful arms wrapped around me, dragging me away.

I screamed and fought, burning everyone around me as my eyes locked on my mother once more. My father released her, and I watched her body slump to the ground. Crimson blood raced across the floor, soaking through her dress.

A sob cracked my chest in half, and with a scream, the violet flames finally erupted from my body on an uncontrolled wave. Fire consumed my vision, my throat raw and the sound of my screams still ringing in my ears as slowly, the world faded to black.

Chapter Twenty-six

Corvinna

Centuries of life in this cruel world had never managed to dull the raging emotions   my mother had always sworn would be my downfall. She used to curse the way I'd freely give my heart, claiming everything I felt ran far too deep for the heir to the Witch Kingdom. All the injustices I had faced in the years since my kingdom fell had only taught me how to control my expressions, to prevent anyone around me from ever knowing how raw my heart truly was.

Maybe that's what led me here, to this moment. Perhaps all the decades of my mother's scorn before her untimely death had not been solely for shaming me, as I had always thought. Maybe she saw in me what I had failed to acknowledge; these emotions, so raw and burning and aching all the damned time, would lead to my ruination.

Because here I stood, my fate sealed with the fallen kingdom, all for vengeance.

Here I stood, on a terrace attached to the temple of Xerexes, Goddess of Death and mother to the fallen people, watching a girl sob and burn over the death of her mother.

I watched Parisa Aldine's body collapse to the ground, watched blood creep across the marble floor. My stomach churned as memories of a different night flashed through my head. Of a High Witch

Queen and her hotheaded, arrogant daughter who felt too much and gave in to every whim those emotions wrought, sobbing in a pool of her own mother's blood.

My past barreled forth to lie beside the present, to watch Aria lose what I had lost, and the guilt sliced into me so deeply I couldn't draw a breath. Two hundred years ago, lost in grief, I fell to my knees before Adriel Elway with a half-formed plan to create the key to the curse. To break the treaty, to launch back into battle, to burn the humans alive for what they had done.

I'd lost everything.

The witch kingdom was gone, and the only other ally I had was this despicable man.

The horrors I had committed at his behest after that moment had branded my soul. Aiding in luring Parisa Aldine from her home, to kidnapping her and forcing her to bear a half-fallen child. Forcing her to go through pregnancy after pregnancy until this one took. locking her in a tower to rot. Allowing Adriel to keep her as his hateful plaything, breaking her slowly over the years.

Then, allowing him to raise Aria, this small child, like a weapon for war. I stood back and watched as she grew up, just as caged as her mother. I stood by and watched as innocence fell from her gaze at far too young an age.

I stood by as her mother lapsed into insanity, and forcing Aria to become her caretaker and protector.

I aided in training her magic, in fighting to make her the perfect key to the curse. She held the weight of all our expectations on her shoulders, and I didn't think I could handle her failure. I had gone through too many atrocities at this point to turn back now. My soul was too ruined, too black to allow this to fail. What was one more act of cruelty when compared to centuries of vile decisions. It couldn't have been all for naught… especially when I had grown to care for the girl.

To love her, as a sister or a daughter or a friend.

And yet… when the time came to mar her soul in a way she would never recover from, to force her to steal the life magic from her mother's corpse, I had betrayed her. I just couldn't let it go. The need for revenge, turning the blood in my veins to vitriol. I had gone so far that her life had meant little when held next to the desire for revenge.

Aria was never a person. She was always a weapon, always a tool.

And I hated myself for allowing that belief to continue on for as long as it had.

"Then change it."

I flinched at the voice, eyes flashing up from the blood-soaked floor. The terrace blurred to a smudge of darkness in my periphery as I beheld Parisa spirit standing before me. Her soul was so bright my eyes ached just to look upon her. The world faded to a buzz in the background, mere shadows moving by in a blur, as I stared into the eyes of the angel I had aided in capturing, torturing, and killing.

My knees felt weak, but I did not allow them to fail me.

"How?" My voice was little more than a rasp.

"Save her."

My eyes darted over to Kellen as he dragged Aria away, enduring her flames until his magic slipped into her mind. Her fire disappeared, her body going limp in his arms as he carried her farther from her mother's corpse.

I looked back to the angel's spirit as the battle raged on around us, everyone else unaware of the soul that still lingered in their presence. "I cannot—"

"I have already begun to process, but you must complete it."

Ice shot through my chest. "What have you done?"

Parisa's lips thinned. *"What must be done. Take her somewhere safe. Let her live in peace, Corvinna. It is never too late to turn back."*

The glow faded, and I watched as the heir to an Archangel's throne faded into the light. The world sharpened once more, little more than a few heartbeats having passed.

Let her live in peace.

I tore my eyes from the space Parisa's spirit had occupied just seconds before. Adriel's eyes found mine across the patio, his satisfied smile the final nail in his coffin.

I beat my expression back into submission, cool and unbothered as I walked through the raging battle to stand by his side. Wordlessly, I drew the vial from my pocket and crouched above Parisa's still warm body.

Her magic was leaking out of her veins with every drop of blood. I could sense it, the life magic meekly rearing its head as she bled out. It was a pity she didn't have more magic, like her father or her daughter. She didn't have enough to save her life, but she had enough to save her daughter's, when the time came.

I dipped my fingers in her blood, unraveling her golden magic from the crimson river, and slowly filled the vial.

And silently, I gave an apology and made a promise to Parisa Aldine.

I am sorry for all I took from you. I will spend my dying breath trying to make it right again.

The battle didn't slow with the flow of Parisa's blood on the terrace floors.

Fallen thieves still clashed with the guards and the elders that had gathered here to watch the sacrifice and subsequent transferring of power. Adriel was drawn into battle, abandoning the angel's body on the marble floor as another casualty in the temple. I forced myself to fade to the shadows, allowing them to consume me until I was little more than a haze of darkness above the battle.

I searched for Kellen, for Aria's limp body in his arms.

I found him in the hall, cornered by a massive, black wolf.

He clutched Aria's limp form to his chest with one arm while he raised his broadsword in the other, standing off against the snarling beast. I landed between them in a blast of darkness. Kellen stumbled back a step, and the wolf lunged, but her jaws closed on little more than dissipating shadows.

"Enough," I said, my voice reverberating through the hall. I spun toward the wolf, my eyes locking on her golden, feral orbs. "Rhea, I presume?"

The wolf snarled in response.

I smiled softly. "If you want to get her out of this hall safely, you're going to have to trust me."

Those clever golden eyes darted between Aria's limp form and me, standing between them. She loosened her stance, apprehension brimming in her eyes.

"Good puppy."

I turned back to face Kellen, finding the tip of his sword angled at my throat. "Are you a traitor now, witch?"

I smirked, waving my hand casually. The darkness settling

around my feet like smoke rose on a wave and knocked the blade
from his hand. "I can't be a traitor if my allegiance has always been
to myself."

Kellen tensed, his hands twitching toward the blade on Aria's
thigh, but in a flash, I disarmed them both. Metal skittered across the
hall, and I reveled in the dumfounded look on his face more than I
should. I stepped in close, forcing him to hold my gaze.

"Do you love her?"

His jaw tightened.

"Do you truly love her, Kellen Ashford, or was it all a ploy to
gain her father's approval?"

He searched my face for a tense moment. "I love her."

I dipped my chin, already knowing his response. "Then you will
help us."

"I will not turn my back on my kingdom."

"Not even for the woman you claim to love?"

"He won't kill her—"

I laughed, cold and low. "There are fates worse than death, you
and I both know that." I stepped in close, my eyes darting to Aria, to
her slackened features. "He won't kill her for this, but he will slide
those last bolts in place in the cage he has been erecting around her
since her birth. He will not kill her, but he'll strip her of anything that
made her mortal until she finally breaks to his will completely. You
are right he can't kill her, but he'll make her wish he would. So I ask
you again." I was so close now I had to crane my neck up to hold his
gaze. "Do you love her?"

His jaw worked, anguish brimming in his gaze as he looked
down at Aria. Finally, he dragged his eyes back to hold mine. "I
won't let you take her."

A smile slowly spread across my lips.

Magic thickened the air, Kellen's eyes glowing before I casually
raised my hand and snuffed the light from the hall. Darkness fell like
a thick blanket, the wolf tensing behind me. "I wasn't asking your
permission, Ashford."

I felt Kellen in the darkness, his magic faltering in surprise,
before the taloned hands of my shadows wrapped around his neck.
I rotated my hand, tightening the shadows around his throat and
pinning him to the floor. Light flared back in the hall, revealing Aria
collapsed in a heap and Kellen's writhing body pinned to the floor by

shadows several paces behind her.

I closed the distance in three leisurely steps, leaning down over the fallen male with a wicked grin. "Wrong choice."

His eyes flared with rage and fear as I dragged my sharp nail down his cheek, leaving a beading trail of red behind. Murmuring a few lilting words in my mother tongue, I spun the blood up in the air between us. His eyes glazed over, going vacant and distant.

I leaned in close, my lips brushing the shell of his ear. "And now, all of your choices will belong to me."

I rose, Kellen rising swiftly behind me, like a puppet jerked up by a string. I picked up Aria, her head lolling against my arm, as I paced back toward the shifter. "Now, shall we go?"

For the thousandth time, I cursed the wards in Calasera for not allowing me to open a witch door to the outside world. How much easier my life would have been these past two centuries if I could merely summon a door and step into another part of the world without entering the Eastern Mountains. I suppose that's exactly why Adriel's wards prevented it.

The shifter didn't hesitate when I asked her to take the form of a wyvern. I was surprised she did so easily, as if she had seen one in person before. Only those who ventured too deep into the belly of the eastern mountains would cross a wyvern in Corvale.

If we made it out of here alive, I'd love to know how she encountered one and lived to tell the tale.

We climbed on the shifter's back, Aria still clutched in my arms, and Rhea took off toward the towering windows at the end of the hall.

The doors to the temple behind us blasted open, shouts of protest filling the hall. I turned to find guards racing after us, led by Adriel. My gaze locked with his across the distance, and I couldn't help the smile I sent over my shoulder, the surprise on his face widening my grin.

Flames came spiraling toward us, but I blocked with a wall of darkness. I turned my attention back to the rapidly approaching window, sending a spiral of shadows toward it. "Brace yourself!" I screamed over the sounds of pursuit and shattering glass, the windows blowing out as the shifter launched her massive, reptilian body into the air.

Wings flew out on either side of us, leathery and dark as night.

Our bodies were weightless for one, two, three heartbeats before Rhea banked upwards with the powerful beats of her wings.

My heart dropped to my stomach with the sudden lurch, and in a few beats of her wings, we were barreling toward the eastern mountains. I cursed as the army leaped out the window behind us in hot pursuit. Bands of shadows secured Aria to Rhea's back as I laid her down, before I rose in a low crouch, facing the fallen and demons swarming behind us.

I raised my hands before me, murmuring a soft spell as I spun the raw magic in my veins with all the intent my mother had drilled into me as a witchling. The army froze, suspended in the air, wingbeats trapped mid beat. Time seemed to slow as one by one, silver magic flew between the army. With a flick of my wrist, their necks snapped in unison. The simultaneous crack of bones echoed across the sky, the bodies plummeting toward the city below.

My eyes flicked down at the castle, grimacing as I watched another horde of black demons fly out.

I wouldn't have enough magic to do that again for several minutes. I turned my gaze forward, Rhea's wings beating harder as she flew toward the eastern mountains. The wind whipped across my face, the familiar sting of flight bringing a small smile to my lips, despite the anxiety coiling in my chest.

If we weren't about to be killed by feral demons, this would be fucking exhilarating.

I clutched Aria close to my chest, raising my hand to cast the witch door as we passed over the border. Thirty more seconds.

The sounds of demons grew closer, snarling cries and snapping jaws mere feet behind us.

We'd have to fly straight through the witch door... and try not to fall when the magic disoriented us. I grimaced, drawing in a steadying breath as the magic built once more beneath my skin. We passed over the border of the eastern mountains, the pop of Adriel's wards thick on my skin. Rhea let out a shriek that echoed off the mountain peaks, and I raised my hand, muttering the spell and sending silver sparks of magic twining before us.

A stone archway appeared, the center little more than a swirling mass of shimmering gray. I masked the location, knowing Adriel's pets behind us would report on whatever they saw.

If this was to work, he could never find her again.

Rhea let out a scream beside us, and I turned to find a demon sinking its talons into her barbed tail. She banked hard, flinging it off. Crimson blood flowed in the wind as she beat her wings faster, spiraling toward the door. I shot Kellen, prone behind us, a sharp command. His face contorted, but he spread his wings and launched off Rhea's back, engaging in battle with the demon closest to Rhea's tail.

In a blinding flash, we barreled through the archway, into a clear sky hundreds of miles away from Calasera.

Rhea faltered midair, her wings coiling around her body in a missed beat. My stomach lurched to my throat as we plummeted toward the ground. I clutched Aria to my chest, eyes locked on the still open witch door in the air above us.

I sent a spiral of magic toward it, closing the portal, but it was too slow.

Kellen and the demon he had been battling came barreling after, plummeting through the sky as the door vanished.

And then we were all falling.

Rhea's massive form fell through the air beside us, her golden eyes wild as she let out an ear-splitting screech.

"Stretch out your wings," I screamed over the wind.

She fought to stretch her wings, her body spiraling through the air clumsily before they finally shot out on either side of her. Rhea banked upwards, drawn away from us on a draft. The shifter desperately pursued us through the air, letting out another shriek of terror.

Fuck, we were going to crash.

Cursing the gods in all their useless glory, I cast a mass of shadows across the ground beneath me. The forest rapidly approached, and I clung to Aria as I sent my shadows spiraling through the trees, blasting them away to form a massive crater.

I drew in a breath and cast out my magic mere seconds before we collided with the earth.

Chapter Twenty-seven

Rhea

I woke on the forest floor, my bones aching as I settled into my mortal form.

Smoked wafted over me in thick, choking waves. My body was bruised from the collision, but I was nearly unharmed, as if I had landed on something far softer than the earth. Sore, aching, dizzy, but otherwise unharmed.

It took only a few moments for the events of the last hour to fly through my head, and I was on my feet running through the smoke. "Aria," I tried to scream, but it came out as little more than a choked whisper.

Smoked burned my throat, and I coughed as I pushed through the clearing, eyes scanning frantically until... *there.*

I dropped to my knees and crawled the final few feet through the smoke, past the small burning flames, until I reached Aria's blazing figure at the center. Ignoring the raging fire that encircled her like a protective cocoon, I reached for her.

"Stop, you fool," a voice hissed behind me, taloned hands dragging me back.

I thrashed against the witch, desperately trying to crawl back to Aria. The witch was stronger than me, throwing me down in the dirt several feet away.

"Make it stop," I gasped out between coughs.

"I'm trying to," she hissed back.

"Why is this happening?!"

Corvinna didn't reply. Those strange shadows wrapped protectively around her body as she pushed forward, bracing her arms against the skin-melting heat whipping off the torrent of Aria's flames. Her figure vanished within the fire, and I watched with bated breath.

In a few heartbeats, the fire receded, until I saw the witch kneeling over Aria's prone form. I stumbled toward them, eyes stinging as black smoke whipped past me.

The witch's hand glowed a soft violet on her forehead, and Aria's contorted features softened. She looked like she was asleep, but whatever Kellen did to her...

"When will she wake?" I asked breathlessly.

"Eventually. I need Ashford," the witch snapped. Her silver eyes scanned the forest beyond the smoke.

"I'm here!" Kellen's voice called.

I whipped around as his form took shape through the smoke. He sprinted across the clearing to stand beside us. Kellen's eyes snapped to Aria, fear flashing across his face as he moved toward her.

I didn't think, not as my eyes fixed on his stupid face, a false look of concern creasing the corners of his eyes. I took two steps after him, gripping his shoulder and forcing him to turn. He spun around, bewildered.

And I punched him square in the face.

Kellen reeled back, looking down at me incredulously. "What the fuck was that for?"

"You don't deserve to touch her, worry about her, or even breathe the same air as her, Ashford. So back it the fuck up before I rip your throat out," I growled, my canines elongating in my mouth.

Kellen rose to his full, towering height. "I deserve—"

"Nothing, Kellen. You deserve nothing. She isn't yours anymore," the witch said blandly.

I spun around to face her. "What's the plan now?"

I didn't know what the fuck was going on, or how I ended up in these woods with the High Witch or Aria's bitch of a fiancé, but I wasn't planning on staying here any longer than I needed to. I was already regenerating my strength so I could transition into something big enough to scoop Aria up and fly far, far away. I didn't trust either of them, but backed against a wall I had no choice but to go with the witch's plan.

Sorrow threatened to pull me to my knees as the image of Aria's mother flashed through my mind. I never met Parisa. I never really liked her, to be honest. Not with how much pain she caused Aria, but... it was her mother. Aria spent her entire life trying to shield her. It was fucked up, backwards, and horribly unfair, but... she was going to be devastated. It might break her, and I needed her far away from these vultures when it did.

"The plan..." the witch trailed off, her silver eyes scanning the treeline, "is for you to wait here a moment."

I watched, jaw gaping, as she walked deeper into the woods. Leaving me alone with Aria and this prick. I turned my gaze back to Kellen, eyes narrowed. He assessed me carefully, dabbing gingerly at his split lower lip. He moved toward Aria again, but I planted my feet firmly between them, baring my teeth.

"You don't—" he started.

"I don't care."

"I love—"

"Not interested."

He threw up his hands in exasperation. "Will you let me speak?"

I examined my nails casually, hoping he couldn't see the way my hands still shook. "I don't give a fuck about any sort of sob story you could spin right now. You don't love her."

"Yes, I do."

My eyes snapped to his. "Oh, really?" I took three steps toward him, closing the distance between us. "You think you *love* her? No, you *want* her. You want what she can give you. You love the parts of her you can control. Did you think she'd be happy with you, married off to some duke and forced to sit up in a manor and rot away?"

His eyes flashed. "I would give her everything."

I laughed in his face. "And the fucking ironic part is the only thing she wanted was to be free. Would you have given her that, Kellen Ashford? Would you have set her free?"

He hesitated, and I scoffed. "Of course not, that would be too selfless. You may have tricked yourself into believing you love her, but I'm not a fool. I know love when I see it." My throat bobbed as I glanced down at her. "You never loved her, not truly. You loved the version of her you thought you could preserve, that you tried to cage. So do us both a favor and shut the fuck up."

We stood in silence, Kellen's gaze hard and fixed on the ground, until the witch returned.

My spine straightened as she walked briskly toward us. She stopped a few feet away, her silver eyes assessing Kellen before darting down to Aria. Her lips thinned, her face hardening as she finally met my gaze. "You don't know me, so everything I'm about to say you're going to want to fight. But I need you to understand this is the only way to keep her safe from Adriel now."

Apprehension coiled in my stomach, but I waited for her to go on.

"She needs to stay here."

I blinked. "In these woods?" How in all the hells would that keep her safe?

Corvinna nodded once. "In these woods. I created a cottage—"

"You *what*?"

"I created a cottage," she repeated, slower, as if she were talking to an idiot.

I glanced behind her, eyebrows raised. She was gone for what, ten minutes? I guess they don't call her a High Witch for nothing.

"So she can live there. I'll create wards around this forest to keep her contained, and to keep everyone else out."

Contained. "How is that any better than what her father would do if he found her?"

Corvinna scowled. "Adriel Elway would torture her within an inch of her life for the trouble she has now caused him, force her to heal, and start over again. Then, he would bleed her magic into the ground and marry her off to this prick behind you before locking her away while this entire continent descended into another dark war. He would clip her wings and lock mantrivar stone onto her wrists until she went mad like her mother. I can assure you, concealing her within these woods in a nice little house is a far kinder fate."

I didn't like it at all. She'll crawl out of her skin being trapped in here, and when she wakes up, her grief is going to eat her alive. I can't let them trap her here in her misery—

"And Kellen is going to complete the glamor over her memories."

I froze.

"I'm going to what?" Kellen snapped, crossing his arms over his chest.

"It's the only way to ensure she never tries to leave. That she can't leave. I can't leave her here to stew in her rage and her need for revenge, it'll only serve as fuel to find an escape. A glamor can protect her. And I can hide the key for her wards in the memories that she can no longer access, making it impossible for her to escape. It'll also make it impossible for her father to find her and break the wards without killing her to retrieve the key."

"No fucking way," Kellen snapped, running his hands through his unbound hair.

"Yes fucking way," the witch said, walking briskly toward where he stood. "It's the only way, actually, so you don't get a say in this."

"She is my fiancée—"

"Not anymore." The witch's body shook with barely restrained magic, her voice layered with the voices of many.

Kellen flinched, his gaze going vacant and slack, just as it had in Calasera.

"I am truly sorry for your loss," she continued, glancing at me now, "but you can't keep her safe. He will tear the world apart looking for her. She must remain hidden."

"What about your vendetta?" I spat. She was just as bad as the king, if not worse.

The witch paused. "That isn't for you to worry about." Her silver eyes flicked toward Aria again, and in that moment, I believed she genuinely wished to help her. Whatever her reasons, true sorrow and regret shone in her eyes.

I still couldn't let them do this. "I could take her to the eastern continent. Or to Casserine, to my people."

Corvinna's eyes flicked over my arched ears, a gift from my mother's Elven blood. "The Elway family has ties in the eastern continent. She would only be safe there for so long, and your own people barely accept you. You left as a child, correct?"

I nodded. "But I could petition the queen—"

"And if that fails?"

"It won't fail." It can't. And if it did… then we would go on the run. I would run to the ends of the earth to give Aria another chance at a different life, out of the clutches of people who only wished to use and discard her.

Corvinna shook her head. "It will never work. Hiding her beyond his reach is the only way. He'll never be able to penetrate these wards, not with a glamor securely in place."

I squared my shoulders, desperation gripping my heart in a fist. "I won't let you do this."

Corvinna barked a laugh. "Why does everyone think I'm asking for permission?" Her shadows rallied behind her, but I shifted fast.

My wolf form came the easiest, and I stood snarling over Aria's body.

The witch stilled, cocking her head to the side curiously. "How about a compromise, wolf?"

I snapped my jaws, advancing slowly. There would be no compromise. I would rip out her throat for even suggesting we cage Aria again. She needed to be free of all of this, and a life on the run was better than a life in a cage. If she were awake, I know she would agree. She would never forgive me if I allowed them to trap her here, without her memories.

I lunged toward the witch, aiming for her throat, but my maw closed on dissipating shadows. I spun, searching the woods for her lithe form, before something slammed into my side. I thrashed against it, but the shadows melted to mist when I swiped my claws or snapped my teeth on them.

In a moment, the writhing mass of darkness pinned me down.

The witch appeared above me. "I can see you're going to be a problem when we leave." She sighed.

She palmed a knife and sliced a line down my cheek. I snarled as pain bit through me, hot blood spilling out on my fur. The witch raised her hands above us, murmuring in that flowing language she had used with Kellen. Dread twisted my stomach in knots as she levitated a thread of my blood, spinning it into a knot in the air between us. With a flick of her wrist, she pulled the knot tight and—

It felt as though a knife sliced through my soul. I howled in agony and terror as that small flicker of humanity inside of me went unnervingly silent. It was always there, whenever I grew teeth or claws or fur, a small thread that led me back to my mortal form.

But… it was gone. Sliced off or locked away, I wasn't sure. I couldn't access it either way. I clawed for it, desperately trying to save the body I called home, the body I was born into, but… it was gone. As if it had never existed at all. I had always run from that form. From the golden eyes of my absent father marring my otherwise Elven features, alienating me from both sides of my kin. But now… gods, how my soul cried in its absence.

The witch looked down on me in pity before she straightened. "Ashford," she called over her shoulder, summoning Kellen to her side. "Glamor her memories."

His face spasmed, as if he were trying and failing to fight against the compulsion. Stiffly, he moved toward Aria's sleeping body.

No no no—

I thrashed and snapped my jaws at the shadows, but they only grew talons and dug into my flesh. I yelped, panting heavily as I struggled to watch Aria. They were going to do it. They were going to place her in another cage, and I couldn't *fucking move—*

Kellen kneeled over Aria.

My heart shattered as silver magic coursed between his palms, the seconds stretching on in agonizing silence. Another desperate yelp ripped from my mouth as Kellen erased everything that made Aria who she was.

Chapter Twenty-Eight

Aria

I *was trapped in a nightmare.*

I stood in a white dress, the world painted in shades of melancholic gray. Trees surrounded me, blasted away from the center as if something had careened into the earth.

I knew it was a nightmare the moment the world began to fracture around me, shadows splintering through the trees, the image disintegrating like smoke and ash around me. Tears silently rolled down my cheeks as I watched the shadows grow, spreading across this barren plain, racing toward my feet.

I was alone again, falling backward into the darkness of my mind. Into the space where my father violently forced me into the world. Into the pit where my mother screamed and clawed her face bloody. I was collapsing into the void that held my worst moments, the moments my father tried and failed to beat the empathy, the warmth, from my soul.

To all the moments Kellen lied to me before he dug his talons into my mind and ripped my trust to pieces.

And worst of all, I knew I'd find my mother's lifeless body at the bottom.

I'd watch my father drag a blade across her throat, vile red pouring down her chest. I'd fall to my knees in her blood and watch the life leave her eyes, over and over again until I lost it. I reached my hands out, screaming into the void that yawned before me.

Screaming for someone, for anyone, to grab on.

To pull me away from the darkness of my soul before it swallowed me whole. Because I was so, so tired.

I had been strong for too long.

And I knew if I fell again, I'd never make it back out.

I didn't want to fight alone anymore. There had to be something... more.

The darkness halted, slowing to a near crawl for several heartbeats. A glimmer of gold spun away from my fingertips, racing through the dissolving world, until... there.

Standing across the yawning distance was a man.

Hazel eyes crashed into mine, confusion quickly giving way to panic. I tried to speak, to call out for help, but my lips wouldn't move.

A shaky smile found its way onto my face as I recognized a coil of gold within his soul, drawn toward the life magic my mother gifted me.

The darkness began to race toward my feet again, and... and the man raced after it. I held his eyes in shock as he fought to reach me across the evaporating plain. He almost made it, his fingers reaching toward me, brushing against my outstretched hand, before the ground beneath my feet gave way and I plummeted.

I fell through my soul to the darkness waiting at the bottom, but this time I wasn't afraid. Despair didn't sink its teeth into my bones. Because I wasn't alone. A soul that matched my own had raced after me, fighting against the impossible darkness for a chance to save me.

I smiled as I slammed into the dark lake of my memories.

For the first time in my life, water raced over my head, drowning me.

And I let it.

Icy water chased away the last traces of violet flames, and I sank.

So deep, so impossibly deep.

I lost my name to the waves.

The darkness shrouded all the feelings in my chest.

The waters rinsed my memories clean.

Down, down, down.

The girl I used to know sank until she rested at the bottom of the darkness, lost to the world.

But even beneath the miles of icy water, even with arms wrapping around her torso and holding her on the silty bottom of her mind, she held on to one truth: there was something more for her than the cage she had always known.

This was not the end.

Chapter Twenty-nine

Rhea

I'll never forgive myself for letting this happen.

I wondered if I'd recognize her when she awoke, if she'd run from me when she saw me in my wolf form. Or if she'd know me intrinsically, like recalling someone from a past life. All the emotions and none of the associated memories.

Kellen moved his hands after a small eternity, sorrow ripping across his features. He leaned in close and murmured something, far too softly to hear in my wolf form. He placed a gentle kiss to her forehead before backing away.

"I'll meet you outside the forest," Corvinna commanded Kellen.

He said nothing further as he flared his wings and took off in the sky.

The shadows receded from my body, but still I lay in the dirt. I couldn't find the energy to rise.

"You can remain here with her, if you wish. You're not a threat to her in this form," she said dismissively. "Or run off into the wilderness like the feral beast you are. Most shifters lose themselves eventually, you're no different."

I would kill her for this.

I watched as the High Witch muttered her spells and spun the air into an iridescent web. She cast the web around us, launching it into the air. It spread out, pastel colors sparking across the sky into the shape of a dome.

I knew Aria often dreamed of a quiet life, but I didn't think she would be content when she awoke. Her heart longed for freedom. And she wouldn't know who she was… she would be forever searching for answers I could no longer give her.

I wondered when the world would stop trying to cage her, and I hated myself for not being able to stop this one from forming. For simply watching as the witch erected the bars around us.

When the spell was done, the witch crouched before me. She snapped her fingers, a rope with a piece of parchment tied to it appearing in her hands. The note read simply *Her name is Rhea.* The witch tied it around my neck before turning to Aria.

Another small slip of paper with Aria's name on it appeared, and she slipped it into her dress pocket. "She at least deserves one small truth."

Her silver eyes fell to me as I slowly rose, head hanging low and a growl rising in my throat. "If you do anything to break her glamor, she will die. Without my aid, the glamor will crush her mind. Let her live, Rhea. Loneliness is a far better fate than death."

Aria's face flashed before my mind, from that night in my living room. The silent, heartbroken confession she had shared over a bottle of wine.

The witch rose, and with one last lingering look at Aria, left. There was a small breeze of a portal being opened, the swoosh of it closing, and then we were alone.

Completely and utterly alone in this forest.

I lay hidden in the shadows of the woods, waiting for Aria to wake.

I watched as her violet eyes fluttered open, gazing up at the clear blue sky, now clouded by dissipating smoke. My heart wrenched when she rose and looked down at her body, past the blood of her mother staining the hem of her gown, unaware of what she was seeing. She studied the rings on her trembling fingers, her brow furrowed in confusion.

If tears could fall in this form, they would have drenched my cheeks. The ring I gave her, and her engagement ring to Ashford, she stared at them blankly. No recognition registered on her features.

My heart cracked in half when she dug her hands into her hair, desperation and panic ripping across her face. I followed silently when she took off running, her once agile and trained body clumsy, tripping over tree roots and stumbling along like a newborn fawn.

When she slammed into the dome, I fought the urge to go to her. I stopped myself.

Not yet... not in this form. It would only scare her more.

I couldn't bear it. I couldn't bear the thought of her looking down at me without recognition.

So instead, I sat behind her in the shadows.

I watched the fight leave her body as she kneeled before the iridescent wards for hours, staring numbly at the world beyond. The sun shifted across the sky, and still I held my silent vigil, bearing witness to her pain.

When she finally moved, wandering the woods with a painfully empty expression on her face, I found the courage to face her.

I followed her to the center of the woods. Her confusion morphed to terror as her eyes locked on mine between the trees. I held my heart together as I silently willed her to remember me, to look into my eyes and remember *something*.

For Aria.

For my soulmate, in all the ways a best friend could become one, I could do this.

I bowed my head low and stepped into the puddle of moonlight between us.

Epilogue

I *no longer floated in a lake.*
The lake was gone, replaced by the burning violet of my soul.
The glamor had finally disintegrated.

I sat at the bottom of my being for a while longer, lingering on the images that had played out before me. My last memory before waking up in the dome was my mother's blood pooling across the floor. I sat there in grief and agony, and found my soul had been split.

There was the Aria before the dome, the submissive fallen princess, the fiancée, the quiet girl that burned inside and never let anyone see it.

And there was... this Aria. The Aria reborn into loneliness. Who survived solely to find out who she had been before. The Aria that fell in love with a man who found her in this place of darkness through her dreams. She was so vastly different from the Aria before, soft in all the ways the old Aria never truly could be.

Both were lonely, both hurting in ways that were so painfully similar.

And now, here I sat, staring at the two halves of my being, unsure how to reconcile them back into one.

I looked up toward the waking world, and a small glimmer of light beckoned me. I wondered what it would be like to wake on the other side of all of this.

I wondered, as I rose to my feet and allowed myself to rise to consciousness once more, what would happen next.

After all that had been taken from me, after all the decisions that had been made for me, what would I do with the freedom to decide for myself?

Who would I choose to be now?

Shadow and Ash Vol. 2
Coming Soon

Find more information at authoremilygrey.com, and subscribe to Emily's newsletter to stay up-to-date on all future publishing announcements.

Acknowledgments

A large part of me still can't believe that this is my second self-published book. Writing An Ember in the Forest was akin to climbing Mount Everest without a tour guide. The process was cumbersome, tiring, far from perfect, and yet... it taught me more than I ever imagined. Writing A Light in the Shadows was such a joy, my self-publishing process now refined, with a worn path to follow from the trek that was my first book.

I am foremost eternally grateful for every single person who has given this series a chance. Every time someone reaches out to tell me how much they loved, it feels so surreal, and I rarely know how to express my gratitude accurately. So thank you for digging a little deeper into Aria's past with me. I wouldn't be able to do any of this without all of you.

Thank you to my wonderful editors. Without your help, this story simply wouldn't exist.

To my family, thank you for your endless support. I never would have taken the first steps toward self-publishing had it not been for that support and belief that my story was worth telling, and that I had it in me to start a business to do just that.

And finally, thank you to my husband for always knowing the right thing to say when I'm at my lowest, convinced that I can't possibly make this work. Sometimes, a coffee and a small distraction is all I need to find my way through the story.

If you're reading this now, book two in the Shadow and Ash series is well underway. And all I'll say to that is brace yourselves; we have a lot to do in Corvale.

About the Author

Growing up in the mind-numbingly boring community of Naptown, Florida, reading and writing fantasy stories became my only outlet for my wild imagination. In whatever free time my toddler affords me, I am an avid reader of all things fantasy, a houseplant hoarder, and an amateur baker; all fueled by my shameless addiction to caffeine. Above all else, I am a writer with a passion for taking the worlds that appear inside my head and spinning them into stories that I hope will one day take up shelf space within the homes of eager readers.